Chronicle

A Princess and an Ooze

Ian Rodgers

For Fantasy lovers everywhere, and for the people who helped make this dream into a reality.

Table of Contents

Chapter 1: How it all began

The first thing I could remember about my life was a conversation. I'd existed before, but it was this point that marked the moment I changed. I'd had instincts and primal, animalistic urges I'd acted upon. Yet I was not aware of them, and could make no conscious, informed decision about these things. I simply 'did.'

However, whether it was fate, a divine will, or mere happenstance, that was when events started for me. For better or worse, those were the first words I'd ever heard, and these were the first two people I had ever met.

"Your highness, please! Such a filthy creature is beneath you! There are so many other wonderful animals here that are so much more befitting a woman of your stature!"

"No thank you, Orleen. I want this one."

"But, but, but! Look at this male Qoatl! Such magnificent plumage! And these feathers become even more vivid in the spring! Such beauty is worthy of one such as yourself! Or how about this

Lily-lynx? Such soft and supple fur must surely be better than that clammy wet sludge in your hands?"

I recalled how hands tightened around me after the older female voice said that, and I remembered the feeling of going 'Squish!' in her palms. Such tiny, delicate hands refused to let something like myself go. If I'd known what gratitude had been back then, I'm certain I'd have felt it.

"Again, no thank you, Orleen. I'd much rather have this little fellow."

"My lady! You are a daughter of high standing! You are Liliana Augustine Roan! To have a creature like that as a pet would tarnish your family's name!"

"If such a little thing could tarnish the name of my family, I'd wonder how we have possibly survived all these years."

"Guh." A strangled grunt was the only response, and I heard something move away from me and the young woman holding me tight. I had no eyes at that point. As such, 'seeing' was an impossibility for me. I also did not have ears, either, so I suppose 'heard' would be incorrect. Rather, I registered the vibrations that passed through the air and my body and translated them into words.

"There, there, little fellow. The mean lady is gone," the person holding me cooed, as if I were a baby. Well, alright, I was technically only self-aware at that moment, but I still remember feeling irked at that treatment. I also immediately remember forgiving her as she stroked my top. I shivered in delight at her caress, and she giggled as I moved around in her hands.

"You're so soft and squishy. Like warm, yet dry, jam. Firm, too. Such an oddly pleasant sensation." A quiet hum of contemplation came from the woman as she stroked me.

"I think for now I'll call you 'Jelly.' We can think of a better name at a later date. What do you say?"

Having no mouth, I could merely make a burbling sound in agreement, and my owner laughed airily.

And that was how I, a mere slime, became the pet of a princess, and Fate began to move.

Chapter 2: A new home, and a new family

"Here we go. This is going to be your home from now on, Jelly." I had been carried away by my new owner a few hours ago, and was now being set down in a room with a plush carpet covering the entire floor.

I had been purchased from a well-regarded pet shop of sorts. Magical creatures were seen as status symbols if made into pets by the wealthy. The store I'd been in before I was self-aware specialized in taming such potentially dangerous animals and then selling them to those who could afford them.

There were all sorts of rare and exotic creatures my owner could have chosen from. The rainbow feathered flying snakes, the Qoatl, renowned for its amazingly colored plumage and ability to blind foes with seizure inducing bright lights. The small and cute Lily-Lynx which only eats flowers and could control plants much like a Druid. There was even a Carbuncle, a rare fairy-like being with a large precious gem set in its body, available that day.

Any one of them would have made a person of her standing an excellent pet. But instead, it was I that caught her eye. I'd been found as a newly spawned little vermin rooting around the store's garbage one day and the owner thought he could try and make a few silver coins off of me as a piece of novelty merchandise. I did not know any of that at the time, though.

I slowly inched my way around a large, wide room filled with well-made objects. I was atop a carpet made of thick, shaggy fur and fibers which lay on top of thick oak panels. Against one of the walls a massive canopy bed sat, finely crafted and with silk and cotton sheets with fine gossamer veils encircling it. Feather stuffed pillows were heaped on the bed like a fluffy mountain range.

In a corner stood a vanity made of soft brown wood with a polished glass mirror resting on its surface, with boxes of jewelry open on its surface. A towering wardrobe stood nearby, with a walk-in closet to the left of the two pieces of furniture. Warm sunlight filtered in through windows set high on the wall, well above the bed and angled so they illuminated everything in the solar rays.

How was I able to know any of that without eyes, though? My body sensed things as both shapes and what they were composed of. It was like an advanced form of echolocation, greatly enhanced with my own innate magical energy. With it, I could tell what was edible, what was good to rest on, and who was around me at any given time. Color was much harder to observe. It took a concentrated effort on my part to grasp the color spectrum. Even then it was dull and muted.

I only had a visible range of ten feet in all directions, though. Within that scope, I could sense intimately who or what was around me. I could tell that there was a frayed, worn edge on the bed's sheets but also that there was a spot of rotting wood on the corner of the wardrobe due to some moisture damage leaking in from the other side of the wall. I could see so much, and more.

And, of course, there was my savior; my owner. She lit up the room, at least to my senses. A faint sheen of magical energy enclosed her skin, like a second body just barely restrained by her physical form. The perfume my owner wore was a light, lilac scent while her dress was of fine, soft wool and cotton. She wore a few pieces of simple jewelry; elegant pieces of silver and semi-precious gems. The one exception was a ring on her left hand that pulsed brightly with sealed magical power; an enchanted item of sorts, likely to provide protection of an arcane nature. But even that glow paled before the intensity of her own existence. I didn't know why she shone so much brighter than everyone else. It was selfish to say, but I felt that it was due to her importance to me.

Beyond ten feet the ability to tell what something was made of decreased rapidly. At twenty feet, there was nothing but emptiness. Between that, things became blurred and fuzzy, but still noticeable. I was also able to "see" through the thin walls of the vanity and wardrobe to examine the items within, but the much thicker walls, floor, and ceiling of the room itself were impenetrable from my senses. I wasn't sure why that was. Maybe there was a limit to the density or solidity I could observe and peer through? Eh, it didn't really bother me.

Giggle! "How cute! Look, Orleen! Jelly really likes his new home!"

My owner watched as I scooted around as quickly as I could, exploring my surroundings under the gaze of her and an older woman who stood nearby. The second person dressed in cheaper clothes that had a much different design than that of my owner's. I assumed it was because she was something called a "maid." Again, information I had no business possessing was somehow in my mind, informing me of this and that. What a maid was, exactly, was vaguer. But it seemed she served my owner, helping in a variety of ways. She had also been the voice I'd heard beside my owner, trying to convince the princess to pick another pet.

"It's certainly… energetic," the woman called Orleen replied. She, like most of the other people I'd met so far, seemed to be keeping their distance from me. I was an unusual creature to own as a pet. Even I knew that!

"I wonder if it can climb walls?" my owner mused.

"I do not know, my lady. I am unfamiliar with the abilities or habits of slimes."

My owner suddenly clapped her hands in excitement. "Look, look! He's trying to do it! Go on, Jelly! Climb that wall!"

Her words had made me curious about what I could do. Until now I had acted instinctively; I just did whatever it was I did without thinking about it. Suddenly though, I was trying desperately to cling onto the granite stones that made up the wall.

It didn't work. I wasn't able to get my gelatinous body to cling or stick to the stone. I felt vaguely disappointed that I wasn't able to meet my owner's expectations, and I slumped slightly.

"Oh, come here, Jelly!" I was swiftly scooped up in my owner's arms. "There, there. It's alright if you can't crawl on walls. You're still impressive. You're a good slime, aren't you?"

I quivered in agreement, and my owner nodded. "That's right! No need to be sad."

"My lady, it's time for supper." Orleen said up after a few moments. My owner just nodded her head in acknowledgement. She turned to the door and strode out, with me still cuddled in her arms. The maid opened her mouth to protest, but thought better of it and instead suppressed a sigh, following her mistress.

I was carried through countless hallways, corridors, and rooms. I had no more than momentary glimpses of the places I passed, but I was able to tell a few general features. Most of the corridors were made of stone, while the rooms tended to be wood paneled. Lamps dotted the walls everywhere interspersed with slit windows. Everything was of exceptional quality. Well-crafted, designed for both looks and sturdiness, even the heavier and more robust pieces of furniture were elegantly made.

My owner moved through and around it all with practiced ease. It was her home, after all. Even if it was expansive, you'd feel rather silly getting lost in your own house. After a few minutes, she emerged into a medium sized room, at least in comparison to other rooms I'd been in so far. It was rectangular and too wide for me to "see" all of it. I was able to get a grasp of its relative size because my owner walked around the edge of it to reach a certain spot.

It was a dining room. I made that assumption due to the wooden table laden with finely made dishware, glassware, cutlery, and platters of rich and hearty food. Four chairs were set up around the circumference of the table, two of them already occupied, whom my owner swiftly joined.

The person seated to the right of her was a woman. Older than the maid Orleen, she sat with poise and grace that I felt my owner try and emulate as she took her own seat. That was her mother, I realized. I could "feel" the similarities between the two. Her hair had immaculate straightness and silkiness and shone like ebony in the light. It was drawn up into a tightly coiled bun. Everything about her demurely, yet pointedly, said 'queen.'

The other person was a younger boy seated across from me and my owner. That had to be her brother. They had a similar "aura" and it made me wonder if it was a lineage trait. His hair was brown like his sister's with the faintest hint of curliness to them.

"Liliana, how was your day?" her mother inquired.

"It went well, dear mother. I went into the Purple District to get a pet."

"Yes, I remember you mentioning that. Did you finish your lessons first?"

"Of course mother," my owner said with only a momentary pause. My owner's mother sighed, faintly disappointed.

"You are already thirteen, my precious Lily," the queen spoke. "You may not like your studies but they are important for your future. After all, you are nearly an adult, and you have responsibilities as a princess."

Her mother's tone was clipped and scolding and Liliana meekly bent her head in acquiescence. The regal woman gave me a piercing and appraising stare when my owner's head was bowed. She said nothing, merely wrinkled her nose before ignoring me for the other occupant of the table.

"I suppose I also have to make sure you did your work as well, Julius," the queen said with a knowing look at her son. As his mother's attention fell on him the prince squirmed.

"Did you complete your lessons before going out to the gardens? And please do not try and deceive me, I can see the grass stains on your pants."

"Yes, mother. I made sure. Even the boring ones," Julius said with a grimace. His mother nodded, pleased.

"Excellent. I understand boys like to be rambunctious, but you are the Crown Prince of Varia. Remember what is expected of you."

Dark green eyes looked down at the table as he nodded. "Yes, mother, I understand."

Despite her attitude and words, I could feel a potent love coming from her directed at her children. As much as she was a queen, she was also a mother. It just appeared she had a harder time expressing that love.

A surge of power cut off my musings as it disrupted my senses. I tensed up, and my owner looked down at me in confusion. Her mother raised a delicate eyebrow at my antics. The momentary flash of overwhelming pressure passed and I relaxed. Still, I warily regarded the man who'd just entered the room. He was tall and broad shouldered, with the same color of hair and the same feel to his aura as my owner and her brother. He was clearly a strong man, not just physically or with magical powers. He had a charisma that was practically palpable. He filled the room with his presence.

He smiled widely at the seated family as he took his own spot at the table, across from his apparent wife with his children on either side.

"Good evening."

"Good evening, father," Liliana and Julius responded politely with respectful nods. His wife silently gave a warm smile.

As soon as he sat down servants entered the dining room carrying trays of food and drink. Eating quickly commenced, and for the first few minutes companionable silence was all there was to be had.

"How was work, dear?"

The king chewed both food and words for a bit before answering.

"Well enough. Geldstein has reported a slight boom in the trade of foodstuff passing through. No doubt Court Darpel will manage to hide all the profits from the taxmen again." A look that was hard to identify crossed his eyes. It smoothed over quickly as it came.

"Then I had another meeting with Duke Tein. He requested another loan."

"That father of mine," the queen sighed with a shake of her head. "I have no idea how my brother manages to keep the territory solvent with his reckless spending. He really should be pushing harder for father to retire already. Maybe you should say something, Tiberius."

"Amos Tein is a stubborn man and nothing short of death will get him to stop working. You know that Amdora. Besides, at least he uses the gold he mooches off of us for infrastructure instead of lining his pockets too much, unlike my other brother-in-law," the king replied.

"Is Uncle Darpel doing something bad again?" I heard Julius whisper, and there was a hint of fear in his voice.

"No, my son, he's just being difficult."

"It's alright, Julius! He would never try and hurt us! Last time was just an accident," Liliana said in an attempt to cheer up her brother. I saw dark looks cross over her parent's faces at that. It seemed that things with extended family were complicated.

"Enough unpleasant matters! If I recall, you were going out to the city today for some shopping," King Tiberius said, dispelling the gloomy mood.

He spared me a searching look before shifting attention over to Liliana.

"So, this is your new pet?"

"Yes, father," my owner said. A thin current of worry appeared in my owner, and I nuzzled her arms in solidarity.

"Where on Erafore did you get it? I cannot imagine any store around here selling a slime," the king inquired. "You didn't go down to the Slope or Wall District, did you?"

"I got him from the Gilded Parlor Pet Shop, down off Kaleidoscope Way in the Purple District," Liliana said. "He was on-sale as a novelty item."

"It looks funny." Julius's honest opinion caused some chuckles.

"He does, doesn't he?"

"Can I touch him?" the prince inquired, quickly switching pronouns when referring to me.

"Sure, Julius! Here!" My owner passed me over to her brother, and his eyes gleamed with interest as he took my body in his hands.

"So soft and squishy," He said with awe. I rumbled a bit at the praise, and he giggled in a way a lot like my owner.

"Should you really be bringing such a monster to the dining table?" the mother asked at last. King Tiberius shrugged.

"As long as it does not make a mess all over the place, I see no reason why it cannot join us every once in a while." At that, my owner let out a breath of relief. Julius passed me back over, and I settled into my owner's lap.

"How did you choose such a unique choice for your pet?" the father asked after a few minutes of some more small talk and dinner.

"Well, I was looking around all the various animals, when I saw a small glass tank in the corner. I was drawn to it, and was instantly entranced by this little guy. He looked so small and sad inside his glass case, and when I picked him up, it just felt right."

"Hmm." A noncommittal hum was her father's response to the story of our meeting. Still, I felt his eyes focus on me several times throughout the meal. That continued up until the end, as if he was judging me.

When supper ended, I was carried back to the room. I'd been fed small little samples and tidbits throughout the evening by both my owner and Julius. It had been a pleasant time in spite of feeling that the mother was not thrilled with my presence, or with her father's constant scrutiny of me.

My owner placed me on a fluffy cushion next to her bed. As I snuggled down into my impromptu bedding and she prepared for the evening I thought to myself (Still a novel action!) and reflected on my first day of life. I was still learning about myself and the world, but I couldn't shake that something important had happened because of me. Change was coming. And somehow I knew I was going to be right in the middle of it all.

The next few days were filled with learning, both about myself and my new owner and home. There was a lot.

Liliana was beautiful to me, and I gathered that the same was true for her fellow humans. Her hair was extremely straight, as if it were perpetually being ironed out, and was a soft, light brown color. Her eyes were glittering green, gem-like in a way. Her nose was like a button, and a smile graced her face almost constantly, giving her a doll-like appearance. Body-wise she was slender with the body of an adolescent just starting to become an adult.

My owner was quite enamored with knitting and embroidery, and had worked on making my bedding all on her own. Whenever she had free time she spent it playing with me, practicing her handicraft skills, or reading books in the impressive castle library. One of them at least.

Called the "Little Library," it was where the royal children had been tutored for countless generations in the castle. It could have desks moved around, and the shelves all contained easy to read materials for all manners of subjects. The room had massive bay windows that let in plentiful light, alongside mountains of candles for nightly sessions.

At one point during a regular trip to the small private library Liliana found me trying to reach for a book. It was not unusual for her to let me pick out something to read. I would gesture to a tome at random and she would then recite it to me, pointing at pictures and words I could not see. But it was the interaction that I craved.

Yet something about this particular book seemed to draw me in. I felt no magic other than the standard preservation and fireproofing charms, and none of the tomes in here contained magical secrets or enchantments. I was pulled towards it none the less.

"What is it Jelly? You want me to read this to you?" I bobbed up and down and she smiled. She pulled out the thick leather clad book and set it down on a nearby table.

"Let me see... Oh, this is a genealogy book of sorts. That is, it records information about my ancestors," Liliana explained. "You know, I don't think you know about the family, do you? Let's start at the beginning then!"

Eagerly flipping through the pages, she stopped at an early one.

"The House of Roan is directly descended from the old Imperial dynasty of Val'Narash, the big continent to the south. Sadly there was an event known as the Great Catastrophe which turned the whole of Erafore on its head. Our ancestors fled to Orria and built a new life here, founding the line of Ar-Varia, or *The Victorious* in the Elder Tongue." Liliana spoke slowly as she recited the words on the page, only altering them in a few places for me to understand them with context. "Much of that early time has been forgotten and lost. In fact, the earliest and best recorded figures of Varia's history belongs to Cyan Ar-Varia, the Savior-King, and his sister, my namesake, Liliana Ar-Varia."

When she spoke the name of her female ancestor, a tremor went through me. I had a connection to that name, somehow. One that was deeper than just my relation with my owner who had the same given name.

"Liliana Ar-Varia is well-known today, but unfortunately the reason for that is a sad tale. About two thousand years ago much of Orria was invaded and conquered by the forces of the Second Elfish Domain. Cyan and Liliana's father was slain in battle and Varia became subjugated. Worship of our gods was restricted. For a dozen years mankind languished under the whips of the elves," my owner lamented, stroking my head comfortingly. "For Liliana this was a hard time for she was a priestess of Cynthia, Goddess of Light. The exact reason for what happened next is subject to much debate, but the gist of it is that she angered the occupying force's leader and was

27

ordered to be executed for some religious matter. Her pet, a loyal Lily-lynx, escaped the capture and brought word to Cyan who had been forbidden from seeing his sister for years and exiled to serve the defenses against the monsters and bandits along the borders."

"Long story short, Cyan was unable to reach his dear sister in time," Liliana said sorrowfully. "He arrived only to find her already dead. He then swore vengeance and waged war for five years to drive the elves from Varia and then from Orria! He was hailed a hero, but he never forgot why he had done so."

"The Church of the Divine Family named Liliana Ar-Varia the Martyred Saintess, Lady of the Lilies, and many other titles. But for King Cyan he gave her the greatest honor he could. He named his eldest daughter Liliana to honor her legacy, and so the tradition has been passed on. The eldest daughter of the royal family has been named 'Liliana' for countless generations."

"And you know what else? There was one other thing that my namesake gave me," Liliana whispered conspiratorially to me. "You see, there exist things known as Bloodline Traits in this world.

Potent magical abilities that can allow a person to wield strange and unique powers obtained from birth and handed down to one's children. I have one. As do Julius and father. Passed down in the royal family from the first of the Ar-Varians, I possess the ability known as *Miraculous Mystery*."

"No one really understands it, hence the name," Liliana explained, leaning on the open book as she looked down at me with a pensive frown. "In moments of great danger or life changing events it is said to activate to save its owners, or to allow us to bless others with the grace of divinity. It is also supposed to nudge me along, giving me hints about what my fate is, and what I need to do."

"Truthfully, I believe when that the day I found you I had been drawn to the pet store. I think I was meant to find you."

I nuzzled her arm. I am thankfully to her ancestors if this was the case. Thanks to her magic, I was able to find a home and a family.

On the topic of relatives, my interactions with Queen Amdora were limited. We saw each other rarely, and only when I was with Liliana. She kept her distance from me and I guessed she hoped my owner would grow bored and discard me eventually. I had no fears on that end. The princess utterly doted on me.

I ended up spending an afternoon with her at one point. My owner had joined her mother for a small tea party with a few other noble ladies when the queen cornered Liliana in the library one day. It was held in one of the rooms of the palace as a sudden squall had made the usual spot in the gardens unavailable.

For the event Liliana was in a sensible powder blue dress with a red ribbon wrapped around her waist like a sash. For accessories she only wore her necklace and the enchanted ring.

Queen Amdora wore much more jewelry and fancier clothes, but did not look overdone. The overly ruffled and laced silver and red dress along with the rings and brooches all emphasized her royal bearing.

In the sitting room hosting the tea party I sat in my owner's lap with the queen on her right. With us were three other noblewomen. Two around the queen's age while the third was probably only a few years older than Liliana. They all gave me strange looks when they spotted me but quickly ignored my presence as they chatted with the royal pair.

"It's a shame Countess Darpel could not attend," the oldest of the three claimed.

"Indeed, Lady Tamira. But my sister-in-law runs Geldstein as much as her husband, if not more so," Queen Amdora stated.

"I suppose operating the richest fief in Varia takes more than a little time and effort," the noble woman conceded. Her companions nodded.

"Doesn't hurt that they are so close to the Crawling Coast. All that maritime trade is only going to grow now that the colonies in Drakon are becoming successful," the youngest guest pointed out. A round of agreements came out that at.

"Speaking of growing, is your son still as excitable as always?" Lady Tamira inquired of the queen. Amdora sighed dramatically at that, making her daughter and I snicker quietly.

"Dear Julius is a little too fond of the outdoors and the stories of adventurers. He tracks in mud and grit even when he steps out for a minute," the queen lamented. "At least my daughter has a level head, if a bit full of those same far-off tales."

"You know I cannot help but notice the critter you have with you, Princess Liliana," the young noblewoman said, bringing attention to me at last. The queen took a sip from her tea to cover her frown.

"Jelly has been nothing but an excellent companion so far," Liliana praised. "He's clean and makes no messes and is hardly a picky eater, Viscountess Silvia. I could not ask for a better pet."

I preened at her words and sat up a little straighter in her lap.

"Still, do you not worry that it might harm someone? Tamed or not it is still a monster," the third woman pointed out.

"I fully trust him. The only incident he's had so far was when he broke a vase practicing his jumping." To demonstrate she placed me on the ground. I was fully on board with showing off and I scrunched up slightly before leaping a foot into the air.

I held back as at full height my bouncing could reach four feet. Aside from squirming along the floor or rolling like a pillow full of gelatin jumping was my only other method of locomotion. By tightly compressing myself I essentially turned into a living bouncing ball.

I moved by inching my body along sort of like a snake crossed with an inchworm, although the speed was quick for such a seemingly inefficient method of movement. I could keep up with a brisk walking pace with no trouble. And hurling myself like a tiny missile was also a decent way to get about.

"And that is not all he can do. Jelly, shake!"

Upon my princess' command I created a stubby little pseudopod limb that reached out to Liliana and slipped into her hand. She then enthusiastically pumped it up and down. I lifted off the floor with each movement of her arm, to the amusement of the guests.

This was another neat trick I had figured out. It was harder than it looked. They were barely useful for gripping anything and I could also only produce three at a time, though from any part of my body. But at least I had the option of limbs with which to grab and interact with. My world was steadily opening up the more I understood myself.

Polite applause greeted me when I ceased performing and Liliana gave me a finger sandwich for my troubles. I took it eagerly, letting my gelatinous body envelop the piece of food. In seconds the snack dissolved inside me and I hummed in thanks. I lacked a sense of taste so I couldn't say if it had been an exceptional sandwich or not. Part of being an Ooze, as well as the fact that my entire body was essential a stomach that could digest anything. From dirt to meat to pieces of the vase I accidentally broke, I had yet to encounter something inedible for me.

"Yes, Liliana's slime has been an easy one to care for. It certainly saves us from buying any specialty foods. And with the price of fodder on the rise that is a good aspect in my books," Queen Amdora said. Her praise was hollow however.

"Brune's ranches would probably pay a premium for feed. My husband has been looking for new business now that some additional fields have been cleared. I should see if he'd be interested," the viscountess mused, and I saw a glimmer of victory in Queen Amdora's eyes.

"I should introduce you to the Linwell Company. They've started doing business in the south recently and I think they'd be glad to help." A thankful nod was the queen's reply, and I saw the queen's game.

Gossip and business were her duties after all. As the wife of one of the most influential men in the world she had her own ways to manage the kingdom and its prominent figures.

"I have to say I am surprised that the little slime has not gotten into more trouble. No offense but seeing a monster roaming around would give me a bit of a scare. And of course our queen is known to have a 'blast first, ask later' attitude in regards to being startled."

"Countess Cleren, please! I'll have you know I have not done such a thing in a long time," Queen Amdora protested. Liliana just smiled and the other ladies smirked.

"I remember when I was at the Royal Varian Mage's Academy with you, your majesty, and I seem to recall more than a few 'mishaps' with your spells when someone bothered you," Lady Tamira chuckled as she teased the queen. "Did they ever repair that scorch mark in the southern gardens?"

"Yes they did. I helped."

"Better watch out there, Princess Liliana. I don't know how well a slime can endure fireballs at close range."

"Thank you for your warnings, Lady Tamira. But I'm sure mother would never try to hurt my precious Jelly."

What looked suspiciously like guilt danced across her features but were gone before anyone save myself could notice. I made mental notes to stay alert around Queen Amdora in the future.

"Don't worry. If you are anything like your mother your magic should be more than plenty to heal any damage she does to your pet," Countess Cleren assured my owner. "Her talent as a mage is renowned for a reason, after all."

A bright smile lit up my owner's face at the compliment. She really looked up to her parents, after all.

On the matter of parents there was only one person I had spent little time with getting to know him. But what I did told me that the king of Varia was an interesting man. When not doing paperwork in his office, King Tiberius met with officers and officials from other nations as well as his own. Much like what his wife did, but in less social settings. The busy king nonetheless tried to spend dinner time with his family. I could tell he was a doting father, and my owner and her brother both loved him dearly.

Each time he looked at me it seemed that he suspected that his daughter had done something to me. I was not a typical example of my species. We both knew it, even he couldn't say what it was exactly, and I felt he was expecting big things to come from my existence. What truly made him a person of interest to me was that he possessed an even greater magical ability than his children. I worried often in those early days that he might take away my newly acquired ability to think and perceive the world around me. Perhaps this was an overreaction on my part, but was a fear that persisted regardless of any logic.

But it was while I studied the family I had been brought into that I learned about myself as well.

My ability to observe my surroundings was constantly working. Even when I slept, if something I deemed to be a danger got too close I'd be forcefully awakened. I learned about that when a cat thought I'd make a nice bed, and I reacted by scaring it off with angry jiggling. Those claws really hurt.

To breathe I took in air through my skin. Even if submerged in water, I could still absorb oxygen to survive, like the gills of a fish only all over me.

But learning about myself and my family took a back seat at times. I was content to spend time with my dear owner, playing with her and her brother, and being fed morsels of food. No one dared to openly speak ill of me, at least around my owner. They assumed I was just a mindless animal, and spoke openly in my presence. Gossip and scandals quickly became as common to my 'ears' as the praise Liliana gave to me. And I liked it. If the loose lips of the servants could potentially give me information to help my owner, then I would take it all. Of course, I had no way to convey any of it. But that was an issue for another time to resolve.

Chapter 3: Lunch in the garden

"Be sure not to go too far, Jelly! Try to stay within the garden!" Liliana called out to me, and I acknowledged her with a jiggle of my body.

I was outside in the royal gardens, a large, semi-enclosed region of the castle that acted as both a greenhouse for fruits and vegetables the kitchens used, and a headily scented spot for tea parties and entertaining guests. It was a fabulous place, filled with healthy plant life of all sorts.

It was late summer, and the normally blistering heat was somewhat muted. Partly because the castle was built along the side of the Starblind Mountains, keeping it cool due to altitude and wind, but also thanks to a handful of runes carved into the walls that regulated the temperature and kept things from boiling over. Runes were common throughout Varia. From simple ones to boil water and create light, to complex ones like those here in the castle that keep summers cool and winters warm. While most peasants couldn't afford something that complex or advanced, magical items were wide-spread enough that even poorer families could have one or two runic or enchanted items with basic effects.

Liliana had brought me to the garden after worrying that I was spending too much time inside the castle. It had been fifteen days since I was purchased, and I had felt a bit cramped at times. So, while she was partaking in some lessons outdoors, Liliana allowed me to roam about in the garden for a bit.

Meandering through rows of hedges, flower bushes, and trimmed trees, I felt invigorated by the nature all around me. I tried to catch a bird at one point just to see if I could. It dodged my limp tentacle easily and flew off with twittering that sounded remarkably like laughter. If I could've shrugged, I would have. I was not really hungry, I just wanted to see if I could do anything with my squishy appendages.

Deciding that it would be a good idea to practice coordination with my limbs I began trying to pick flowers. After an hour I successfully managed to do so without dissolving the target while it was wrapped by my limb. My control over my bodily functions was progressing well. I bobbed a bit in place, proud of my latest achievement.

For lunch I gulped down some berries that had fallen from their branches. They were called "blueberries," I believe, and were a bit on the spoiled side. That was what I get for grabbing food off of the dirt, I suppose. I didn't mind, though. I couldn't really claim I had anything like the ability to taste food. I preferred some kinds of edibles, true, but I could, and often did, eat anything offered to me.

Mold and bugs were devoured and digested just like bread and soup. I have to say I did not like spicy foods. They tingled, for lack of a better word, as I dissolved them, and mint did the same thing. Such foods tended to be overpowering for humans as well, so perhaps I'd inherited my owner's food preferences? Sugar was one thing I could "taste," and was something I enjoyed immensely. It wasn't a common addition to any meal, and even the heavenly caramels Julius offered me were a rare treat.

Salt was another story. I was like a slug or snail whenever I came into contact with salt. I am mostly liquid and mana with only a bit of solid mass holding me together. I shrank and contracted, my body drying out, when salt entered me. My owner and I panicked a bit when that first happened. The heavily salted pork she fed me cut my size in half when I ate just a forkful. Julius and the King just laughed. It was a funny event as I look back, but I wished Liliana's mother hadn't looked so eager during my plight.

While lost in these thoughts I came across something that I sensed was out of place. It looked like an ordinary rose bush, but under my unique gaze I could tell it was anything but. Oh, it had been a rose bush not too long ago, but now it had something growing beneath it. A parasitic worm had attached itself to the roots of the bush and was slowly altering the plant in subtle ways. The thorns of the roses were now producing a paralytic toxin, while the pollen contained hallucinogenic properties. None of these changes affected me, but to a human it would be dangerous, if not outright deadly. The creature currently responsible was easily three times my size, and looked to be mostly a mouth, sharp teeth, and stomach. If I had to guess, it would emerge from the soil to devour whatever was rendered unconscious by its altered roses. As a result of the changes the plant itself didn't look too healthy. There seemed to be considerable strain on the bush due to the mutations it was undergoing.

I wobbled indecisively. I understood that I could not leave this dangerous creature alone; at the very least I had to inform a gardener somehow. Fighting that creature was likely a bad idea, as it was much larger than I was. But I was unable to communicate by vocal means, and the odds of no one paying attention to my warnings even if I could were high.

I sighed –somehow- and did the only thing I could think of. I began to eat the rose bush. I tore branches and blossoms off as quickly as I could, devouring them so the pollen and poison did not continue to cover the area. I then nibbled at the roots, making them bleed sap. Hopefully that would kill the bush sooner and the monster taking up residence in the foliage would leave.

As I digested the meal I could feel the poisons and chemicals I had ingested sloshing around inside me, their matter slowly assimilating into myself. It was unlike any meal I'd had before. There was a vivid bitter taste to these substances.

I couldn't help but feel uneasy about the whole situation as I digested. Something had drawn me to the bush, I was certain of it. A tug on my soul, a warning bell in my head.

Satisfied with my work I wiggled away, pausing by another plant, an un-possessed rose bush, to snag a few stems.

I returned to Liliana, her lessons close to finished, and presented her the bunch of roses clutched in my tendrils. She took them with undisguised glee, petting my top fondly.

"Are these for me?" I nodded and she laughed happily, touched by my gesture.

"Thank you so much, Jelly. This is a lovely and kind gift. Let's just hope the gardeners don't get too mad at you."

I shivered at that, and Liliana smiled comfortingly. "I'll get some water and a vase for these. Thank you again, Jelly. You're a doll."

She scooped me up into her arms for a quick hug and nuzzle, and I forgot my earlier discomfort. This was a good day, all things considered.

"Anything to report on the home front?" King Tiberius asked, making his way down the halls of the castle to the dining room. Aides and servants scurried around him, carrying documents, notes, and other items of business for him to look over later.

"The head gardener would like to speak about a recent matter," an aide spoke up, and a man in dirty, grass stained clothes stepped up hesitantly.

"Your Majesty, earlier today the princess's new pet was in the royal garden, and it, well, made a commotion and uncovered a problem."

"How so?" The tone was clipped. Tiberius was not a harsh man, but he was curious as to why this matter was being brought up to him at all. Certainly, the little slime had few allies, but to actively bother him about it was discouraged by the staff.

Noticing his lord's tone, the head gardener quickly explained.

"At first we thought it had attacked and destroyed a rose bush. A silly act from a monster, you know. But on inspection, we found that the plant had been taken over by a Rose Worm."

The king's expression sharpened. He gave full attention to the man in charge of the gardens.

"A Rose Worm? Here?"

"Yes, my king. We dug it up and quickly killed it. And from the looks of things the slime noticed the infestation and ripped out the infected parts of the plant before anyone could get hurt by them."

"What was a Rose Worm doing in my garden? And are there any others?"

"As soon as we found the first, we checked all the rest of the rose plants. We found two more, all in the early stages of corruption. They were eliminated quickly, needless to say. We're not sure how they got in. The magical wards should have repelled any kind of monster, including the princess' pet, from even approaching the castle's perimeter, let alone the interior parts of it. I'd like to request that someone examine the garden to see if they can find any breaches or issues with the magical defenses."

"It seems that the slime noticed something was wrong with the bush, and likely acted to protect the princess," the head gardener continued. "If it hadn't, we'd probably have had some casualties before we noticed anything."

"Thank you for the report. I'll send word to the Academy to send a mage or two down to check on the barriers as soon as possible," Tiberius stated, as scribes scribbled down notes to do as their king wished. "You have my thanks for the swift actions of you and your staff. Take the evening off once you're finished checking on the garden."

"Glad to be of service, my king." the gardener bowed deeply before walking off in a hurry.

"See to it that he and his men have an extra glass of ale for their dinner as a reward for quick thinking. And inform the Academy I want a team inspecting every inch of the castle's wards and interior for anything unusual," Tiberius ordered once the gardener was gone, and a servant nodded before dashing off in the direction of the kitchen, while another went to fetch a messenger hawk.

The king sighed, massaging his forehead, before putting on a smile as he approached the dining room where his family waited. He was glad Lili's pet had uncovered a hidden threat, and was fairly certain that the slime knew what it was doing. Whenever he watched it, the blob seemed to know he was observing it, and not just like an animal would acknowledge another person. There was something human in the way that tiny monster seemed to stared back, and Tiberius had a feeling it knew that he knew.

He strode into the room his family sat in with his usual flourish. Giving his son, daughter, and wife smiles, he absentmindedly continued to ponder the Ooze's situation. He had seen a lot in his many years. From cursed artifacts to rebellious lords. Yet he had never seen a slime act this way before.

There were too many inconsistencies with how it acted for it to be an ordinary Ooze. There was always a chance that someone had tampered with it to create a hidden assassin. An extremely small chance, admittedly. But eight years ago someone had tried to murder his family by setting fire to their vacation manor. And before he had married his darling queen his own siblings had tried to usurp the throne from him. He had become overly sensitive to anything that might harm his family as a result.

As long as it didn't become a threat to his family, he had no issues with it. In fact he thought it was a good influence on his daughter. Teaching her responsibility and what not. Still, cross him, and the monster would learn why Tiberius was king.

Chapter 4: Bath time for a slime!
There is nothing better than a warm bath!

Liliana was a princess, and it was expected that she be clean and fresh scented as often as possible. Possessing wealth and resources, she was able to bath every day if she so wished. That could be seen as expensive and wasteful, however, and so every two days she was allowed to fully immerse herself in the soap, suds, and waters of the royal bath. On alternate days she was wiped down by her maids and spritzed with perfumes.

Liliana loved having me accompany her into the baths. The maids in charge of her had at first protested. They argued I would make the area much messier, or even melt into a puddle thanks to excess water. But she resisted, insisted, and pouted, and finally her servants gave in. Maybe they hoped I would dissolve. But it didn't happen, and soon I was being scrubbed by a bristly brush and lathered in soap alongside my owner, who took a great deal of pleasure in being able to clean me herself.

And I admit, it felt pleasant. I had no nerves, but I could still feel. The sensations of cloth, brush, soap and water passing over my body created a wonderful feeling all over.

My first bathing experience occurred on my second day in the castle. Until then I'd never had a bath, or actively cleaned myself, at least to my limited knowledge. It was a novel experience.

My body was self-cleaning to a degree. I could, and did, just absorb dirt and grime that accumulated upon me, and assimilate it. But there was something soothing about the act of bathing, and I let my owner enjoy herself as she cleaned me.

The day after my garden adventurer was bath day. My owner happily carried me into the bathing room. It was a large, stone room, with a tub made of polished white marble set into the center. It was a foot off the floor, and twelve feet wide. It could fit the entire royal family in it with only a bit of a squeeze. I wondered if that had happened at all when she and her brother had been younger. Did humans even do communal bathing?

Water was added into the bath via a contraption that pumped up cold water from one of the many wells connected to the palace and into a brass heater. In a room directly below the bathroom, a boiler heated it with a harsh burning wood fire. If it was summertime a series of etched runestones could activate to boil the water with magic. Then the steaming hot water was redirected back up another pipe and into the tub in the floor above. A complex but ingenious system.

Beside the marble tub were stone trestle-tables and benches with many grooming implements laid alongside glass vials of shampoo and blocks of scented soap. Dry towels were kept in a smaller adjoining room, since the humid bathing-room air could quickly dampen fabric.

My owner entered the bathroom from yet another adjacent room where she'd undressed, wrapped only in a towel to preserve her modesty. A few maids entered with her. Since full baths were uncommon for non-royalty, it was a treat, even a reward, for servants to assist in the main bathing room.

These helpers wore loose fitting robes and underclothes in the presence of their lord or lady. The servants got cleaned by proxy while washing their mistress. It was a luxurious experience compared to what they could expect in their own homes. A trio of maids accompanied Liliana, including Orleen. She was the head maid in charge of caring for the princess. The other two were just a lucky pair who'd been selected for that day.

"My lady if you don't mind, I will hold your pet for you while you get in," Orleen said as she directed the others to fill the tub. Liliana shot a glance that was almost suspicious at her chief maid, but consented and passed me over.

I wondered why Orleen was volunteering to be the one to hold me. Usually she fobbed the job off onto one of the other girls. I got my answer when she whispered to me "Thank you."

I remained still, but inside I buzzed with confusion. Had Orleen, the stern older maid, just thanked me?

"Yesterday, you ate a rose bush. A monster known as a Rose Worm had attached to it." Oh, so that's what that monster was known as. A fitting name.

"My husband works as a gardener in the area where they keep the roses. I don't know if you knew what you were doing or not, but you prevented him, and so many others, from being harmed. Thank you."

Orleen began to absent mindedly pat my 'head' while I remained still and silent. She eventually broke the mood with a small chuckle from under her breath. "It's funny. Here I am thanking a slime that doesn't even understand me, or knows that what it did probably many lives. If the other servants could see me, they'd all laugh."

In response, I gurgled and rubbed up against the hand that was petting me in a manner I thought was a comforting one. She froze, before stiffly resuming her patting.

We spent a few minutes in companionable silence before she brought me back to my owner so Liliana could have her fun with cleaning me. As Orleen retreated a few feet to stand watch, I thought back on what she had said. My actions had alerted the staff to a problem, and in turn they managed to prevent a disaster. Maybe that was why I had been given that mind. To protect people. Not just my dear owner, but others as well. I'd acted to defend Liliana, and in doing so I potentially saved the life of a man who had a loving family. If that wasn't a good reason for my new found gifts, I didn't know what was.

I snuggled deep into Liliana's arms as she rinsed lather from my body. I had saved a life, something that might not have happened if I'd not been my owner's pet. What else was I going to change with my presence? A warm glow filled me.

Chapter 5: Two mages and a potion tasting

Did you know that potions of healing taste like strawberries?

That odd bit of knowledge came to me when I accidentally slurped up the contents of a spilled bottle.

I could actually taste magic, and it translated into flavors and sensations I knew of, but had never experienced. Somehow, whatever force gave me a mind and ability to instinctively "know" information taught me what certain foods taste like, even if I cannot taste them normally. If I ate an actual strawberry, it would have no real taste. But the magical potions brewed for healing? They do taste like strawberries, and I knew that even if I did not know what that fruit really was like. Was that another connection to my dear owner? Do healing potions usually have the flavor of strawberries to them, even for human patients?

Wait, I'm getting a bit off track. Let me explain how I first managed to snag a sample of liquid magic.

You see, I inadvertently created a stir in the castle when I uncovered that infected rose bush and ate it. It seems the culprits responsible, a species called Rose Worms, should not have been able to enter the barriers that surround the castle. It protected the castle from weak monsters and magical beasts.

But the Rose Worms, which fell into the category of magical beasts, had somehow gotten into the garden. That was why the king had immediately summoned a team of wizards to investigate the cause. Either the barrier had faded, broken, or someone had smuggled a trio of dangerous monsters into the palace. Needless to say, no option was good, but the latter was the worst of them.

Liliana had wanted to see the mages arrive, and so was standing in the back of the main hall with me in her arms, an eager smile on her face. Julius had also pleaded to see the visitors as well and he was standing next to his sister.

"Do you think they've been on adventures?" Julius wondered, shifting from foot to foot in his excitement.

"Certainly! They probably go on all sorts of missions and jobs all over the world!" Liliana assured. "I bet they've seen tons of monsters as well!"

"Wow! Monsters! Maybe they've seen lots of Jelly's family, too!" Julius mused excitedly, shooting me a wide eyed look.

That's probable. Oozes were the most commonly encountered monster amongst adventurers, or so it was said. And talented magic users were well respected for the variety of uses for their spells. Odds were though that any mage who'd encountered my kind had made short work of them. Hopefully none of them would attack me on sight.

As I was thinking that morbid thought, the doors opened and a pair of men in robes were escorted into the hall. The first person to enter was a bit on the pudgy size, with a hint of a belly poking through his robes.

He was the oldest of the two, and carried himself with practiced ease. He had training in courtly etiquette, and it shone through his measured steps and calculating gaze. He was also the oldest person I'd ever seen so far. His beard was a luxurious veil that buried his chin, neck, and chest in grey. His head, though bald, was covered by an absurdly large, pointed hat.

In his right hand was a smooth wooden stick that had a band of gold wrapped around the tip. It had a slight crook at the top that clutched a thumb sized opal stone. It was a wizard cane, the defacto symbol of a mage and the medium through which one might channel and cast their spells.

The other was thin as a rake, noticeable even through his billowing clothes. His skin was the pale color typically associated with a lack of sun, and his face looked as if he skipped more meals than ate. He had wispy scraps of a beard on his chin, and appeared to be a decade or so younger than the king. Though telling a person's age with my "sight" was a series of trials. He did not have a staff, instead opting for a silver wand stuffed into a pocket on his robes.

Both of them radiated magic, their bodies aglow with their own mana and the sealed power of the various enchanted items on their person. The older one had more magical power, but his follower was not far behind.

King Tiberius approached the duo and gave them a short nod which they returned.

"I'm glad the Academy could dispatch you so quickly. I hope I do not need to explain how this situation had concerned us all."

"Of course not, your majesty. You are an important figure, and an important patron. Any threat to you and your family is worth the expedience," the oldest wizard spoke, his sentiments echoed by a bobbing head from his companion.

"Please, no need to stand too much on formality, Renos. That the Academy chose to send an old family friend and the most skilled shield-mage alive is a welcome surprise." The wizard called Renos just nodded his head again at the praise.

"I suppose I should introduce the man beside me. This is Petrus Goyn, one of the best apprentices I've taught in a while. He is as skilled at barriers and wards as I am, and with training I hope to have him surpass me, and eventually succeed as the next head of the Magical Defense Department."

"It is an honor to meet you, your majesty. I hope to live up to my mentor's praise." The young man called Petrus bowed low, and the king nodded in approval.

"A pleasure to meet you as well. Now, I believe we should get started."

"Please, show us to the garden, and we'll check the wards," Renos said in agreement, and they moved on. Liliana and Julius tagged along from behind, chatting to each other about the two wizards.

"Here, the royal garden," King Tiberius stated, leading the group into the sweet scented air of the walled region.

"Petrus, scan the area."

"Yes, Sir Renos." The young man hurried off into the gardens, waving his wand in slow, measured movements. I felt strands of magical power coiling and shifting into odd, complex shapes as he worked. That was how I perceived spells; as a tangled mess of luminous shapes interlocked and working in tandem to produce a result. I was most intrigued. I wanted to learn more!

"And these young ones behind us are your children, I presume?" Renos uttered without turning around. Ah, so he had magical senses as well. That was good to know.

"Yes!" Liliana declared proudly, before stepping forward and bowing her head to the elder wizard. Julius followed my owner's actions, bowing and greeting the master mage.

"It is a pleasure to meet you!"

"A pleasure to meet you as well, Princess Liliana, and you too Prince Julius. And that critter in your arms?" Renos greeted before catching sight of me.

"This is Jelly! He's my pet!" Liliana said, happy to show me off to someone. And, to my surprise, I did not see any hostility in the wizard's gaze. Merely curiosity.

"It's not often I see such a well behaved Ooze. You must have quite the talent in raising animals," Renos praised, peering at me. I felt magic flicker behind his eyes as he examined me. A clear sign that a spell was being used on me. A type of magical analysis, most likely. I did not react. No matter how much my primal side was shouting at me to attack and then flee, I remained calm. His job right now was to protect the royal family, and if it helped Liliana I would put up with the scrutiny. For now.

"It looks healthy. And remarkably well trained," Renos concluded, flashing Liliana a warm smile.

"How can you tell he's both of those things?" She asked, a barely perceptible tilt to her head.

"For the first part, you can tell an Ooze's state of health based on the sheen of their body. Judging by the shininess of your pet it is nice and happy. On the second point, Ooze are not exactly fond of people using magic around them. Even something as basic as a light-making spell, or *Detect Magic*. They tend to act violently towards those who do. A defense mechanism for their kind, since offensive spells are one of the few things that affect their gooey forms," Renos explained, impressing Liliana and myself with his knowledge.

I had known that, but on an instinctive level. This might be connected to the information that popped into my head.

Baths and people were related in some way to what Liliana herself knew. Things she did not know, like this background on my own species, was bereft from my mind. Curious.

"Jelly had always been well behaved. He's always calm and nice," Liliana assured, and Reno nodded in response.

"Her pet was the reason we uncovered the Rose Worms in the first place," King Tiberius interjected. "It vandalized a bush that was undergoing the mutation process, which alerted the gardeners that something may have been wrong with it. The rest is as you know."

"I see." Renos shot me another searching look, though without magic this time. "Yet more proof that your 'Jelly' is a loyal pet, Princess Liliana."

Liliana nodded happily.

"You know, my student, Petrus, is fascinated by magical creatures. I think he'd like to meet Jelly sometime. He is a very interesting Ooze," Renos continued, off-handedly and indirectly asking my owner her permission to study me. That did not go unnoticed by the king or me. It flew right over the children's heads however and Liliana just looked thrilled to have someone else interested in me.

"Sir, your majesty, I think I found something." The king and the elderly mage looked up sharply at Petrus' call, and quickly walked over to where the younger wizard was standing. Curious, Liliana and Julius followed behind once more, and I am brought along for the ride. Not that I mind. I am just as intrigued by what we might learn.

Petrus was standing at the edge of the gardens, near to where I'd found the Rose Worm in the first place. He was near the wall that encircles the lush habitat, beneath the boughs of a gnarled old peach tree. The student glances over at us as we approach, and his gaze lingered on me for a moment before turning back to his teacher and the king.

"The wards have been worn thin here and here. It looks like the rains from a year ago washed away a portion of the foundation stones next to this tree. And then, a root from the tree jutted out and created a bridge of sorts. The root blocked the barrier from fully forming. There is a tiny gap where a Rose Worm could, and apparently did, wiggle through. Here, you see this?" Petrus pointed down at the soil, where a bulge could be seen. "That is displaced dirt where something the size of an adult Rose Worm tunneled through. All in all, a simple problem to fix, and one I've already remedied. I moved the root and reestablished the wards so this would not happen again." King Tiberius looked relieved, as did the mentor. It was just a coincidence.

"Mister Goyn, Sir Renos said you liked magical creatures. This is Jelly, my pet Ooze!" Liliana spoke up once she had confirmed the mood was back to normal. The man blinked but turned a smile onto my owner as I was held out to him.

"An impressive looking specimen!" He praised, and I preened slightly. His words were sincere, and the two royal children escort him off to show me off. We moved away from the king and the older mage, and soon they were beyond my sensory range.

Now we finally came to the event that gave me my first taste of delicious potions.

Liliana and Julius led Petrus to a gazebo-like building that sat in the center of the gardens. It was a few feet from an artificial pond that doubled as a water source for the plants, and was surrounded on all sides by waist high flower bushes.

The gazebo was painted white and had enough room to fit a table and ten chairs; perfect in every way as a location for a fancy tea party. Right now there were only five chairs around a smaller table, and they were quickly occupied by three buttocks.

"What's it like being a mage?" Julius asked, looking up starry eyed at Petrus.

"A lot of hard work, actually. It's fun and rewarding, but you have to study to be able to perform spells properly," Petrus admitted. The young prince grumbled about lessons and mean teachers.

"What do you do at the Academy, Mister Goyn? Do you go out on adventures?" Liliana asked next, and the mage leans back in his chair, trying to get comfortable.

"I'm a senior student up at the Royal Varian Mages Academy. That means I'm apprenticing directly under one of the various professors and mages there. Master Renos is my mentor and also the head of Magical Defenses. He and I specialize in wards, barriers, and magical methods of protection," the novice wizard explained, seeing the uncomprehending faces of his listeners. "And I haven't gotten to go on many adventures yet, though I do accompany Master Renos on his jobs often. Once I complete my studies underneath him I'll likely register with the Adventurer's Guild to get some real life experience in the field for a year or so."

"That sounds like a lot of fun," Julius said with a longing expression. My owner nodded in agreement. I knew that the two long for freedom of sorts. They were cooped up in the castle almost 27/6. They took whatever escapes they could from their gilded cage. Stories about adventurers and heroes always enthralled them. I didn't mind listening to them either, but I have to admit I disliked the stories with lots of monsters being vanquished. It could have been me in those situations, after all.

"So, you wanted me to meet your pet?" Petrus asked, shifting focus onto me. Liliana nodded and held me out to the mage, and he gingerly accepted.

"He's rather heavy. Does he eat a lot?" He asked, weighing me with his hands. I huffed internally. No one likes to be called fat, good sir! And I'm not fat! I am pleasantly plump! At all times!

"Is that bad?" Liliana asked, her question to his question an admission of sorts.

"No, just don't overfeed him. Oozes grow in size when they eat a lot, and it can be permanent. They often don't stay this small for long."

"How big will he get?" Julius inquired, and Petrus shrugged in reply.

"What sort of things do you know about Oozes, sir Petrus? The books I've found in the libraries are not exactly well informed on this subject," Liliana asked as the mage examined me.

"That's understandable. Unfortunately, Oozes are so well known there is rarely any research done on them. Only the more obscure subspecies and variants get any attention. As for what I know: an Ooze, also commonly referred to as a slime, is what is known as a monster. That means it is more magic than solid matter. They're merely amorphous blobs of magical gel and goo, created when wild, ambient mana gathers and coagulates," Petrus explained as he continued to poke and prod me.

"An Ooze is a fairly common monster. A single Ooze is an annoyance at most but they can also be considered dangerous for a few reasons. One of which is, ironically, their universality and rate of reproduction. In regions that have suffered cataclysmic magical damage slimes emerge constantly until the mana is used up. Next, their semi-solid nature allows them to resist most physical damage. Only extremely violent attacks and magical energy could harm us in any meaningful way."

"And the third reason for their infamy is in their adaptability. They can live anywhere. From swamps to tundra to caverns below the surface of the world. They can mutate, changing form and function to fit into their new ecosystem. An Ooze from a swampy area would likely become darker colored and able to resist poisons. In colder regions they'd become immune to lower temperatures and even siphon heat from other living things."

"Oozes have no eyes or mouth or features of any kind. They move around with what we assume is a form of echolocation, like a bat," the senior student continued as the royal children listened closely.

"They are roughly spherical in shape. At the center of their body lies their core; a nucleus of sorts, made of the same material as the rest of the body, but harder. Not too hard, as it is able to bend and shape itself if need be, but clearly different. It is much darker in color, so it stands out amid the opaque material that comprises an Ooze. It contains what I tentatively would refer to as a brain, a stomach, and a few other organ-like features. Not exactly like that, though, as these "organs" are all one but also distinct. It 'grows' the sludge their body is composed of like a film that constantly overlaps its core, and absorbs the nutrients from whatever it eats via the digestive fluids inside the gel. In short the core is the most vital part of an Ooze. If the core were to be damaged for any reason it would heal slowly. But if it were broken or removed from the body for too long it would perish. Such a glaring weakness is yet another reason why slimes tend to be regarded so lowly as monsters."

Petrus nodded to himself when he was done with me, lowering me to the table. I burbled in appreciation. As informative as his lecture had been I felt weird being handled by someone other than the princess for so long.

"He appears to be a normal Ooze. Greenish blue in coloration, no larger than two and a half feet in diameter and width, and weighing no more than twenty pounds," the wizard supplied. I briefly worried that I'd grow too large for Liliana. Hopefully I'd stay fun-sized for a long time.

That's big," Julius said in child-like wonder, echoed by his sister.

"Hardly. Some Ooze sub-species can grow enormous. In fact, the largest Ooze type is the Lake Ooze. They can grow as large as their namesakes, which can be several hundred feet to actual miles," Petrus taught, and I was impressed. This man knew a lot about my kind. The kids were too from the looks on their faces.

"Neato! Could Jelly get that big?" Julius asked eagerly, but Petrus shook his head.

"Unlikely. While it is possible for standard Ooze to change and mutate based on their habitat, they rarely become too large. Most Ooze are born as their type and never change."

"What sort of new form could Jelly become?" My owner inquired, and he shrugged.

"No idea. But if he stays in this sort of environment," at that Petrus waved his hand to indicate the lush greenery around him, "he could become a Green Ooze; an Ooze directly tied to plants and natural life. Or, more rarely, he might become a Healing Ooze."

"What's that?" Liliana asked. I notice a change in her as she registers the name. Was her power reacting to what Petrus had mentioned? Why, though?

"A Healing Ooze is a rare breed that only appears in places of potent light magic or after a regular Ooze has consumed a lot of recovery magic and items. Like a healing potion, for instance." Petrus reached into his robes and removed a small glass vial filled to the brim with a pale red liquid.

"Healing Ooze are able to produce their own curatives, and are prized because the rare Elixir can be distilled from the essence of such a creature."

As soon as he pulled out the potion, my senses became fixated on it. In the open, its magical signature drew my attention to it, and I could not look away. It was so tempting, so tantalizing!

Without thinking, I lunge at the vial, knocking it from Petrus' grasp. Orleen and her counterpart that watch over Julius gasp in shock at my sudden actions. Petrus gave a startled yelp and began to instinctively charge a spell of some sort while Liliana shouted at Petrus and I to stop. He did, reluctantly, and I landed hard on the hard stone floor of the gazebo. The potion bottle did too, and broke apart. I greedily lapped it all up, shards and all.

As I do so, a burst of flavor strikes me. Until now, I had not "tasted" what I ate. For the first time I understood why humans and other sapient creatures were so obsessed with that most heavenly of senses. The liquid turned to strawberries in my "stomach" and I hummed loudly with pleasure.

"Well. It certainly seems like he had a favorite food now," Petrus joked, visibly trying to calm down. Liliana let out a sigh of relief that I had not been hurt, and that I hadn't been trying to hurt someone.

"Oh, Jelly! That was a bad thing to do! Very rude!" She scolded, and I shrunk in on myself. Partly due to my owner's disappointment, but also because of a thrill of worry in my mind. I had acted, for the first time since I had gained this new outlook, solely on what my instincts and primal reasoning told me to do. And that frightened me. Could I attack somebody if my baser side took over again? And why had it done so now? Was I reacting to the odd movements in my owner's magic, or was it entirely me? I did not know, and I wanted, no, I needed to find out.

"I'm so sorry for that, Sir Goyn! Please, let me reimburse you!" Liliana said hurriedly, fumbling at the pockets in her dress to pull out a coin purse, but the mage quickly stopped her.

"No, no, that was my fault! I should have remembered that Oozes are attracted to magical items they find intriguing or delicious," he explained, waving off my owner's attempt to pay for a replacement potion. "And at least this way you know about his tastes now, so you can prepare for this not happening in a worse setting."

"Of course! Thank you for being so understanding, Sir Goyn!" Liliana said, changing his term of address while giving a short curtsy.

"Don't mention it. Actually, it might be best for all of us to keep this incident between ourselves," Petrus urged. Everyone agreed, though the staff hovering nearby did so reluctantly.

"Petrus! It's time for us to prepare to leave!" Renos called out, approaching the group from beyond a hedge wall accompanied by King Tiberius.

"Of course, Master Renos. I bid you farewell, Princess Liliana. Prince Julius. Hopefully we can meet each other soon." With that, the kind young mage left to rejoin his mentor, fading from my senses as Liliana continued to admonish me quietly. I wobbled in apology as I mentally vowed to resist my animalistic impulses at all cost. I owe my loving owner that much at the very least.

"You said you had something else to tell us?" King Tiberius queried, handing Petrus a tumbler of whiskey. The men were in a study, where the king was offering the mages a congratulatory glass for their efforts. A pair of butlers stood at the edge of view, as well as Sir Blaine, commander of the Dire Swords, the loyal personal guard for the Varian royal family.

"Yes, your majesty. It's about the wards." Petrus took a small sip to steady his nerves before continuing. "You see, everything I told you was the truth. Rain had eroded the wall, and the root did grow out to block off the barrier. But, the thing was the root could not have grown in such a way naturally. It was too straight. And I could sense extremely faint traces of a spell in the tree."

"This was planned?"

"Why did you not inform us sooner?"

Two angry voices spoke out at the same time, overlapping. King Tiberius shot a look at Renos, and the pair quieted down.

"It seems that this was not an accident. Moving a single root using magic is something any mage, from Druid to Cleric to Paladin to Sorcerer, could perform with ease. And I felt that leaking information that this was a man-made situation would be a poor idea. We were in the open, servants and staff and your own children listening in. I maintain it was best that this knowledge be kept from more people, lest there be panic."

Renos opened his mouth to scold his student, but Tiberius waved a hand to cut off the esteemed mage.

"He made the right choice. This information was too sensitive to be allowed in the open. This was a plot, we know that now. But the perpetrators think we do not. That is the way it should remain. If you could be discreet in this matter with the Academy as well, Master Renos, I would be grateful."

"Understood. I will make sure this information does not circulate. And good job, Petrus. You did well today."

"Thank you, mentor."

"By the way, what did the two of you think of my daughter's new pet?" the king inquired after a lull.

"More than just well trained, that little Ooze was disciplined. It should have made some sort of movement when I used my Analysis spell, but it didn't even flinch! If I wasn't a fool, I'd swear that slime was watching me as well," Renos said, leaning back in the chair and taking a mouthful of fiery alcohol.

"I agree with Master Renos. That little Ooze was definitely an oddity. Also, I think you might want to stock up on healing potions soon," Petrus mused.

"What do you mean?" Tiberius asked, a firm tone entering his voice.

"Only that Princess Liliana may want to start feeding them to uh, Jelly, was its name? I dropped one of my vials of a minor healing potion earlier, and it slurped it right up, and seemed to really enjoy it. I then may have mentioned that an Ooze that consumes large quantities of restoratives and light magic may mutate into a Healing Ooze," the young mage assured his liege, noting the shift in atmosphere. Tiberius sighed in relief.

"Was that all? I'll try to accommodate her to a degree. And I have to agree with your earlier assessments of the slime. It was definitely odd. Personally, I believe it may be due to *Miraculous Mystery's* influence."

"Ah, that explains it. Her magic may be altering the Ooze in subtle ways, maybe even allowing her to exert unconscious control upon it, managing its actions. It might explain why it was so calm," Renos muttered.

Petrus, not completely in the know about the ancestral magic of the royal family, remained silent and enjoyed his drink. Vices such as alcohol were in limited supply at the Academy. The professors and staff preferred to have their students learn in a clean environment. He gratefully took the little pleasures he could get. It was also a very good vintage. Petrus quietly hoped he hadn't been dragged into something dangerous. But knowing his luck, it probably would end up becoming such.

Chapter 6: The azure teacher

It had been three days since the mages had visited the castle

and I had learned about my love of potions. Liliana had taken it upon

herself to obtain as many as she reasonably could to satisfy me. I

wasn't complaining. They were delicious.

"Here you go, Jelly. Open wide!" Liliana said in a sing-song

tone, holding out a healing potion vial an inch or so above me,

making me jump for it. I liked the exercise, and she liked seeing me

leap about like a bouncing ball. It worked well for us.

"Please refrain from doing these antics at the dining table,

Liliana," Queen Amdora tsked, wearily attempting to curtail her

daughter. She knew it was likely futile, but she was a mother, and

was thus obligated to at least try.

"Your mother is correct, my flower. You shouldn't play with

your pet at the table." King Tiberius looked up for a moment from

where he sat, backing up his wife. A barely perceptible nod passed

between the couple. I smiled in my mind. They might not have had a lot of time together nowadays, but they were still deeply in love. Even I, a magical being with hardly any social skills, could see that!

At her father's words, Liliana meekly complied, a hint of a blush dusting her cheeks. He was the only person who could effectively tell the royal children what to do with any degree of success. A talent many a servant envied.

"How have your studies been going?" the king asked after a moment, and the two youngsters winced.

"They go," my owner stated evasively.

"Yeah, that!" Julius agreed. King Tiberius shook his head in mock despair.

"Such a response! What will ever become of this kingdom with such whimsical princes and princesses? Oh, woe to be!"

"Father, stop!" Julius complained, sticking his tongue out at the melodrama. Liliana pursed her lips in childish revulsion. King Tiberius just laughed, and the queen even gave a short chuckle. I stayed put, content to bask in the atmosphere. I felt at peace when I was around my owner's family and they were all joking around like this.

"Speaking of lessons, I have a dance tutor coming over for the two of you in the coming week," Queen Amdora mentioned in an offhand manner, abruptly shifting the mood.

"The two of you need to work on your dancing skills for the ceremonial ball this autumn. You haven't had much of a need to practice dance and footwork before as you've yet to attend many high profile events. But this year's Adventurer's Advent is not something we can have you miss, or do poorly in," their mother explained in a kind but firm manner. Liliana and Julius perked up at the mention of the party, but I remained in the dark. What was this Advent they were talking about?

"Ah, yes, speaking of which, I need the two of you to promise me not to bother some of the guests too much this year. I know you were both excited to meet the adventurers, but you clung to them like adorable puppies. Especially you, Julius. You are ten years old now. You need to start conducting yourself as an heir should. I understand it is a heavy burden to put on your shoulders this early, but I know I can trust you on this. Both of you, in fact," King Tiberius said, and his children bowed their heads in acceptance.

From my owner I felt a rush of pride that her father had such high expectations for her. Yet this was mixed with the natural tingle of fear at the thought of failing her parents.

I nuzzled her gently to reassure her, and she squeezed me tight in response.

"This is the one thousand year anniversary of the founding of the Adventurer's Guild, right father?" Julius inquired, and I finally started to connect the dots as the king nodded.

"Indeed it is. And even though it's a few months away, we need the preparations to go well. Both in personnel matters and those of decorations." He gave weary sigh at the thoughts of all the extra work he'd have to do. "I'll also have your history tutor focus a bit more on the background of the Guild for a bit. A reward for all your hard work so far."

"Do you think the World Paladin will show up?" Julius asked eagerly, to which his father merely shrugged.

"He's an X-Rank, son. He probably has a lot of problems to take care of."

"Aww." Julius pouted but quickly turned his frown upside-down as he began to talk with Liliana about a variety of people and places and events I had no idea about. I just listened quietly, soaking up what I could about the subject that so fascinated my owner and her brother.

"Who did you hire to perform as their dance instructor, my lovely queen?" King Tiberius asked over his children and their conversation.

"Bluemont, dear. She'll be here a week from tomorrow."

To my ever-lasting surprise, King Tiberius' face went pale, as did the ones from several of the nearby servants. They were all older staff, who had been working in the castle for many a long year. If this person was able to elicit such a response, what kind of tutor was this 'Bluemont' woman?

"She's still alive?" He croaked, pleading eyes begging his wife that it was not so. "It's one of her daughters or granddaughters, right? Not her?"

"Don't be such a baby, Tiberius," Queen Amdora smirked, giving her husband a wicked smile. "You know full well that a lady of her caliber will live forever as long as there are children to teach. No force on Erafore could convince her to retire and die."

King Tiberius sat back in his chair and slumped a little, eyes staring into nothing.

"This is revenge for not having gone to bed yesterday, isn't it?" He whimpered earning a laugh from his queen.

"Don't be silly, Tiberius! I asked for her the day before yesterday! This is revenge for using the last of the pear-scented soap last week."

I was royally perplexed at this point. This Bluemont person must be some sort of incredibly strict task-mistress to make a king fearful like this! I hoped my owner could endure her lessons!

True to their father's orders, the tutors switched their lessons about somewhat, teaching the two all about the history of the Adventurer's Guild. It was relevant for the royalty of Varia to know this, which was a surprise when I learned about that.

"Can you tell me what year the Adventurer's Guild was founded, princess?" The history teacher inquired. He was a portly man who wore a comical-looking flat board hat over a bald patch, along with a mixture of black robes and white tunic. He was enthusiastic about his subject, and Liliana was also eager to dispense her gained knowledge for him.

"The guild was founded in 2309 AC, which was also the year of its founder, King Gregor Roan's, coronation."

"Indeed! And what exactly makes King Gregor's ascension to the throne so unique?"

"King Gregor was the first king in over six hundred years who did not come from any pre-established noble family. He was a commoner who gained fame for being an amazing warrior. He slew hundreds of Goblins during one of their periodic invasions, including their warlord. Not only that, Gregor saved the lives of the Dwarven royal family, earning their respect. and he killed a dragon solo!" Liliana's eyes gleamed with awe and respect. I too was impressed. This man sounded like a true hero, definitely the stuff stories were made of.

"Indeed. Your ancestor's deeds were so outstanding he was elevated to the nobility several times in the course of ten years by no less than six different countries. The family name of 'Roan' was given to him by the king of Brune when he was first knighted. His actions so impressed Queen Liliana the Youthful of Varia that she married him. An act that completely surprised most of the world. In this way, the last living descendant of the Ar-Varia family accepted an incredible man as her husband and establishing your current lineage. He becomes known as the Hero-King thereafter. But can you tell me why he founded the Adventurer's Guild?"

"Well, the land of Orria was in terrible shape. In 2195 AC there was a series of volcanic eruptions in Suld that blanketed the southern lying regions in ash and destroyed the harvest for numerous countries, creating a long lasting famine. A demonic insurgence in the Starblind Mountains destroyed the Royal Varian Mages Academy in 2241, crippling the supply of magical artifacts, enchantments, and runes across the land. And later in 2288 the Second Elfish Domain attempted to invade several human nations on their border. This all meant that Orria was in extreme disarray." The princess took a deep breath.

"Gregor felt the only way to establish a lasting peace was to create a group of mercenaries who focused entirely on taking care of monsters and magical issues. Too often conflicts between nations resulted in fewer soldiers able to defend towns and villages from wild beasts, curses, and vile creatures, who took the weakened lands as ripe targets. To this end, Gregor made contracts, deals, and treaties with untold dozens of nobles and merchant groups across the world. The Adventurer's Guild was made to be a force dedicated to protecting the world from the inhuman and the impossible. But this also meant that the guild was forbidden from partaking in conflicts, feuds, or wars between countries or internal factions."

If I had eyes, I would have been using them to stare at my owner. This was the first time I'd seen Liliana not only focused but speaking in almost a single breath. Her tutor didn't seem surprised and just gave her a wide, approving smile.

"Very good and precise! Yes, you are completely correct. I think you could probably teach me a thing or two about this particular topic. So, how about you answer this final question, and I'll let you go free early today?"

"Of course!" Liliana said excitedly.

"Alright then. So, final question; what was the gift that the King Upon the Buried Throne, lord of all the Dwarf Clan-holds, gave to Gregor for saving the life of his entire family from a cult? And how are our relations with that great nation in Par-Orria?"

"It was not just one item, but three! The dwarf Ancestor-King presented Gregor with three whole suits of Berserker Armor! Two of them are still kept in the castle armory, while the third set, his personal one, was lost. They say he sealed it, and a large portion of his wealth, in a hidden vault, which only a true hero can find."

"And thanks to his actions, the dwarves had been close allies with Varia for many years. The majority of dwarves reside in the

92

Towering Peaks in Par-Orria to the east but they have a strong presence as merchants, adventurers, and of course craftsmen in cities across Varia and our closest neighbors. With an alliance that has lasted a thousand years humans and dwarves have become close friends."

"As usual, excellent answers. Well-spoken and with such enthusiasm! You're free to go, Princess Liliana. Enjoy the rest of your day."

"Thank you!" Liliana shouted in joy, rushing over to my corner and scooping me up before dashing out the door. Her wild run quickly mellowed, slowing to a brisk walk. It was not dignified for a lady to run. If any of them more stern servants encountered her, they would undoubtedly scold her.

"You must think I'm pretty unladylike, huh, Jelly?"

Well that came right out of nowhere! I shifted in Liliana's arms so I could give her the impression of staring up at her in confused shock. She seemed to notice my bewildered attention, and continued speaking.

"I mean, was it really OK for me to be this interested in heroes and adventurers? The stories and legends are something I've grown up on. How could I not love hearing about the good the Guild had done, knowing that it was thanks to my family that so many have been helped and even saved!" Her smile, at first radiate, quickly turned bitter.

"But some of the staff think I shouldn't be so focused on them and this subject. 'It isn't ladylike,' they say. And then I feel a bit embarrassed being so excited about adventurers like this. Is it wrong of me to be so happy when I talk about them? Is it wrong for me to want to know more about them?"

Liliana had stopped walking and leaned against the balustrade of the stairs leading up to her room. She looked down at me, and I could feel her sorrow and her conflicted emotions. One the one hand, this was her legacy. Her ancestor created an institution that even I, a monster, respected. But, there were the expectations for a lady of her class and social standing to not be overly dedicated to something that was seen as not the most glorious of professions. For every adventuring hero, there were a dozen more who were just monster hunting mercenaries that saw their job as just that; a job.

No matter what though, I felt that it didn't matter what others thought of my mistress. As long as she didn't try and run off to become an adventurer herself, I doubted any of the staff would push too hard on her hobby.

I relayed my feelings to her my rubbing up on her arms. I gurgled happily at her, and she giggled at my antics.

"That tickles! Carefully, or I'll drop you!" She said playfully. I didn't stop and grew two tentacles to tickle her with, and her giggles grew louder.

"OK, Ok, Jelly! I get it! I'll cheer up!" I finally settled down as I sensed her mood improve. She let out a contented sigh, and slid down onto the floor, holding me closer.

"Thanks, Jelly, for helping me. The others may say you're just a monster, but you are so much more than that to me. Thank you."

I just nuzzled closer, basking in her warmth. I doubted I had solved her issue, but at least I'd made it a light burden on her shoulders. She's too kind and gentle to be sad. I think a lot of the people around her will agree with that.

She wiped her eyes off and stands, a determined stance to her steps.

"Let's go, Jelly! I hear the kitchen is baking ring cakes!" I bounced in excitement. Now that sounded like a good way to end a day of hard work!

It was the day of reckoning; in just a few minutes the Baroness Bluemont would arrive and I'd be able to see what all the fuss was about. In a manner of speaking. Servants and staff were fretting around the place, getting things in order, and I was able to eavesdrop on some of their conversations about this mysterious tutor while I hung around in my owner's arms.

Baroness Bluemont came from a minor aristocratic family that had dedicated its daughters to the cause of "Proper Education."

For generations this family had raised and trained the best teachers and personal tutors for the upper crust of society. Any child who came under the wing of a Bluemont emerges as a well mannered, properly trained gentleman or lady.

And this particular Bluemont was the most famous in a very distinguished family. Rene Lasfel Bluemont; current matriarch of the household and renowned for having taught the current king of Varia and his father the ways of etiquette. And not just Varia's royal family, but the current kings of Tashel, Brune, and Larate had been taught by her. Countless noble scions and the wealthy offspring of merchants and guilds had passed under her tutelage. Her methods were known and respected as far as the Second Elfish Domain of Par-Orria and Distant Qwan in the east.

So why was she so frightening to these people? I couldn't understand their panic. Was she the harshest of task mistresses? Did she use the cane? Even King Tiberius, normally unflappable, was shifting from foot to foot due to nerves. I trembled.

We were currently in the Lesser Audience Hall, a room reserved for small, informal meetings. Unlike the throne room, which was made to be spacious and imposing, this place was cozy and much less intimidating. It was where the king met the mages from some time ago, and where he preferred to greet important individuals one on one without fanfare.

The royal family was all dressed up today. The king was wearing his usual outfit, but had taken care to polish the buttons and shine his boots. Queen Amdora was in an outfit that resembled a wedding cake more than anything. How she could even move was anybody's guess. Young Julius was in a fetching jacket-and-pants ensemble, all in varying shades of blue. It sort of made him look like a pile of blueberries from a distance. Lastly was my owner. She too was in a dress that seemed far too heavy and expansive to move in, the white fabric emphasizing her pale skin.

Behind Liliana and Julius were their maids. Orleen stood close, the air of nervousness sweeping her up along with her counterpart, a slightly younger woman. Her name was Jean and it was she who took care of the prince. It seemed that neither had been in the castle when Lady Bluemont had been around before. Understandable then that the tension from the longer serving staff carried over onto the younger members.

We did not have to wait long as soon there were footsteps on the other side of the door. It creaked open a smidge to allow a hasty, whispered conversation to pass between heralds.

"Announcing the Baroness, Lady Rene Lasfel Bluemont!" A servant called out as the doors to the hall were pushed open. King Tiberius went stiff, his children echoed his worry with nervous expressions. Queen Amdora just smirked at their discomfort. I remained unmoving in Liliana's arms, warily watching the entryway.

"Oh, little Tiber! It has been so long! Are you doing well?" A tornado of a woman swept into the Lesser Audience Hall, bustling over to the reigning monarch of the country and embracing him with a bone crushing hug.

I must say, she was not at all as I'd expected, and my owner and her brother shared my surprise.

Unlike the rail-thin, prim and proper task-mistress I had been picturing in my mind Lady Bluemont was a short and portly old woman with apple-like cheeks in a flowing yellow dress all but choked in white and yellow ruffles. Her hair was composed of dark grey curls that bounced as she moved. A plethora of jeweled accessories covered her fingers and decorated her neck. She smiled widely as she remained wrapped around King Tiberius.

"It has been a while since I have seen you! Oh, how you have grown! Let me get a good look at you." She reached up and clasped the king's cheeks in her hands, dragging his head down to be level with hers. She hummed and hmmed as she looks over him, before releasing him with a grunt of approval.

"Glad to see you've grown into a fine, strapping lad! And such lovely facial hair! I do love a man with a beard," Lady Bluemont said with a wink at the queen, who laughed at that.

"It had indeed been a while, Baroness Bluemont. I am so glad you agreed to tutor our children," Queen Amdora said, holding out a hand to the famous woman who took and eagerly shook it.

King Tiberius was still reeling from the attack on his personal space, and so stayed as far away from the conversation as he could.

"These must be the little dears I'll be teaching, then?" Bluemont inquired, turning to face the royal brood.

"Indeed. This is Liliana and Julius. Say your greetings, dears."

"Greetings, Baroness Bluemont. It is a pleasure to meet you, and welcome you into our home," my owner said, Julius only a syllable behind.

"Very polite! Good, good, I see I won't have to worry much about proper greetings. Posture could use some work on the both of you. And you're both far too thin. Do you feed them properly, little Tiber?" Their father only grunted at that as the tutor continued to examine her new charges.

"Nibbles? I made them myself." Out of the blue, the elderly teacher reached into a pocket on her and removed handfuls of sliced, dried fruit, offering them over to her two new students. Blinking in surprise, they only hesitated for a moment before reaching out to take some of the offered meal.

Out of the corner of my senses, I noticed King Tiberius shiver in some unknown emotion as he spotted the candied fruits. Further away, I could tell that some of the servants' expressions took on wary looks, eyes locked onto the snack. But none of the Dire Swords made a move so they weren't toxic or dangerous.

Ah. So that's the story.

My intuition was proven correct when my owner's face scrunched up in barely contained and suppressed disgust. The little pieces of fruit were unnaturally flavored and unpleasant to eat. And from what I'd so far gleaned of this woman, she would likely take every opportunity to feed people her homemade 'nibbles.'

Surprisingly, Julius actually seemed to like whatever these dried fruits were. He shocked everyone when he reached for a second handful. When this happened, Lady Bluemont chortled good-naturedly.

"Eat up, you two! Children need energy to do well in school!" She urged.

"Of course, Lady Bluemont," Liliana choked out.

"Please, call me Rene. No need to be formal to me. Too many rules stifle learning," the unusual aristocrat implored. Her gaze then shifted to me, and I pressed myself back into Liliana.

"And who is this little one?"

"This is Jelly. He's my pet, and friend," Liliana stated proudly.

"I see. Shake!" I jerked in surprise and instinctively extended a pseudo-pod out to Lady Blu- I mean Rene. She gripped my tiny limb and pumped it up and down before releasing me. She then passed me a few slices of her dried fruit snack. Confused, I none the less accepted, and swallowed them into me.

Despite being as magical as a chair, an explosion of flavor filled me as I "chewed" the fruit slices. I gleaned a few unique properties about this food as I digested it. While dried, it had a massive boost to its sugar content. The reaction of my owner made sense, as did the faces the people nearby made when they saw the edibles. Most people would find it sickeningly sweet, and almost unpalatable. But a second, much more interesting facet of the fruit was that it contained small traces of natural anti-toxins. They were potent and lingered for a while after consumption. Eat enough of them and you could potentially survive consuming all manners of non-magical poisons, be they fast or slow acting.

Ah, now it makes sense!

From what I already knew Rene Bluemont had taught generations of notables and their children. And sadly such people are often the target of assassinations. Poison being a time honored, popular and common method of carrying out this heinous act. So, to prevent her charges from dying, she made them eat a homemade anti-toxin. I wondered just how many of her students had had their lives inadvertently saved because of this. I wondered if any of them even knew.

I offered the kind elderly woman a happy, thankful burble, and she replied with a grandmotherly smile.

"It's nice to see that at least two people here appreciate my cooking," she said jovially. Julius nodded and eagerly took another handful. Well, it seemed the prince had quiet the sweet tooth. Interesting.

"Now, I know we've just met, but I need to get a sense of what I need to work with. If you two darlings wouldn't mind, I need you both to show me what you can do already." There was a twinkle in her eye as she said this, her enthusiasm practically overflowing.

"I have set up a space for your classes, Rene," Queen Amdora cut in before anyone did anything right then and there. "Perhaps it would be best to perform their evaluations in there first?"

"Splendid idea, your majesty! Come, children, let us see what our classroom will be like, and then we shall begin some simple tests." Like a sugar-scented whirlwind the elderly lady practically carried off the prince and princess, their maids trailing behind anxiously.

"Hmm, not a bad room. Plenty of natural light and floor space, and not a whiff of mildew," Rene commented, nodding in approval. She clapped her hands and eagerly turned to face my owner and Julius.

"Let us start off with some bows and curtseying. If you cannot manage this, you'll never be able to make it in high society," Rene lectured. "Oh, and I'll have to ask that you put your pet slime down for this. It can stay in the room, but you'll need your hands free."

"Yes, Rene," Liliana intoned obediently. She passed me over to Orleen who proceeded to gingerly place me onto the floor. I sighed internally. Even though the two of us had bonded somewhat over the Rose Worm incident, my owner's personal maid was still not entirely comfortable or keen on holding me for longer than necessary. It's not like I am dirty. I suppose some people just don't appreciate the soft suppleness of my body.

I settled down to watch my owner perform the various gestures and actions known to and expected of a person of high standing. Seeing her focused on her work only made my own drive to improve grow.

I had been working on a surprise for my owner. I hoped I'd be able to show it off soon. They'd love it.

Chapter 7: A slime and his body

The past few days had been nothing but torture for me. So far, I had spent a lot of time watching my owner and Julius learn how to bow, curtsey, ballroom dance and more. Interesting the first few days as I got to see some new movements and activities. But now it was excruciatingly painful being hardly able to do much but watch the two people closest to me be scolded in a passive aggressive manner by an grandmotherly tutor who kept offering sickly sweet snacks to everyone nearby.

Lady Bluemont, or as she preferred, Rene, was very good at what she did. She knew her subjects and how to best work with the strengths of her students to improve their coordination and success rate. In the two weeks since she began teaching, Liliana had dramatically improved; where she used to be unable to bend her knees too far, now she could almost reach a 90 degree angle with her knees. In regards to dancing, Liliana was already decent, but far too fast and eager to move for the more sedate ballroom dancing that a noble most often performed. As such, it was a strain to get used to more measured steps.

Julius was doing well too. He could perform a deep bow with an almost perfect 90 degree angle on his spine, and had gotten a lot better on coordinating his feet when dancing, only stepping on Rene's toes two times out of ten, instead of five. He only really needed work on his balance. He was quiet good at memorizing the forms he must take and use, and was steadily getting better at the stances.

And of course all credit had to go to their tutor. Rene's secret to this improvement; stretching and an odd body workout called 'Yoga.' It looked painful, and each warmup session tended to end up with lots of pulled muscles amongst her students. But it limbered them up, and made it easier to work on using muscles for longer periods of time.

This martial art work out style originated from a far off continent in the east, beyond the Deepstar Ocean; Distant Qwan, a mystique-filled land full of interesting goods and ideas. Even the dried fruit Rene so loves originally came from this nation, and had been replanted and grown here in her own personal greenhouse.

So why, then, did I remain in the classroom with my owner, when I could leave whenever I want?

Because I was studying on my own. I was observing how Liliana and her brother moved, both in short bursts of rapid movement, and slow, measured paces. I was beginning to understand how the human body moved, and how it looked as it did so. Soon I would be able to show off all my hard work!

"That's enough for now." At Rene's declaration, I glanced over to where my owner stood, panting lightly and coated in a sheen of sweat.

"Thank you," she gasped, giving her teacher a short bow, before beckoning Orleen over. The maid quickly approached and passed her a towel to wipe down with. A grateful sigh escapes Liliana's mouth.

"You are doing well. I am glad to see that your actions and movements have improved," Rene praised, giving my owner a smile and holding out a handful of dried fruits.

"Yes, all thanks to you," Liliana responded, hiding a grimace as she took one of the little snack foods. Far too polite to outright refuse, she resigned herself to having one of the overwhelmingly sugary tasting fruit slices.

After exchanging some more farewells, Liliana scooped me up and carried me, somewhat stiffly, back to her room. Her chipper mood was muted somewhat and I could tell that the daily training was starting to get to her. She only had one day a week off, the rest all involving her studies. Mornings were reserved for the non-physical classes; history, letters, law, governance, and arithmetic, one of each every day. But the late afternoons and early evenings all belonged to Rene and her classes. Cramming so many in seems odd to me. Why had their parents waited so long to teach them this, when the event looms so close? I couldn't fathom the thoughts of my owner's parents.

It was barely evening and yet my owner flopped face down onto her bed with a groan of pleasure mingled with a sigh of bone crushing weariness.

"My lady, that is quite unseemly," Orleen scolded. But there was only the barest trace of disapproval. I could tell she said it merely because it was expected of her. She'd been with her ward all the time and had seen, and even participated with on occasion, Rene's lessons. Orleen understood how hard her lady was working, and was careful not to be too harsh when my owner wanted to relax.

"Sorry, Orleen, I'm just so tired today," Liliana apologized, words muffled by the pillow she lay down upon.

"You've been working hard, my lady, and I understand your desire for some personal time, but you can't let all of Lady Bluemont's etiquette teachings go to waste so soon after learning them," the personal maid admonished. Liliana somehow managed to look meek and chastised despite remaining face down on her bed.

"I'm sure with a good night's rest you'll feel much better. But until then, you need to get ready for dinner."

My owner complied with the request, changing into some new and better clothes than the exercise outfit she'd been in earlier, and departed with Orleen, leaving me behind.

I did not mind. It gave me more time to practice in private.

The next morning came soon and Liliana awoke in a slightly more chipper mood than the one she'd fallen asleep in, but a sense of dread for the afternoon still loomed over her. Sensing that, I rolled groggily out of my bed. Today's as good a day as any to show off my new trick, and hopefully it would improve my owner's disposition. I really disliked seeing her depressed. As she swung her feet off the side of the bed, and Orleen stood nearby ready to help as always, I trundled over and reached out for her with a tendril.

"What is it, Jelly?" Liliana asked, looking down at me as I tugged at the cuffs of her pants to get her attention. My ability to touch and manipulate with my pseudopods had gotten better through trial and error, and I could now grab people's attention without melting the article of clothing I snagged. Pleased that I had her attention, I took a deep breath (figuratively) and concentrated.

The surface of my body wobbled and jiggled violently, unlike anything my owner and her maid have seen me do before. Then, I extended my body five ways, creating a quintet of new pseudopods. Slowly and shakily, I felt my body rising vertically, as I flattened out bits and pieces of myself to create a new shape for my body to balance out the five new limbs I was generating.

It felt like several long minutes had gone by since I started, but in truth no more than a few seconds had passed. To those observing me, I underwent a rapid transformation.

"Sweet and Holy Cynthia, Selika, and Nia!" Orleen shouted, taking several steps back until she was pressed up against the wall in her shock. Liliana just stared open mouthed at me. Their reactions were not surprising. I had a body now, after all.

To be accurate, I had changed my old body to resemble the form of a biped. Two stubby tendrils became 'legs,' and a second pair of them acted as 'arms.' A fifth pseudopod pretended to be a neck and head. I shifted my core around so it now rested where a brain might be in my new 'head.' I now looked like I had a giant cyclopean eye sunk into my skull. I had yet to figure out how to give myself eyes or any other facial features, so it was just a smooth, flat surface for now with my core suspended in the middle.

The sensation of molding a new form for myself was not one that I could describe fully, since it wasn't anything new, per say. It was just like growing new tentacle-limbs, but required far more focus and attention so they do not merge back into me. And as could be seen I had managed to create more of my limbs at once. My new limit was seven, and they could stretch and act a lot like freely than they used to. I am also still the same size, sort of. My mass was still the same, just more distributed. I now stood about two feet tall and half that wide. My limbs were all stumpy and small, but functional none the less. I kind of look like a creepy doll of sorts.

Anyways! It was time to test the body out. Carefully, I lifted one leg in front of the other, one after another, until I'd taken several steps and was fully facing my owner. As she stared on, I gave a short and pitiful bow, before holding my hand out and beginning to shadow-dance with myself. All those days spent watching my owner in her dance and movement lessons had paid off as I now imitated those same actions in front of her, performing a crude but playful recreation of her own efforts.

I took another bow, before Liliana started clapping her hands excitedly.

"Oh my goodness! Jelly, that was amazing! How did you do that? Was this what you've been doing while watching me practice with Rene this whole time? Amazing! Amazing!" Liliana cried, giddy with joy as she praised me. I put an arm behind my head and shuffled my feet, imitating a bashful expression. At that, my owner squealed loudly in glee and swept me up, hugging me tight and praising my efforts more and more.

I felt a warm glow build inside me, and I basked in her adulations. My impromptu plan had certainly cheered her up.

Orleen was still trying to merge with the wall in surprise, so Liliana had to call one of the other maids to help her dress herself today. She managed fairly well, deciding to go with a simple sun dress and skirt that were both pale yellow with emerald green patterns woven along the edges. She rushed down to the room where breakfast was served, startling her brother and father who were currently inside partaking of the morning meal. Unlike dinner, which every member of the royal family participates in, breakfast was more up to chance for members of the family to eat together, and lunch was almost always served and eaten separately from the rest except in certain cases like tea parties or luncheons with guests.

"Father! Julius! Look at what Jelly learned how to do!" Liliana cried, presenting me to her sibling and parent like I was an astonishing object. Which I was, of course, but still.

While she dressed and then dashed for the dining room, I had returned to my rotund form in order to conserve energy. It took a lot of effort to maintain my bipedal shape, and I'd had a feeling she'd want to show me off.

Placing me onto the table in full view of her gathered family and a handful of staff, Liliana beams proudly. They all look on politely. The princess had shown me off often enough before, showing off my astonish ability to leap, my limbs and their range of control, and my willingness to eat even the most stinky of cheeses without complaint.

Today I blew away their expectations. Like earlier in the bedroom, I concentrated and focused and soon grew into a biped form.

It was times like this that I was glad I had the capacity for retaining memories. Because the looks on the faces of everyone was priceless!

Thanks to my physical training, my sensory powers had expanded in correlation as well, and now I am able to not only "see" almost one hundred feet around me, but also perceive colors more clearly and analysis things under my direct scrutiny. That worked well, as I could "see" everyone in the room simultaneously, and thus also their reactions.

King Tiberius' jaw was slack, and his eyes were fogged over in stupefaction. The servants all had different reactions, some dropping what they'd been holding, others started screaming and backpedaling into a wall, yet others swore out loud in shock and reaching for concealed weapons. Only Julius remained unterrified, shouting out "Cool!" before leaning in for a closer look. I showed off my new range of movements and he was quick to praise me.

I looked around at the rest of the people and scoffed mentally at their overreactions. Sure, it might have looked weird, and yes, it was a surprise, but was it really so shocking for a slime like myself to take on a humanoid-ish body and do some ballroom dancing on a table?

...On second thought, don't answer that.

"What is going on in here?" Everyone shook themselves out of their stupors or excitement to look at the source of the disapproving voice. In the door way Queen Amdora and Lady Rene were both standing there, looking onto the scene before them with confusion and suspicion. They hadn't seen me yet, as Liliana was blocking their line of sight to me.

"Oh, mother! And Rene! I was just showing everyone Jelly's new trick!"

"Is that so? Then please, enlighten me as to what could be so stunning," Queen Amdora dryly stated. Her daughter nodded eagerly and stepped aside so the two women could see me.

I gave the queen and tutor a friendly wave. The queen's face paled rapidly, and for a moment I thought she'd faint. She quickly rallied herself, however, and shakily stumbled over to a vacant seat at the table.

"Is it too early in the morning for a stiff drink?" She asked one of the servants, who just shrugged helplessly.

"Make it a double," King Tiberius ordered, giving his own request, and the servant hurried off to fetch some liquid courage.

"How interesting," Rene mused, her own surprise quickly giving way to a scheming grin.

"Congratulations, my dear. You and your brother now have a new partner to practice with."

Uh oh. 'Maybe I should have thought this through?' I wondered as I start to dread the next few days. Based on the eager grins of Liliana and Julius, and the smirk on Rene, I could safely assume boredom wouldn't be much of a problem from that point one.

Here's a little exercise for you folks out there. Try balancing a plate on your head while standing on one leg. Then, move forward by merely shuffling your one foot. Move too fast, and you just stumble and everything falls down. But if you don't move, then someone comes up behind you and starts poking your back.

That was what it was like for me trying to practice bipedal locomotion. I needed to focus on creating each legs, then maintaining it, then actively lifting it and moving it in front of each one after the other. By the gods. This wasn't quiet torture, since I was willingly doing it to myself, but it sure wasn't pleasant.

Without any muscles or bones or tendons or nerves, the strain on my body was of a different variety. When I grew tired, it became harder to not only maintain my pseudopods, but also my sensory abilities. When I over reached not only did I revert back into my spherical form, but I also became unable to see more than a foot or so beyond me. Moving also got harder, since I used up stamina to maintain my new form, which I also needed to move it, or myself *au naturel*.

But I was improving. Under Rene's tutelage I learned how to save energy when I moved. I used up less stamina and mana with my movements by cutting down on excessive actions.

I was eating more as well. Before, I only needed a pound or so of food a day. Now, I had to consume five times more food to make up for the nutrients and energy I loose while training. The healing potions helped a lot. I recovered faster when I drank them, and I processed their magical energy better than solid foods.

"No, no, not that like! You're putting too much thought into you actions, Jelly. You need to be graceful and fluid with your steps. Try following your princess's lead this time." Rene interrupted my musings with a clap of her hands, grabbing my attention.

I was currently in the dance room with my owner and Rene, being taught how to move properly. Queen Amdora had been opposed to this. Rene was being hired to teach her children, not their pets. Besides, it's not as if I would be allowed at the party anyways, she argued. Rene had a counter for that. I should, in fact, attend the ball this autumn. Nobles showed off their wealth and status all the time, and pets were a prime way to do so. But how many people can say that their daughter not only tamed a slime, but taught it how to formally dance? It would greatly increase her reputation, something that as a princess Liliana needed to foster sooner rather than later.

Somehow, Rene's words won over the queen and she grudgingly conceded, allowing me and Liliana to practice together. My owner was overjoyed, and even now still remained chipper. In fact, her attitude and level of improvement have steadily been on the excellent side ever since I started learning alongside her.

Liliana gave me a curtsey that I returned with a squishy bow. She began to dance. One, two, pause, sidestep. One, two, pause, sidestep. Over and over she repeats this, and I imitated her to the best of my ability. I managed to repeat the forms, but never perfectly copy. Most of that was due to my size and shape. Even as a biped my limbs do not have the joints needed for some of the more complex dance steps. But, I struggled on.

Despite all my complaints and gripes, I was starting to get better. I started a week ago, and I already could see clear signs of this improvement. My control was slowly growing, my discipline and willpower were boosted, and the look of joy on my owners face proved to me that this was the right way for me to progress.

"Hmm, I think you should try to lift your legs a bit higher when you move, Jelly. Keeping yourself grounded was good and all, but dance requires limbs to be limber." Rene gave a titter at her word play before turning to face Liliana.

"Princess, you are doing well. Though perhaps you should try and slow down more. Though he was not dancing with you directly, Jelly was none the less your partner. You cannot go too fast, or you'll leave him in the dust, and then he'll scramble to catch up and increase his chances of making a mistake. Remember, dancing is a team effort. You and your partner have to understand your paces, and work together to produce harmony," Rene explained. Liliana nodded in understanding, her resolve unwavering.

"Good. Now then. One more time, from the top!"

And that was how the rest of the day went. We got released close to five in the evening, and my owner and I took the time off before dinner gratefully.

Liliana looks down at me and flashes me a sincere smile. "Thanks, Jelly. Class was a lot more fun with you around."

I burbled happily, content to let her talk with me. She continued speaking to me, discussing the lessons from her other classes, the weather, and the upcoming festivities. To my surprise, I learned that there was a second event coming up besides the mid-autumn Adventurer's Advent, but not one that requires dancing.

Known as the Reaffirmation of Faith, it was a holy ritual that took place at the Temple of the Divine Family on the last day of summer, which was fast approaching. I was not sure what it entailed, as Liliana did not speak much on it, but from what I gathered it was a vital ceremony for all of Sanc Aldet and culminated in a city wide carnival and party. My owner mainly lamented that she never gets to see much of or participate in the activities of the festival.

Hopefully this year would be different for her. After all, if she did well in dance class then her mother promised she could explore the fair. Under guard of course, but still wander freely. I was certain she'd be fine. Her knowledge and poise in public and formal settings was already impressive for a girl of only thirteen springs, and she knew when to restrain her exuberant emotions.

If I may be so bold, I must say that Liliana was an all-around outstanding lady.

Chapter 8: The smiles of Goddesses

Well, there I was, being held in the arms of my owner as we descended from the castle towards the Temple of the Divine Family for the Reaffirmation of Faith.

The days passed in a semi-lucid blur to me. Rene Bluemont drove the two of us, plus Julius, hard, but the results showed themselves every time they needed to present themselves before others besides their families. Liliana and Julius' grace and poise almost 'oozed' through. I'm sorry, that joke was in poor taste. I fear Rene has been influencing me too much lately.

Back to the current state of affairs: The weather was starting to have a cool snap to it, and the royal family was heavily dressed up in the finest outfits they have. Or, one of the finest sets. As wealthy rulers, they had a lot of gold to spend, and much of it had to go to maintaining appearances. While it could be said that the astronomically rich and well-off could afford to live frugally, and the Roan's tended not to overindulge in their lifestyles, formal occasions demanded excellent attire.

Julius was wearing a deceptively simple blue and purple tunic with the crest of House Roan, a rearing stallion before a golden flame, worked elegantly into the breast pocket above his heart. His brown hair had been slicked down with gel of some sort and combed over. He was fiddling with the silver buttons around his collar, trying to loosen them, all the while his mother fussed with him, trying to fix imagined issues.

Queen Amdora was stunning, lavishly dressed in a dress that was more of a wedding cake than anything else. It was dark blue with silver and gold accents along the hems, while a large golden set of rings studded her fingers. Her nails had been painted a deep crimson, and her lips and cheeks dusted with rouge. The queen's hair was tightly coiled into an odd three style bun, which draws the hair from her face and reveals the entirety of her regal expression. The overall effect of her outfits made the queen appear both serene and stern, but with nobility and kindness creeping out from her eyes and faint smile.

King Tiberius's choice of clothing was somewhat more subdued than his wife's. He wore a tunic of rich, purple fabric tied around his waist with a leather belt dyed an ocean blue, accompanied by a large golden buckle shaped into a roaring flaming holding it up. A much larger version of the family crest was woven onto his chest and onto the back of a cape made of silver and gold silk. Black leather gloves and boots cover his hands and feet, while a large signet ring of platinum dominated his right index finger. Atop his head was a crown, made of thin bands of gold that looked as if they'd been tied together like string rather than a metal, while a stylized flame of yet more gold dominated the center of the headpiece. Clasped in sockets along the crown was a number of rubies and sapphires, cut and polished to a shine, each one filled with mana to power a number of spells and wards woven into the crown's surface.

Last, but not least, a scabbard and sheath hung at his waist, made of tooled black leather, with a hilt of vividly bright silvery metal standing out starkly. It was the famous long sword of the Savior-King; *Soul of the Ruler*. Made of mithril and adamantium, with a jeweled pommel of orihalcum and layered with ancient, potent enchantments, it was almost a sacred artifact. It had bathed in the blood of king and country's enemies for over two thousand years, and despite being concealed in an almost equally magical sheath, I could taste the power of the blade from where I sat. It was like a natural disaster; terrifying, unstoppable, and made all the more frightening for the fact that it was a necessary part of the world.

Shivering slightly, I forced my attention away from the blade and onto my owner. For her part, she wore a dress much less imposing than her mother's, but still very frilly and fancy. It was a baby blue dress with long silver edges, under which she wore short leggings. Around her neck she wore a simple necklace of braided silk, on which three ornaments hung. In the middle was a golden dove, wings spread for flight. To the right was a stylized bolt of cloth, made of fine silver. And to the left rested a blooming lily flower crafted from silver. These three tokens were symbols of the goddesses worshipped by Varia and the majority of humans, and soon enough we would be entering their hall of prayer.

As we rode through the streets my owner chattered to me as she pointed out this and that beyond the window.

"We live back there, in the Palestone Castle. It's been there for countless generations here in Sanc Aldet. That's the name of this city, which is the capitol of Varia!" Liliana explained to me. "The city is pressed up against the Starblind Mountains, with the upper parts settled on artificial plateaus. That makes up the Purple District. It's where all the best stores are, the aristocrats manors, the Grand Library, assorted schools for the nobility and elite, and of course the Temple of the Divine Family!"

"Down below is Erafore's third-longest set of steps, the Footsteps of the Gods, which separates the Purple District from the Slope District. All of the guild halls, merchant houses, and less fancy stores can be found there. It's partly on the slopes, hence the name, and touches the foot of the mountains. But don't worry, it's not that steep! It was carefully made with dwarf architects so it isn't in danger of falling off the mountain any time soon."

"And then at the very bottom is the Wall District," the excited princess pointed out, again at something I was unable to see. "Housing for the majority of the city is down there, as well as warehouses and markets. A lot of goods pass through here from the

Red Road leading back out to the kingdom or into the various stores here. It's also surrounded by a massive defensive wall which gives the third part of the city its name."

"Liliana, we're here," King Tiberius said, drawing my owner's attention, as well as mine. Smiling demurely, my princess nodded and prepared to greet the crowds.

The royal carriage approached the Temple of the Divine Family and once we rolled to a stop the family stepped out, one after the other, led by the king. Immediately my senses were flooded by the sea of people that waited beyond. The massive cathedral was hard to miss as well now that I was out of that moving box.

This days was an important one, and the common folk came out in droves to catch a glimpse of the regal ceremony and the royal family. They were kept at a distance by the cities peace keeping guards, and a few units of royal knights. Flanked by members of the royal guard, the so-called Dire Swords, we were allowed a glimpse of the monolithic building as we were escorted up to it.

Vast and numerous blocks of marble and granite composed the body of the church, with a set of large steps leading up towards a pair of doors hewn from oak so large and thick that they could each probably be used to make a house. Intricate carvings of myth and legend adorned the surface of the wood, busts of angels and saints stared down from on high, while angelic warriors stood guard over the building in place of more common gargoyle statuettes and figures.

We were greeted at the door by two people, both in elegant white robes. The one in the lead was a middle aged man, leaning on towards portly and with the beginnings of a double chin. His outfit, while simple, was obviously well made and tailored, and likely cost more than the pair of shoes my owner currently wore. His robes trailed slightly to the floor, and upon the front and back was a golden five pointed star set in the doorframe of a stylized house; the sigil and crest of the Divine Family when the deities were all represented as a whole. In one of the house's two windows was a small dove, not unlike the stylized one around my owner's neck. This showed which god he directly served under. Though united, they were still five distinct deities. Finishing off his attire was a mantle of deep red, draped around his shoulders and fastened by a silver cord.

This man was Cardinal Wollend, head of Varia's religious order, and representative of Cathedral City in the walls of Sanc Aldet. I knew of him, and his companion, thanks to the castle gossip. I found that as certain events approach, so too did talk about subjects pertaining to the event in question. In this case, I knew that the Cardinal only got his position because of his status as a noble, and as a relative to a high ranked clergyman in the main sect as well. Not surprising. He left most of the day to day operation to his second in command, Bishop Hanless, who was the man standing a few feet behind the Cardinal.

The bishop was an older man, with an austere feel to him. He wore delicate white robes as well, with the same symbols upon it, though he wore a rosary with five tokens in it rather than the red cloak of his superior, a golden sword and a silver halberd joining the dove, cloth, and lily similar to what my owner possessed. There was a sense of humility from the man, and he looked at us as if we were grandchildren he cared dearly for. From what I heard, Bishop

Hanless was much better regarded than the Cardinal, for he actively supported the local communities with charities, and was once a traveling Cleric who accompanied a famous adventuring party long ago. He had long since retired from that past, but his worldliness carried over, and the bishop was well loved by both fellow clergy and the people he tended to.

They both give deep bows to the royal family as we near, before King Tiberius bade them to rise.

"Once more we are honored by your presence, King Tiberius, Queen Amdora."

"As we are as well, Cardinal Wollend, to be in hallowed ground for such an august occasion," the king replied neutrally to the fawning cardinal. We were lead down an aisle of lovingly carved wooden benches and pews, most of them already full with various nobles and notable persons. It was traditional for the royal family to arrive last, and then for the monarch to open the ceremony with a speech of some sort.

The interior of the church was just as awe inspiring as the exterior, perhaps even more so. The ground floor was vast, and filled with benches and seats. The second floor was similar but with more lavish seats, while the third was all but empty save for a large section dedicated solely for the royal families use. Lesser nobles and the wealthiest of the bourgeoisie sit on the ground floor, while higher nobles and important guests of state were allowed up on the second floor. The view from the second floor and up was likely spectacular. As we proceeded I spotted Lady Rene Bluemont sitting up near the front of the church in a powder blue dress who gave us a polite nod of acknowledgement as we passed by.

King Tiberius stepped up along the center aisle as conversation stops. He led the rest of us on to the front, where the altar stood, and then waited as his family was led up to seating on the third floor of the church, where the royal box awaited.

Besides the seating, there were long rows of marble pillars lining the aisles. There was lots of space, and the stained glass windows, all depicting the lives and times of various saints and heroes, let in light in blinding amounts. Statues of heroes and angels

136

stood in alcoves here and there, with rows of white votive candles before them on stone plinths, all lit with faint flames. Further back in the more shadowed recesses of the church were small booths with curtains; confessionals for the parishioners who visit.

But what truly drew the eyes was a set of five massive statues standing above an altar carved from purple veined marble. It was my first time getting a good look at the depictions of humanity's major gods. The largest of the five was a pair, standing slightly above the trio below, and were made of almost solid gold. On the right was a beautiful, motherly woman, with bowed head and long locks of slightly curly hair. Her symbol, the golden dove, appeared on her bosom made of a solid chunk of topaz. In her right hand she held a sword pointing down, while her left hand clutched the right hand of the other golden statue.

"The golden woman on the right is Cynthia Goddess of Light, Mercy, and Healing. She is the Holy Mother, who protects and guides mankind," Liliana murmured quietly to me as we approached. I did nothing, merely watching in awe as the imposing figures loomed into my vison.

"The one next to her is her husband, the Knight-God. He is the god of war for mankind, and safe keeper of the souls of those who die in battle. Honor and courage are his aspects."

Also almost entirely made of solid gold, the figure beside Cynthia was a male wearing an all enclosing suit of baroque, ornate armor that included a helm that hid his face from the world. He was utterly featureless save for the armaments he carried. In his left hand was both his holy symbol, and his sacred tool; a sword. Long sword, short sword, great sword, scimitar or falchion, all blades were the Knight-God's domain, though the one depicted here was a simple long sword, pointing up towards the ceiling.

"And lastly, the ones below are their children. From right to left are Selika, goddess of the dead and eldest child. Those who died due to accidents, suicide, or because of injustice are her primary concerns. Then there is Kardale, only and middle child, and the god of Justice and Order. He carries the word of law, and judges those who sinned accordingly. He and his servants hunt the criminals and monsters who hide in the darkness of the world, dragging them into the light. No transgression shall be permitted under his watch, and no lies can be told on any tongue that wagged near him or his effigies."

"And last but not least is Nia, Goddess of Love, Purity, and Innocence. Marriage is her remit, as is the protection of maidens. She unites lovers and punishes lechers, adulterers, and other such cruel people who abuse. Kind and gentle, she takes after her mother most of all. Some say that my ancestor, Liliana the Martyred Saintess, had her soul used to give birth to the youngest of the pantheon," Liliana whispered, introducing me to the final member of the Divine Family.

Liliana turned a bit so I could get a good look at them. Each was carved from pure white marble and embossed with silver and platinum, but had their own unique style. Selika on the right looked out with a stern expression on her face, a cowl covering her head. She wore a modest flowing robe bereft of embellishment. Her symbol, a bolt of white cloth, rested under her left arm while in her right hand she clutched a quarterstaff.

In the center stood Kardale. He too had a stern face, set in a neutral expression. He wore the robes of a judge over a suit of armor. In his right hand was a halberd, symbol of his might and favored weapon of his Paladins while in his left he held a book of laws.

Lastly, standing on the left and directly beneath her father was the youngest daughter, Nia. She clutched an unstrung bow and a spring of lily flowers in her hands before her chest. She wore long robes but went bareheaded, her long hair curling majestically like her mothers. A peaceful expression graced her face as she beamed down onto the assembly.

I continued to stare at the figures even as Liliana took her seat with her family in the royal box. There was an odd, niggling feeling in the back of my mind as I looked at them, especially the depiction of Nia.

As I focused on them I felt a strange magic fill the air. It was unlike any I had encountered before, and seemed to be seeping into the area from nowhere in particular, but focusing primarily on the statues. The magic felt smooth but also dangerously hot, like liquid fire. It caressed me as it passed over everyone in the cathedral, and though I tensed it did nothing to me. In fact, it felt as if it was merely curious, and was observing me as I did the same to it. Looking closer, there appeared to be five distinct trails of mana gathering from thin air, and each was linked to one of the five statues.

Ah. I see. It seems the Divine Family was watching the proceedings from wherever they dwelt. I settled into my owner's arms, content to know that while some (or rather, most) of the people who spotted me in here frowned in disgust and disapproval, the gods themselves were permitting my entry into their home so I relaxed, at peace.

King Tiberius had remained down below in front of the altar, staring out over the congregation with an impassive expression. He cleared his throat, and what looked like a candle-stick with a rune studded orb on the top was placed in front of him. Each rune possessed specific magical effects, and as the king spoke the device let his voice be heard throughout the church and into the teeming crowd just beyond.

"People of Varia. I am King Tiberius Augustine Roan, the Lord Protector of the Sydrae Oldlands, Master of the Golden Flame and Sovereign of the City of Light, our beautiful home. I stand before you as your monarch. To most of you, I am a distant figure of authority, hidden away up here in the Purple District. It is only days like this one that allow me to walk among my people, and for that, I am thankful, to see how beloved I am." King Tiberius' speech stirred the crowd beyond the walls of the church, and echoing roars of approval from the people just outside seemed to shake the very foundations. The personages inside applauded in a much more muted manner. Their approval was clear though, and the king continued.

"My ancestors have ruled this kingdom for countless generations. From the days the first human refugees fled the Great Catastrophe that sundered Val'Narash, to the time of the occupation of Orria by the elves, to the dreadful world spanning war four centuries ago, my family has guided and protected the land and the people. And now, it is time for us to reaffirm our devotions. In praise of those who have given their lives for ours over the countless generations, from militia soldier to noble general, I bow my head in thanks."

"It is not just I, who reaffirms the love and devotion to the Divine Family and our city this day, but all of us, commoner and high-born alike. We all live in this city, a bastion of peace, propensity, and progress for the entire world. Today, we are all Varians. Let that simple truth unite us all, as we give praise to everything that allows us to be happy and free in our own ways." Thick tendril of golden light suddenly emerge from the eyes of the five statues as he said this, and reverent mutterings slide about before all noise ceases, only to be replaced almost immediately by chanting. The clergy began to hum and sing a collection of hymns, and their voices soon became the tempo that the radiance soon followed, pulsing and flickering in time with it.

The light bathed the king and the closest seats of the congregation, some of it trickling out and spilling forth to encompass all of the building and a good deal of the front steps as well. A harmonic tune filled my head, and I hummed along with it. For a moment, I felt something pat the top of my head. I looked around in confusion. It couldn't have been Liliana, as her hands still held me. And I had not sensed any other living being approach. As I glanced about, I saw a pair of ethereal beings form nearby. The first and shortest resembled the figure of Nia, but composed of shimmering silver magical energy.

The second appeared to be Cynthia herself, but formed from radiant gold, as if sunlight had been made into a solid material. As I stared at the mother and daughter duo in shock, Nia giggled soundlessly as she caught my gaze and raised a finger to her lips. Winking once, she and her mother faded away along with the light that had once filled the room.

The light receded, and the moment was over. A reverent silence remained however, the heads of the people still bowed as the chanting quieted down. After a moment, Cardinal Wollend stepped up beside the king, who made room in front of the voice enhancing artifact.

"May Cynthia bless our souls, so that we may know a portion of her kindness, and that we may spread her wisdom. May the

Knight-God keep us safe and our courage and honor strong in the face of adversity. May Selika guide our loved ones safely beyond to the Heavens and allow us to rest easy knowing they go where they deserve. May Kardale watch over us and judge our actions, rewarding the good while punishing the bad. May Nia hold our hearts, and ensure that love ever exists within us. We pray to the Divine Family for all of this, and more. Glory be to the Family!"

"Glory be!" The congregation responded, and the words boomed out across the entire city, carried aloft by the lungs and tongues of nearly seven million people.

In my mind, I smiled. So, this was faith, huh? I could see why humans found it appealing. Glancing up at Liliana's beaming face, I nodded to myself. Yes, I could see why.

Chapter 9: A picture and a premonition

Now what? That thought passed through my mind as the ceremony wound down. After the speech, the golden light, and the chant, there was only some token posturing on behalf of Cardinal Wollend and a handful other notables, though the person my owner paid the most attention to when he stepped up was an elderly half-elf man with thinning greyish hair atop his head. His grey hair and lined face spoke of long, harsh years in the outdoors, and the thin, almost invisible scars poking out from under his collar told of battles long gone. And to my eyes that man burned with fathomless vitality and power.

"My dear Lily, come say hello. I'm sure you remember Silas Revel, Grandmaster of the Adventurer's Guild?" King Tiberius said with a twinkle in his eyes as he introduced his child.

"Ah, Princess Liliana, a pleasure to see you again."

"And you as well, Sir Revel!" My owner said happily, an awe-struck look on her face. "I've read all about your adventurers and quests and have some of your merchandise as well! You're the oldest living X-ranked Adventurer alive, and you earned your rank and the title of *Phantom Blades* during the goblin invasion of 3211! Oh, I wish I'd brought my copy of *A Darkling Bridge* to sign!"

On my end I was impressed by the deeds this man had managed. Not just anyone can become X-ranked. There were less than a dozen active at any time.

"That's quite alright. Why don't I send you an autographed, first-edition copy? I'm sure there's space for it in the castle." Silas chuckled seeing my owner's face explode into a beaming smile.

For an instant I'd swear both the king and queen had jealous looks on their faces when they overheard that, but it was gone before I got a better look.

"You look like your great-grandfather when you smile like that," Silas said softly, ancient memories filling his head. "He too was enamored with adventurers and heroes, something that has lingered to this day it seems."

Now I really wasn't seeing things as Liliana's father and mother both blushed momentarily in the background.

"It was an honor to fight alongside him against the goblins, and a blessing to have his friendship. He would be proud of how beautiful and kind you and your brother are," Silas praised.

"Thank you, Grandmaster Silas. I'll do my best to live up to the pride of my family," Liliana promised, and I made a gurble of agreement. The aging half-elf just smiled fondly at my owner and gave me a pat on the head before heading off.

I decided that I liked him. Anyone who was a true and loyal friend of my owner and her family was a person I could get along with!

Now that the ceremonial portion was over, it was time to move on the next step of this holiday, and it was the part my owner loved the most. It was time to explore the stalls, booths, and activities! And this year was Liliana's chance to see more than ever before.

The royal family split up somewhat once the meet and green was over. The king and queen, accompanied by servants and a squad of Dire Swords, made their way through the crowd of guests and greeted everyone who approached, be they noble or commoner. This practice had earned them great favor in the past among all sorts of people, and I could easily see how beloved the royal family was in the eyes of the citizens.

On Julius' side, he planned on going around the various places that were selling candies and sweets. Something I had learned was that Julius had an extremely sharp sweet tooth. He was someone who could stomach the sickening sweetness of Baroness Rene Bluemont's special snacks, so something like a dozen ring cakes or an orchard of caramelized fruit was fairly tame. Plus, his figure didn't seem to be affected. Could it be related to his own *Mysterious Miracle* ability? Eh, whatever. I could do the same. Wasn't that hard. Though some women clearly watched the prince with envious eyes as he stuffed himself with seemingly no ill effects.

He was with his head maid and a duo of stern Dire Swords, with an extra trio hidden in the shadows. He was the heir and future king, after all! Such steps are only natural.

For Liliana and myself, we were browsing the accessories sold here and there. Lots of clothes and jewelry abounded in prices ranging from outrageous to clearance sale. Our escorts were Orleen, of course, and a duo of dour faced Dire Swords of our own.

We were only walking around the Purple District, as even during a festival a princess would not casually descend to the lower, and much less safe, levels of Sanc Aldet. Even so there was a whole plethora of goods here. Close to the Temple, and the vast and wide stairs that descend to the Slope District, the goods were an eclectic mix of middle class items and lower grade artifacts normally available to aristocrats and nobles. At this time, wealthy merchants and well to do adventurers were able to sample the bounty of the upper class, while those of the Purple District could amuse themselves with simpler items as a novelty of sorts.

It was around this unique border that Liliana explored, since she had always had an interest in all the aspects of her people.

"Do you think this looks good on me?" the princess inquired, examining her appearance with a plate of polished brass that was doubling as a mirror. Around her neck was a lovely pearl and opal necklace. It was high quality, though the merchant selling it was trying to gouge the price.

"It fits her highness so well! A vision of loveliness!" The seller praised, nodding his head rapidly to my owner. It wasn't hard to recognize Liliana as the princess, and even if someone didn't know, the armed guards flanking her at all times insured that she had the presence of a VIP.

"It does look lovely, but perhaps a tad on the expensive side," Orleen said, offering her input. The look she shot at the merchant made it clear she knew what he was trying to do with the price.

"For you, my lady, I am more than willing to offer a generous discount! How about a ten percent cut? Only nine gold!"

"I don't know, that certainly seems excessive for opals of that lackluster cut and polish," Orleen mused, and Liliana took an almost unnoticeable step back. She'd seen this side of her maid before, and knew it was best to let her haggle to her hearts content. I, for one, was most impressed by the rapid fire exchange of numbers and arguments that went on. Watching Orleen, I quietly learned from her mastery of the market, and from Liliana's whispers as she explained the currency to me.

Money was fairly straight forward in Orria. Each kingdom minted their own currency, but it all followed a fairly stable monetary system. The coins were made of copper, silver, gold, and platinum. A day's wages for a simple laborer tended to be about twenty copper. The price of a loaf of bread was about five coppers. And the conversion rate was also fairly simple; it was a hundred copper coins to a single silver one, but only ten silver coins to equal a gold coin. Fifty gold coins makes one platinum coin, though that particular currency was only rarely used, mostly by nobles and large scale transactions.

"Another side effect of the Adventurer's Guild wide spread presence is that the economy tends to be fairly stable all over, barring a war or major natural disaster," Liliana continued, and I finally realized why she so clearly remembered her lessons on economics. "Because Adventurers travel so much more and in far wider scope, a stabilized monetary system was all but insured so they could continue to buy goods and sell treasure and loot. Their needs force certain goods to retain a standardized value across national borders."

After a moment of intense back-and-forth, Orleen smiled primly and removed a purse from her waist, counting out a number of small golden coins. The merchant accepted with a smile and nodded politely to the woman who had bested him.

I stole a glance at the currency, intrigued. I have only seen it from a distance, as Liliana did not often carry her own money with her. Most of her allowance was entrusted to Orleen. She understood monetary issues and the worth of a coin, but an old law prevented any noble not an adult from carrying more than five silver coins at any time. Odd, but it was observed stringently by the upper class.

Traditions were, if nothing else, adhered to rabidly regardless of how ridiculous they seemed.

We moved on from the jewelry stall, grabbing some lunch as we did. It was a piece of cooked meat wrapped in crusty bread and stuck on a skewer. Liliana, through Orleen, purchased everyone in the group a skewer. Her Dire Swords bowed their heads in thanks before discreetly checking for poison in their share as well as their princess'. I swallowed my portion whole, wooden stick and all, and hummed contentedly as I digested the meal.

"What next should we visit, Orleen?" Liliana inquired, wiping some grease off her mouth with a handkerchief.

"It's up to you, my lady. Though, if I may offer a suggestion?" Liliana nodded at her, and the maid cleared her throat.

"I heard that there was a group of artists down near the fountain. Perhaps you might enjoy having a sketch done or seeing a performance?"

"Wonderful idea! Lead the way, Orleen!" My owner cheered happily, passing me her now empty stick. I took it anyways, eating it. No need to make trash. Seeing this, the two guards shared a look, before the one on the right shrugged and politely offered me his own used skewer. I did not mind helping out and snagged it, which was followed quickly by his partner's.

"You have a most useful pet, my lady," the right most Dire Sword said with a chuckle. His comrade shot him a scathing look, but let it go. They were tasked to protect the royal family. If the princess did not reprimand them for conversation, it was not his problem or duty to scold his partner.

"Thank you! Jelly is indeed the most talented!" Liliana beamed, and followed after Orleen with an upbeat mood to her steps. At the fountain, which was a large marble pool with a marble statue of Nia spouting water from her hands at the center, there was indeed a large number of artistic and creative people mill about. Not just painters and sketchers, but bards loudly trying to tell tales and songs, acrobats and jugglers showing off their techniques, and so much more happening at once.

Eyes wide and gleaming Liliana swept through, trying to take in everything at once. She quickly returned to Erafore with a sharp click from Orleen's tongue. Settling down, the princess looked about, trying to spot a free, or moderately less busy, artist to capture an image of her and her pet.

"There, he seems mostly free," the Dire Sword on our right spoke up, pointing over at a young man who only had two other customers. With a bounce in her heels, Liliana heads over, but was not in a hurry. There was so much to see, and we enjoy watching a fire eater compete with a sword swallower as we wait. I was particularly impressed with the two performers. I knew for a fact humans could not naturally consume flames or metal, so watching these two men do so, or at least pretend to do so, was most amusing.

"My lady, are you interested in a picture? I have charcoal, ink, or pastels!" A youthful voice called out, and as one the princess' group turns to see who it was that cried out for their attention. It turns out to be a person none of us, save myself, had noticed. The man was tiny, less than half the size of Liliana, and whipcord thin. Their hair was a shocking orange, and they wore simply made clothes stained on the edges with paint and ink, much like his fingers. He sat on the lip of the fountain, with an easel and bunches of art supplies close at hand. He gave a winning smile at our group, and I could feel Liliana become excited.

"Oh my! A gnome!"

"Indeed I am, my lady. Was it perhaps my size? Or the hair?" The miniscule man said with a kind laugh. My owner's flashed a bit red but kept up her smile seeing as the Tiny Folk artist took no offense.

"We don't usually see gnomes outside of Tantara or Par-Orria. Apologies for my excitable behavior."

"It's no problem. I understand my people tend to be rather isolated. Not me, though. I've taken a liking to travel, and recording what I see there. So, perhaps my nomadic talents might pique your interest?" The young looking person inquired as he swept a hand around at his creations.

"Was this your work?" Liliana asked, looking at a nearby finished picture. It was an intricate charcoal drawing of the fountain

157

and surrounding area, with great detail laid into the entirety of the features. It was carefully done, and clearly of a high grade.

"Yes, indeed! Every stroke and every smudge! I must say, young lady had a fine eye. Would you care to have your image captured? I have good rates, and excellent skill."

"I don't see why not. One ink portrait, please." So saying, Liliana stepped demurely up to the miniscule painter and took a pose with me in her arms; perched on the edge of the fountain, staring off into the distance while she fondly pat my head. The gnome quickly got to work and had a brief outline done in minutes. Once that was completed, he informed my owner she could move around again, and her shoulders sagged a touch in relief.

A quick arch of the back removes the tiny aches in it, and she peeked over the shoulder while the artist works. She said nothing, simply watched, and I did as well. The gnome politely said nothing as well, focused instead on his work.

About thirty minutes later, the short man let out a sigh of satisfaction, and leaned back slightly to admire the drawing. Liliana and I did so as well, and I was impressed. I'd gotten better at seeing things with my echolocation, so I could now comprehend certain kinds of pictures and writing. With my senses, I could trace the ink and the indentations made by quills or brushes, and "read" whatever they made. It took a bit more effort but I was able to appreciate this well-made portrait. Judging by his steady strokes and careful lines, this gnome had considerable skill. Not master class, or even an expert, but definitely a cut above the average street painter.

Liliana gave it a nod of approval. Growing up surrounded by luxuries, it would be weirder for her not to have developed a sense of taste and how to gauge talent and craftsmanship.

"Very well done. And I'm glad to see you gave care to the depiction of my dear Jelly, as much as my own profile. Thank you," Liliana praised with a tilt of her head. I burbled in agreement. I have to say, this fellow really caught the majestic curvature of my body!

"Your words are too kind, my lady," the gnome replied with his own bow of the head. "I am most pleased that you find my work satisfactory."

"Of course! Here, the payment." At this, Liliana reached into her own purse and removed a single silver coin. A considerably generous tip for a work that should only be a dozen or so copper!

"Thank you, my lady!" The artist profusely gushed his thanks, bowing his head rapidly. Liliana waved her hand placating, and with a smile nodded at Orleen who accepted the parchment from the Tiny Folk.

"He was rather talented, don't you agree?" Liliana queried once we are some blocks away from the fountain area.

"Indeed, my lady," was the monotone response from her Dire Knights, while her maid merely nodded. As we move on, I detected a familiar presence, and wiggled excitedly.

"Oh! If it isn't Princess Liliana!" My owner turned her head, as do her companions, and a lanky man in mages robes appeared from the crowd. He pushed his way through with the occasional apology, and nodded his head in respect once he got close.

"Sir Petrus! How are you?" Liliana extended her right hand, and he demurely pressed his forehead to her knuckles in greeting.

"I am well. Yourself, my lady?" The student mage asked, giving nods of respect to her escorts.

"I am doing well, thank you for asking. Are you enjoying the festival?"

"So far so good! It is a very lively gathering, the likes of which the Academy's city cannot hope to match. And I see you're partaking of its activities," Petrus said, glancing at the rolled up portrait.

"Indeed, here, take a look. This drawing is of decent quality, wouldn't you say?" At her mistress's request, Orleen gently unrolled the artwork, showing it off to Petrus who bobbed his head in appreciation.

"A very lovely work. But fragile. I fear it won't last the rest of the day in a crowd like this. Perhaps I might intrude, and cast a protection charm on it?"

"Oh, would you? That would be most wonderful!"

At her approval, Petrus took the portrait carefully and muttered a few words over it while running a glowing palm across the surface. It flickered with light for a moment, before the glow receded. Once done, he passed it back.

"There, the ink won't smudge for a week and the paper will remain crisp and mostly dry," Petrus said with pride.

"That was impressive! I did not know there was magic like that," Liliana noted, and the apprentice shrugged.

"It was a fairly simple spell, and one that almost all students at the Academy learn. It's useful for keeping our notes intact and the books damage free. Always a problem when we have to share resources in the buildings," Petrus explained, with just a hint of annoyance being expressed at his living arrangement.

"Regardless, I am most grateful for keeping my purchase safe." Liliana gave Petrus a thankful nod, which he returned with a deeper bow.

"Not a problem at all, my lady. Now, I must ask your pardon, but I have someone to meet up with. Please excuse me."

"Oh course, no problem at all. But, will I see you at the Adventurer's Advent later?"

Petrus ponders the question for a moment, before giving a nod. "Most likely. Master Renos will be attending as a representative of the Academy due to the headmaster being busy, and as his disciple I'll likely have to accompany him."

"Then, I look forward to our next meeting," Liliana said, nodding politely before moving on deeper in the event. As we leave, I see Petrus give a lingering look back at us. Or rather, at the portrait. Was there something about it he recognized?

"Look, Jelly! Ring cakes!" My owner's joyful exclamation shook me out of my musings. Questions later, pastries now!

"Well look at what the cat dragged in! How's school life treating you, Petrus?"

"Well enough, Marl." The thin, almost starved looking mage approached a gnome painter who was sitting at the edge of the

Purple District's fountain, doing some sketches of the surroundings while watching the people go by. The mage gave a friendly wave to the Tiny Folk. At least, that was how it appears to any passerby. The gestures spread a thin sheet of magic around the two, forming a sound reflecting barrier.

"Pleasantries aside for now, though. I found what it was Master Renos wanted." Marl the gnome reached into a pouch at his feet and removed a rolled up scroll bound in string, passing it over to Petrus. The mage took it and quickly unfurled it, eyes skimming the contents before closing it.

"Just as he feared, then?"

"Yup. Something is going on out along the western border, centered on the Edelstein domain. That blasted Count is up to something. He's been gathering all sorts of records and data, and of the sort he has no real business obtaining. Maps of the castle walls, details on the composition and locations of the wards, and entire ledgers worth of profiles on the staff." Marl looked pointedly at his friend. "We need to let the king know as soon as possible about all

164

of this. And worse, I have a feeling in my gut that this is just the tip of the iceberg."

"I understand. I will relay this information post haste," Petrus nodded, rolling up the scroll and tucking it away in his own robes.

"You know, Marl, Renos is still waiting for you to come back. You have a real talent, and I think…" Marl raised a hand to cut him off.

"Please, Petrus, don't do this. I've made my decision. The wizarding way is just not for me. I feel a greater connection to my art than I do to my magic, and I enjoy applying one to the other in my own style. I want to explore this new path. But give my thanks to Master Renos for still thinking of me."

Visibly working to keep his mouth closed, Petrus nodded his head tightly.

"It is your choice, after all. Just know that you're welcome any time at my studio."

"Thanks, Pet," Marl said softly. At the nickname, the mage heaved a sigh, but smiled faintly none the less.

"Keep an ear to the ground, Marl. The Academy and the Crown may need your services again in the near future."

"Sure thing. And watch over the princess and her little squishy pet, got it? She's a real gem."

Petrus laughed knowingly at that. "Isn't that the truth!"

Chapter 10: A display and a dark plot

The day was winding down, with dusk just approaching. The mountain tops were stained a fiery red as the sun set, though I cannot see it, and I gave a content sigh as I watched the final events of the day with my owner. The royal family and I were sitting in an elevated stand overlooking a large, cleared out section of the Slope District. Here, a large impromptu arena had been established and now a series of people in armor and 'unique' outfits were demonstrating their admittedly impressive skills.

Bursts of magic, combat drills, and more exploded across the field, drawing 'ooo's' and 'ahhh's' from the audience, which was full to bursting with the citizens of Sanc Aldet.

"Father, why is this competition part of the festival? Isn't it a bit more violent for a religious event?" Julius inquired from his seat between his father and mother.

"The Reaffirmation of Faith is a holy day, despite all the fun and games that goes on after the morning ritual. This event was originally made to show the devotion the gods' Clerics and Paladins, but it wound up becoming akin to an unofficial muscle flexing on the part of the church, and by extension, Cathedral City," King Tiberius explained for the benefit of his son. Julius gave a slow nod.

"Cathedral City is an independent city-state run by the Church, right?" Liliana asked.

"Yes indeed, Liliana. But it also acts as a location for all of the sanctioned god's to be worshiped. Gaea, Akasha, Balcom, and other deities have important temples there. Thankfully Varia and the religious headquarters are on good terms. As such, this posturing takes on a somewhat friendly tone. Plus, quite a few of the participants are members, or ex-members, of the Adventurer's Guild," Queen Amdora explained, picking up the explanation from her husband for her children.

"Not only in the church, a great deal of groups and factions send their people to train in the guild. The youngest children of minor nobles and aristocratic families, trainee knights, and students from the Mage's Academy all used the Adventurer's guild as a stepping stone in their careers. And famous adventurers could become high ranked in the church or institute of their choice once they retired, much like Bishop Hanless."

The priest in question was currently acting as a referee and commentator for the display down below to make sure no one went overboard.

"And a wonderful display from Cleric Elati of Saluda, the *Storming Falcon*! Her sword dance was as beautiful as the wielder!" The bishop announced, giving a send-off to the B-ranked adventurer who had just presented.

Though Queen Amdora scoffed earlier and mumbled about how it was shameful for a woman to wear so little, she, along with the rest of the family, had watched closely and appreciatively. Observing this, I started to understand where my owner and her brother got their enthusiasm for adventurers from.

"And now, we come to a highlight of this display. Our kingdom's very own Captain of the Guard, the Commander of the Dire Swords, the world renowned disciple of the Knight-God, please welcome Sir Blaine ArLeon the *Purple Blade!*" Bishop Hanless called, voice carrying to all the area thanks to the device from earlier. At the introduction, Liliana and Julius began to applaud with extra vigor as the familiar figure of their long time guard enters. Though he always attended to their father, Sir Blaine took the time to get to know the rest of his charges. He wasn't that close, but he was considerate of my owner and her brother's preferences for defenders and accommodated when he could.

He was also an imposing man, on par with King Tiberius for charisma, and a peerless swordsman. He was all but unmatched in the capitol, and the Adventurer's Guild graded him as a lower grade S-rank warrior.

"Sir Blaine has trained as a Paladin, but chose to dedicate his life protecting the kingdom, and later, the royal family instead of being an adventurer or an elite in the Church," Bishop Hanless revealed to rapturous applause. "Much of his Paladin magic remains and his connection to the god of war allows him to be a master of both offensive techniques as well as defensive ones."

The commander of the royal guard entered from the side and took a stance in the center of the arena, striking an impressive figure. He wore the blue and gold uniform of the Dire Swords with a crimson cape fluttering serenely in the evening breeze. Chainmail sat beneath his tabard, small glints showing it off as he moved. Dark brown boots and gloves covered the feet and hands, and a leather belt and scabbard completed the ensemble.

As roughly a fourth of the entire city watched, Sir Blaine took a careful stance, slowly drawing his blade. The setting sun reflected off the ensorcelled steel, turning it blood red, which only enhanced the intimidating effect. Motes of blue light begin to gather at his feet, and lazily started to spiral around him. Then, he lifted up in the air, propelled by the magical energy coalescing upon him. His sword became wrapped in pulsing ropes of energy that glow a faint gold, and it left trails of golden after images in the blade's wake. Sir Blaine proceeded to perform sword drills in midair, floating lazily about as if he's just defied gravity and was totally unimpressed with his results. Which was what he was doing, technically. Furthermore, under my scrutiny, I noticed a trickle of magic pool behind and around his eyes. On the visible spectrum, this resulted in a glow that was almost lost amid the rest of his magic. Curious. I wondered what he was doing with that spell?

Though his movements were impressive, and his control over his weapon enviable, what I was truly intrigued by was the magic he was using.

My owner possessed curiosity as well and looked to her mother for an answer.

"Sir Blaine is using what we call Divine Magic," Queen Amdora began, unable to say 'no' to her daughter's pouting face. "Amongst the four types of magic, Divine Magic follows very odd rules. Occult Magic, sometimes also known as Arcane Magic, is the type used by Wizards, Sorcerers, mages in general, and people who studied spells and used their own magical power to produce spells. It is what I used when I studied at the Academy Divine Magic on the other hand involves praying to a deity and having them bestow a portion of their might upon you in the form of spells or unique abilities."

"So all you need to do is pray? That's it?" Liliana asked, and I leaned in a bit.

"Basically, yes. For Occult Magic, a spell can be cast over and over as long as you have the ingredients or magical power to do so. As such, Divine Magic has an advantage in that area, as you don't need to know any magic or spells to use the gifts of a god. However once cast a certain number of times the knowledge of the Divine spell will be forgotten. You can no longer use that spell, unless you pray again to the god who gave it to you."

"Amazing," Liliana whispered, and I couldn't help but nod.

Magic was so wide spread across Erafore that even a peasant could, and often did, use magic, be it in the form of enchantments, runes, or cantrips. All living things possessed souls, which produced mana, which was the raw fuel for magic, which when manipulated created spells. But not everyone could study and memorize spells, or gather the materials needed. Which was where the gods apparently came in, offering immediate access to spells in return for a few hours of prayer and obeying the laws of the deity.

That was why the talent show began to really interest me. After all, only the most devout practitioners could afford to waste spells when showing off like that. Thanks to their reckless spending I was getting insight into the nature of the previously unknown magic.

Where Petrus' magic was drawn from within himself and fused with the magical energy beyond his body, thus creating an Occult-style spell, Sir Blaine and the rest of the so-called Clerics and Paladins had the magical power seemingly pop up out of nowhere. It leaked into reality from a place I could not comprehend or even analyze as the portals it came from appeared and vanished far too fast for me to get more than a quick glance.

But the attempt of trying to catch a glimpse of that mysterious realm kept me attentive at least. I did not know enough about fighting or the exploits of these people to be engrossed in the displays. It was their spells that I was observing. I really wanted to learn as much as I could about magic. After all, as an Ooze I am about 90% solidified magic. The more I knew and thus understood about that force of reality the better I could potentially manage my own existence.

Could I even use Divine magic anyways? Because I was born from magic itself, or rather the residue of it, I didn't know if I had a soul. Was that what my owner's ability did to me? Did she perhaps give me a soul, or allow a nascent one to be nurtured in the body of mine?

"What an amazing display of divine blessing! Able to maintain two Divine spells at once! Sir Blaine is truly worthy of his position as commander of the Dire Swords! We are all glad that his majesty King Tiberius is under his watch." His routine completed, the armored knight returned to the ground as Bishop Hanless promoted his feats. Mentally, I applauded the man. He was incredibly talented, and seeing him use three spells simultaneously was a treat in and of itself! And the fact that no one seemed to be able to tell that a third spell had been used further cemented his skills in my mind.

He made his way back up to the stand where we were and he took a stance behind King Tiberius. He leaned his head down, ever so slightly, and started muttering so only the king could hear. Well, the king and myself. Unconsciously I leaned a bit over to listen in.

Again, I marveled at how sensitive my body was. Through the way the voices travel through the air, I could hear practically everything going on in the arena and audience at once. I couldn't feel pain in the traditional sense, but focusing and comprehending each and every conversation was like trying to create, maintain, and use dozens of limbs at once, while also balancing a plate on each one. Doing so made my mind feel weak, and the energy that sustained me started to degrade faster. As such, I had to willfully ignore more than half of what went on around me at a time, lest my mind tear under the stress. Still, I thought I could allow one more talk to enter my consciousness. After all, this one seemed serious, given how stiffly Sir Blaine was holding himself, and the minute creasing of King Tiberius' brow. Knowing about it could help my owner at some point.

"My king, it was as our informant said. At least two men under Count Darpel's command were using magic in the crowd to analyze the contestants, myself included. And another one was further back, trying to dismantle some of the wards around your carriage. I fear we may have a potential coup in the making."

If it was possible to go pale, I would have. Okay, what? What was that? Was there something happening in the backgrounds I was not aware of? I mean, I cannot be everywhere, but I do have some pride as a gossip-gatherer, and I have heard nothing about a revolt or rebellion!

Though the name 'Darpel' rang a bell. That was the family name of a count from a prosperous territory who married one of the king's older sisters. It seems the man was bribing some of the staff for information on the castle and the people within. I returned my 'ear' to the pair nearby and listened in some more.

"Damn him and damn my sister! I let them live last time, but they get no second chances! Inform the Dire Swords to keep a sharp eye on the people we've confirmed as being on his payroll, and if need be find a way to eliminate them. I will not have another conflict like the last time my siblings tried to take my crown! I will not have my wife and children put into danger!" King Tiberius hissed, a seething fury bubbling in every syllable. An imperceptible nod was the only response from Sir Blaine and he took a step back, making a complicated hand gesture to one of the closest Dire Swords. That man then nodded and wandered off to do something. Pass on the orders, I supposed. I slid my gaze up into the grinning face of my owner, and steeled my heart.

If anyone dared to harm my Liliana, they will see how dangerous a slime could be!

Chapter 11: Danger senses, awaken!

Well, yesterday was fun, but now our noses were back to the grindstone! I didn't have a nose, obviously, but I could grow something that looked like one. In fact, I was now able to create fingers and toes on my bipedal body, or as Liliana calls it, my Gel Doll form. I'd gotten better at controlling that odd shape, and now I could walk without doing a shuffling hop every time I need to move. I still need some help with balance, but other than that I think I'd improved. I could perform the Leol Waltz without much problem and only a smidge of aid, and the Swan Step was so simple even my lack of coordination was easily remedied. And that's good. These two dances were the most common for younger and unmarried nobles to do when on the dance floor, so if my owner wanted to show me off, I could follow her lead and dance without shaming her.

"Very good, very good! Princess Liliana, your grace and elegance is really shining through! Your footwork is light and steady, therefore I think the Swan Step is the best choice of dance for you." Lady Bluemont mused, overlooking my owner and I's practice. "I recommend focusing on your balance if you want to improve with the Leol Waltz, though for the limited time you've had so far, I must say I am proud and impressed by your growth."

"Thank you, Rene," Liliana replied with a curtsey. Her smile became strained as she accepted one of the tutor's dried snacks, but she did her duty none the less. I burbled with appreciation as well, and took my own share of the tasty treats with much greater enthusiasm.

"Tomorrow, we'll be doing something different. Instead of practicing our routines, a tailor will be here to take your measurements, my lady. We'll be able to do live dress rehearsals once this is done. And he can find something for Jelly to wear as well. Though I do not know how well he works with garments for pets," Rene informed, shooting me an appraising look as she finished speaking.

"Now then, I want you well rested for tomorrow. Picking out the right dress may seem easy, but it can be fraught with peril." Liliana chuckled, clearly thinking it was just a joke. But not me. I could tell that Rene's emotions were stable. She believed in what she was talking about. Huh. As a being that had never worn clothes before, the concept had always intrigued me. I wondered what I could even wear? My body was far too slippery and oddly shaped for most fabrics, so would anything even stay on me? What if it was absorbed into my body and dissolved, like the dirt and other things that ended up lying on my form? A question for another day I supposed.

"Thank you for the lessons, Rene," Liliana said in farewell to her tutor, giving a slight bow before scooping me up. As I was bundled up into her arms, I reabsorbed my limbs back into myself, returning to my blobby orb shape. Despite all my training, that was still the form I am most comfortable with.

"Tonight is bath time! I must admit I am glad. Dancing is surprisingly strenuous. I've worked up a slight sweat." My owner chattered a bit to me, and I listened politely as did Orleen.

An hour and a half later and Liliana was washed and scrubbed and ready for dinner. She carries me to the small dining room, where surprisingly, only her father was waiting. It was rare that the king was first to the table. As usual, Sir Blaine stood a few steps behind his liege, while a scribe looked over a collection of documents in his arms.

"How are you, my flower?" King Tiberius inquired, giving his daughter a bright smile.

"I am well, father," Liliana replied, nodding respectfully. King Tiberius nodded as well, and he turns to the handful of papers sitting before him on the table.

"Rene is doing a good job then?"

"Oh yes! She is very good to me, and is very talented. I've learned a lot under her!"

"And does she still give out her 'treats?'" the king asked, his voice steady, but with a haunted look in his eyes. Liliana's own expression darkened a tad and her own eyes mirrored her father's.

"Yes, father, she does." Nothing more was said, but a companionable silence descended upon the room, parent and child sharing a moment of understanding through similar hardships.

"Dear, have you seen Karina? She had not been around for a few hours, and I'm concerned," Queen Amdora asked as she entered the dining room a few minutes later, her gown billowing slightly as she entered. Her husband glanced up and nodded in confirmation.

"Yes, I have seen her. I sent her off on an errand."

"Oh, I see. And when will she be back?" the Queen inquired, a hint of annoyance in her tone at her personal servant being ordered by someone else.

"Not long, I should think. Another day or so, I would imagine," King Tiberius mused, sharing a covert look with Sir Blaine, who offers a minute nod. That byplay passed right by my owner's notice, but not the queen's. She too nodded mutely in acceptance, her annoyance now supplemented by worry.

I also felt a touch of concern. Karina Ashbell was a half-elf and was not just the queen's personal maid but also her primary

183

defender. A trained assassin sworn to serve and protect Queen Amdora, she was only ever away from the castle if she was needed for darker, bloodier matters. How did I know that? Being able to hear and sense practically everything around me helped a lot. Karina's footsteps are much lighter than a normal maid's, and her muscle tone was one born from rigorous training with weapons, not lifting loads of laundry or carrying and using cleaning tools. Plus, I once glimpsed her pin a cockroach to the wall with a fork with pinpoint accuracy from half a room away. She did not like bugs. At all. I kept that lesson close to my core.

"Well, be sure to let me know when she returns," Queen Amdora informed her king and husband, who agreed. She then settled into her chair, and now it's me, her, my owner, and the king, waiting for Prince Julius. It was not long before he entered, a dazzling smile on his face and grass and dirt stains all over his clothes.

"I see you've had some fun today outside," King Tiberius chuckled, looking the disheveled appearance of his son. The queen was not as impressed. Her mouth was compressed into a thin line, and a disapproving glare nails her son. Julius shrank back slightly, his smile wavering.

"And how exactly did you get this messy?" Queen Amdora demanded.

"Um, well, I was practicing my swordplay, but a rabbit popped up, and I sorta… chased it around for a while?"

A heavy sigh escaped the queen's lips before she sat back and restored her primness with a deep breath. "Next time you get so dirty, make sure to clean up before attending dinner, Julius dear."

"Of course, mother." The prince acquiesced meekly, before sitting down at the table. The exasperated look from the queen was now directed at Jean, his maid, who lowered her head in embarrassment.

"Please try and help my dear son maintain a degree of decorum, Miss Jean," Queen Amdora politely but firmly instructed, with the maid bowing her head quickly in acknowledgement.

"Well, since we are all here, let's begin dinner." At the king's suggestion, a nearby servant hurried off and almost immediately more staff bearing platters power walked in. As they set the table with delicacies and savories, Liliana removed a pair of small glass bottles from her pouch around her waist. I bounced slightly in place as I sense my owner pop the stopper from one of them.

My meals lately have consisted of vial after vial of healing potions. A dull red in color, held in tiny glass containers, these little alchemical wonders were absolutely delicious to me. They were only Minor-grade potions, but that was enough. A single Minor healing potions could almost instantly heal cuts and bruises, and could be applied directly to the wound for quicker results, or drunk to spread the effect to any and all cuts. Somewhat expensive though. That tiny bottle of fairly ordinary but efficient medicine costs a whole silver coin! And for the common worker, with only a few dozen coppers earned per day, that was a luxury. Still, not terribly expensive for them, which was good, I supposed. I'd had Minor-grade potions so far, since even as a royal pet I am not exactly worth the gold coins for the highest quality stuff. But the magic in them (strawberry flavored) was good enough for me!

I reach out a pseudopod and slurpped down the contents of the offered potion through it. Liliana and Julius both giggled at that.

"Oh, you're acting just like a baby, Jelly," Liliana teased. Ignoring her comment I continued to drink unabashedly, and once I finish the first bottle, I gurgled and reached pitifully for the last potion. Laughing at my antics, the princess passes me the vial and I uncork it myself, holding the bottleneck close as I greedily drink the succulent juices.

As I had my meal, the royal family began theirs as well. Steam wafted through out the room, and it was only strict disciplines and iron wills that prevents the servants on standby from salivating and staring longingly at the feast before them. I extend some pity and sympathy for them. Really, forced to watch but unable to actually touch the food must be torture.

As I was pondering this, without warning, my core started to itch! I froze in my owner's lap, bottle of potion mostly drained. My sudden stop did not go unnoticed. The guards went stiff, as did the more perceptive servants, and of course the king and queen. Only Julius and Liliana remained ignorant of the sudden shift in mood. I ignored everyone's attention at me, and expand my senses as far as they would go, trying to find the source of the irritation. My core had never done that before, and I was worried as to what that means. The itch was also less of a physical sensation, and closer to how I assume shivers might run down the spine of a person.

After a bit my extrasensory scanning came to a halt, unable to find anything out of place nearby. As much as I had improved, I still did not have total control, and my 'sight' did not go through thicker surfaces like the stone floors and walls. Whatever I just sensed, it was too far away for me to detect. But that just raised the question of 'why did I react in the first place?' I settled down, albeit reluctantly, and the dining room's company relax as well. Some of them keep their attention on me, but as I have made no additional moves, are content to assume it was just an 'Ooze thing.'

Dinner had come and gone, and now I was resting on my cushion that doubled as a bed. Liliana had wanted to give me one of those basket-beds for felines, but I was perfectly happy with my fluffy pillow, so she did not push the matter. I listened for a moment to the sounds of my owner breathing softly, and I felt at peace as well.

Yet I could not sleep! The itch in my core had not left, and I could not find any succor! At length, I slid off my bedding and squirmed my way towards the door of the room. Carefully, I squeezed my mass through the tiny opening under the door and slipped through with nary a problem.

As long as that 'itch' remained, I felt I would not have any peace, so I sought out the source. Inching my way along the hallway, I hugged the wall, careful to avoid the passerby's. Even at the dead of night there was activity in the castle. Not just guards patrolling the areas, but also servants scuttle about, keeping fires going, closing and opening windows to control the temperature, airing out and cleaning older rooms so not to disturb people who might use them during the day, and a whole plethora of odds and ends that needed doing, regardless of whether it was the sun or moon in the sky.

Avoiding them was easy, though perhaps not surprising. In the dark I was nearly invisible, and the torches and lamps the various wandering workers carried cast extremely long and thick shadows here and there which meant I could just stop moving next to a suit of decorative armor or a plinth with a valuable vase and blend into the darkness created by the passing light. I do not make much noise either, just a low 'squig squish' as I move, so staying put when someone walked by was enough to get me unnoticed around the castle. I'd done that before, at least during the day; exploring here and there, learning the layout of the castle.

Day or night meant little to something that 'saw' through a form a magical echolocation, and I made my way deeper and deeper into the depths of the royal palace, following the sensations tickling my core. It was like that peasant child's game, "Hot Hot Cold," or whatever, I had seen the staff's children playing in the outer courtyard. When the sensation dwindled, I would wander about till I found it again, and then followed the itching as it grew stronger. As a result of that, it took me much longer than I'd originally planned on.

I ended up in the depths of the castle's cellar, or one of them at least, where large containers full of produce and salted meat were being stored. My core hadn't stopped annoying me; in fact I could feel my very essence quivering thanks to something in the air. I opened my senses as wide as possible, now that I was closer to the source of my irritation. What I saw made me cringe.

Oozes. At least a full dozen of them, lounging about in the slightly musty darkness of the food cellar, and amusing themselves by rolling over the food and consuming it. At first glance they looked like me; round body, squishy, with a semi-solid core resting in their center. Closer inspection revealed some very key differences. Mainly that these Oozes were far more acidic and full to bursting with toxins than I was, or ever had been. On the color spectrum, they'd be acid green, appropriately enough, with darker green cores, and they were slowly filling the basement air with an airborne poison of sorts.

I glared at these intruders, vaguely understanding why I was feeling the way I did with my itching core; it was a danger sense, more specifically a sixth sense related to the wellbeing of my owner. If these things were left unchecked they'd poison all the food down here, and that would endanger Liliana.

Even if the food went untouched, the fumes the toxic Ooze were leaking would drift slowly upwards into her bedroom. Not just hers, though, but Julius' and her parent's rooms as well! Now that I was oriented, I clearly realized that this was no accident. Several vents, cracks, and airways lead from that room up through the castle and filtered into over a dozen others, including the royal chambers where my owner and her family currently slept.

Left down here long enough the poison would build up and reach them! I doubt that even Rene's homemade anti-toxin snacks would do any good against the secretions of a Poison Ooze, for there was quiet a lot of magic in the poisons that I could detect, and I had no idea how'd it react to the Aruga fruit slices she'd been feeding us.

Giving a vague approximation of a growl I rolled towards the intruders. As I gave the impression of a glare, one of them perked up and turned to 'look' at me, and I felt its senses brush against mine. Something tried to enter my mind at that point.

I froze, worried it may be an attempt at mind control, but relaxed when I felt 'confusion' and 'caution' push upon my thoughts. That was not a mental attack; that was the Ooze in front of me trying to communicate with me! But I have no way of doing so in return. None that I could remember, at least. Whatever Liliana had done to me at the pet shop seemed to have stripped away my natural ability to 'talk' with others of my kind. A brief flash of sorrow and regret flashed through my mind, but I squashed it under righteous fury and protectiveness towards my dear owner.

What happened next was over very quickly. In response to the mental probe I lashed out, propelling a tentacle out of my body as fast as a whip and piercing the offender's body and core. I then ripped my limb out, the Poison Ooze's core still impaled on the end, like an olive stuck to a cocktail stick.

Immediately the other Oozes became hostile, spitting globs of stinging acid and venom my way, which I dodged quiet easily. I was far faster than any of them, and over and over I thrust a tendril towards them, stabbing through their slimy flesh and impaling the core, before proceeding to rip it out and consume it in my own body. It was over in less than a minute.

I gobbled down their cores, feeling a tiny bit of shame at doing so. Again I ignored those feelings and proceeded to slurp up the quickly dissolving remains of their bodies. Without the cores, an Ooze would begin to rapidly decay, becoming a slurry of liquid magic. That goo could be just as deadly if left alone, especially considering it was from a Poison Ooze, and I neutralized the toxins left within the remains inside my own body.

Then, I sucked in the air around me, turning myself in a giant pseudo-lung that purified the air the Oozes had tainted. I finished up my cleaning of the area by devouring the bits and pieces of preserved food that had been touched by the foreign Oozes as they'd dwelled down here and sliding over the Poison Ooze's slime trails.

As I cleaned the cellar I found the source of the infestation: a box. Wooden paneled on the outside but thin sheets of lead had been slipped inside to make it impossible to detect the Oozes or their poisons. And upon it was an emblem. Two griffons in flight upon a red shield. The mark of Edelstein and its ruling family.

In a shriek of rage I lashed out with a limb and smashed the wood to pieces before I began to furiously devour the container that had nearly delivered death to my owner and her family. Even as the lead, a well-known magical inhibitor, burned my body as I dissolved it I kept feeding.

Perhaps I should have saved it as evidence. But I was blinded by rage at the sheer audacity of it all! Not even a nail was left behind as I scoured the room clean of the murderous intent.

After heaving up and down as the anger faded the tingle and itch of warning in my mind disappeared altogether. Only partially satisfied with the conclusion, I made my way back to my bed, and my owner. She was safe now, and I was going to have a well-earned nap!

Chapter 12: A day of dress up

I woke the next morning feeling refreshed, and also slightly stronger than before. My mana had grown significantly, and I could feel a new pair of traits swirling about in my gelatinous body; poison and acid. I could now generate a toxin similar to the ones produced by the Poison Ooze I encountered last night, but much weaker, as well as manifest a stronger version of my 'stomach' acid externally. They were very similar abilities to the Poison Ooze's I had found last night. My hypothesis was it was due to the dozen Ooze's I slew and devoured down in the cellar. Something to consider for future consideration.

Only a hint of regret still lingered about me due to what I did. They were members of my own kind, but they were also unintelligent and a danger to my owner and her family. Their deaths meant little when I weighed it against that.

Enough depressing matters! Liliana was awakening as well, and it was time to start the day.

After getting dressed she cuddled me close as per usual on her way to breakfast. Her schedule had been cleared so instead of an Arithmetic lesson with the very old tutor for that subject, the entire day was dedicated to preparing a dress for the ball that was fast approaching.

"Good morning, Rene," Liliana called out to the elder woman in the dining room. Her instructor in all things high society looked over and smiled warmly, nodding in greeting and motioning for my owner to take a seat next to her. Breakfasts and lunches were disordered affairs, and while it would be improper for a minor aristocrat to sit at the table when the king himself was present, Rene was permitted by King Tiberius to sit in the Minor Royal Dining Room when she wished. Regardless of his inability to deal with her boisterous personality she was an important guest, and a family friend.

"Are you all rested up for today?" Rene inquired, looking the two of us over as we sit down across from her.

"Indeed! I had a very good sleep last night. And Jelly looks rested and ready to go as well!" Liliana declared, holding up out to her tutor with a wide grin on her face. I uttered a burble of assent, and Rene's mouth crinkled with a smile.

"Good to know. When you've finished eating we'll be meeting the tailor in our usual room."

"Um, is there anything you can tell me about the person I'll be meeting today?" Liliana asked as a platter of eggs and crispy meats were placed in front of her. I snagged one of the bacon pieces and nibbled on it, still somewhat full from last night. I didn't want to seem too suspicious, so I just slowly savored my food.

"I do in fact know the man, I've been using his clothes ever since he opened his shop."

"A man?" Liliana paused mid-bite, and Orleen raised an eyebrow at that. Even I stopped my eating.

"Oh yes, my grandson, Renard. He's quickly gaining a lot of renown for his high quality products. It's a bit of nepotism I suppose, using my own family for the resources, but there's no one I'd trust more to make sure you have the perfect dress," Rene explains, and my owner and Orleen relax. I nod as well, fully understanding and reading between the lines a bit more.

I had noticed before with Baroness Bluemont, but in certain aspects she was extremely paranoid. Especially when it came to her young charges. Feeding them antidote laced snacks, and making sure only someone she could fully trust and rely on made their more important possessions; Rene Bluemont was someone who puts the children under her care first, and would not let anything happen to them if she could help it. Even if that means managing everything to an absurd, seemingly fatuous, degree then so be it. In that regard I find common ground with her. My owner's safety and wellbeing was number one at all times.

"He's scheduled to arrive in about an hour or so," Rene continued, spearing a hunk of meat from her own plate. "So please be prepared by then."

An affirmative nod was all she gets from my owner, whose mouth was currently full of breakfast. In her place I gave a coo of understanding, which earned me a grandmotherly smile.

The rest of the meal passed by uneventfully, something I'm grateful for, and Liliana rose out of chair ready to face the day. With Orleen a few steps behind and Rene accompanying us, we all arrived at the classroom with time to spare.

To our surprise, there was already a group of people inside. One was a member of the palace guard, whose face clearly expressed how little he wanted to be here. He was reluctantly holding a large wooden chest while standing awkwardly to the side. A pair of maids, also seeming to have been roped into whatever this was, were heaving a wardrobe into place, slightly to the center of the room. A third maid was trying to wrangle a full body mirror into place against one wall, and all the while the fifth and final person was busy giving orders to them all, trying to coordinate the set-up.

Out of all of them, it was that bossy man who caught my 'eye.' Though to be honest, his very looks seemed to scream at me, demanding my attention. Ever seen a peacock? It's that oddly flamboyant bird, whose males all have extraordinary feathers and plumage. I vaguely remembered that there'd been one at the pet store I'd been picked up from, and without a doubt this person before us reminded me of that beautiful avian. He wore a dark green tailcoat with slightly puffed up collar and cuffs made of white silk over an orange tunic. Silver buttons pinned his shirt up while a crimson sash-like belt held up navy blue trousers, though they had no frills on them. Only a tiny amount of dark brown hair graced his head, and most of that was on his upper lip forming a softly curving moustache. His top was shaved bald and possessed a waxy gleam, though he covered that up with a red velvet hat resembling a troubadour's cap.

"No, no, no! Are you trying to blind us with that mirror? Put it down just under the window, not across from it! And give it a slight tilt upwards, if you please! And you, my good sir! Don't just stand there slack-jawed and scowling! Put that trunk down next to the mirror and come help these two ladies set up the wardrobe!"

The glamorous man had to be Rene's grandson, the tailor Renard. There was no room for doubt on that front. And indeed I was proven right when the elderly tutor steps into the room and cleared her throat with a soft "A-hem!" which catches everyone's attention. The bald, well-dressed man turns with a flourish of his robes and a bright smile makes its way across his features.

"Ah, grandmother! It has been too long!" Renard made his way over to us, bowing before his grandmother and kissing her hand in greeting. He then repeated the gesture on Princess Liliana, but with a deeper and more submissive bow.

"It is a pleasure to meet you at last, Princess Liliana. I do hope my grandmother's lessons have not been too hard on you?"

"Not at all, Ren- Lady Bluemont had been extremely kind and a most wonderful tutor," Liliana professed, stumbling a bit with the name which caused Renard to chuckle softly.

"It is fine to call her 'Rene' in my presence princess, since it is likely what she herself requested. I do not mind, and I am sure she'd much prefer the informality."

"Of course. And it is a pleasure to meet you, Sir Renard. I look forward to having you prepare a proper dress for me."

A light and airy laugh came from the tailor as he nodded in understanding.

"Yes, I shall create for you the finest gown you've ever seen or worn! You will not be disappointed!" Renard bustled around the room, shooing the male guard out of the room while instructing the three maids in setting up the various needs. From within the chest an impressive collection of measuring tools and cloth samples appears, while the wardrobe produces a foldable screen to change clothes behind and a number of partially made dresses, just waiting for the finishing touches.

"First, let's get some measurements…"

The next few hours were a pastel colored blur, interspersed with praise and criticism, both often at the same time. Liliana was put into proto-type dresses one after the other, while Renard hummed and hawed over which looked best. Orleen and the three other maids were taking on the task of prepping the clothes and helping the young princess put them on. Even these simple gowns required a full ten minutes of grunting, swearing under the breath, and pins and needles pricking the fingers to wear.

As I watched this from a stool in the corner, I wondered if I was a male Ooze, since this all seemed rather pointless and over the top for just scraps of fabric that covered the body.

Yet despite my obliviousness towards fashion I could also see how some pieces of clothes accent and enhance my owner's natural and inherent beauty. For example, big, puffy dresses looked ridiculous on her slender frame, so Renard had put her into a selection of dresses with much less fabric that also had more straight edges to them. If I could nod my head, I would, as I could tell that this tailor understood his work intimately. No wonder he was in such high demand amongst the socialites of the kingdom. He could make a dress that suitably complemented the person wearing it.

"And voila! I do believe I have found the perfect dress for you, Princess Liliana!" Renard exclaimed happily. I returned focus onto him and my owner again, to see her in a lovely outfit that was modest yet regal.

Princess Liliana wore a milk white gown that descends below her knees, the hem just barely trailing along the floor. Her sleeves were a dark white, almost silver, which darkened ever so slightly to create a distorting effect on the light, making the fabric shimmer. There was a small cut above her shoulders, leaving the barest hint of skin bare. A powder blue waist sash wrapped around her hips and tied neatly in the front, while a similarly blue colored wave pattern decorated the front around her chest. The end result was simply astonishing, and I knew for certain she would turn heads come the ball.

"The full dress will be complete tomorrow. Last minute adjustments and such. Now, my dear grandmother wanted me to take a look at your pet, and see if I could do anything for him…"

I shuddered all of a sudden as the eyes of the entire room turned to me with a childish, predatory glee in them. If I had had a spine, chills would be running through it. A part of me started to understand what was about to happen. I understood that look with an instinct ingrained into all males regardless of species. It was the look of someone about to play dress up with an unwilling playmate.

Oh dear.

Chapter 13: The adventurer's night

Here we are, the day of reckoning! Heh, sorry, just wanted to give the event a touch more awe. It was the day of the long awaited Adventurer's Advent Ball, a huge event that would be held in the castle's opulent ballroom, but the fever pitch of excitement had spread to the rest of the city. Adventurers from all over the kingdom, and even some beyond, have traveled to the Guild's main branch to party it up. Of course, a handful of the highest ranked members had been invited alongside the various other high profile guests to attend the main party here in the castle. It was intimidating to have to be in their presence. I could feel their power pushing down on me thanks to my unique senses.

I was being carried into the main foyer where the guests were mingling near my owner, and already we were getting appraising looks. I too returned the appraisal, examining the outfits being worn by the guests.

I was biased when it came to that particular subject, but I had to say that my owner was without a doubt the most beautiful girl attending!

She wore the powder blue and milk white gown from the other day's dress-up with her long hair kept loose but tied by a pair of purple ribbons to ensure the strands do not fly this way and that too much when she danced. Silver and gold jewelry bearing the emblems of the Divine Family decorated her in a tasteful fashion. Her necklace with charms shaped like a golden dove, silver lily and silver bolt of cloth were prominently visible, while a badge with the scales of justice was pinned to her chest and a second, slightly larger badge with an image of a straight sword on it rested down near her waist on the right, where a sheathed blade would normally hang. As she was not yet an adult and a noble woman to boot actually wearing a sword would be a *faux pas*, so aristocratic girls tended to wear a badge with a sword image on it to honor the Knight-God. Or so Rene had explained when her grandson showed off the designs.

With a faint scent of lavender soap lingering from her bath and lilac perfume gently spritzed on her, Princess Liliana descended like an angel onto the room. Her steps were cautious, but why wouldn't they be when she's in those pointy heels?

I too was dressed up in a snappy little black bowtie. Renard had wanted to make me a tiny suit to wear, but it would only fit my bipedal form, and it was easier for me to just stay round and spherical unless I had to dance, so the idea for dressing me up was scrapped. Still, he did insist on the accessory, which I admit I liked.

The entire royal family of Varia was accompanying us, King Tiberius leading the way with Queen Amdora on his arm. The king was wearing the same ceremonial outfit he'd worn during the holy day a few weeks back, while the queen wore an expansive cloud of silks and cloth and ribbons. It was a dark blue dress with purple and gold trim, and her stern face was graced with a serene smile as she politely greeted the various well-wishers alongside her husband.

Little Julius was looking around nervously, dressed up in an adorable black and dark blue uniform. A 'tuxedo' as it was called by Renard. He also had accessories bearing the marks of the Divine Family, but instead of being made into necklaces or badges, they were silver and gold buckles on a thin belt. He was being escorted by Rene Bluemont and his personal maid, the two of them in charge of the youngest child and heir to the throne. As for the princess and I, we just had Orleen with us as an escort.

The area holding the Adventurer's Advent Ball was an extremely wide room with a vaulted, arching roof and art work dotting the walls. It served as both a dance floor and a mingling ground, with groups that entered stepping down into the area splitting off to find allies or acquaintances. Here and there servants in primly starched uniforms wander about with trays laden with drinks and tiny nibbling food.

I looked around the room, noting the placement of the dozen or so Dire Swords standing guard, as well as the numerous guests and serving staff wandering about. While not as nervous as her brother, Liliana was still hesitant to wander too far from her parents, and was hovering about nearby. As a result, she ends up drawn into a couple of conversations and introductions. One such example was rapidly approaching, in fact!

"A thousand greetings and a hundred blessings, King Tiberius," a short and stocky individual exclaimed with a bow as he approached us, flanked by two men.

"And a ten-fold return of respect, King Redarik," the Varian ruler replied, bowing his head in response. I look over the man with a curious eye. This was the first time I'd ever met a dwarf. One of the races that lived alongside humanity, dwarves were a fairly decently sized people. On average, they stood two feet shorter, but were slightly wider in the shoulders with thicker muscles and flowing beards. The one before us stood exactly five feet tall, a head or so above his two guards, with coppery skin, flint grey eyes, and fiery red hair that reached his belt and was intricately braided. The two beside him had similar skin and eyes but their hair was black, and though just as delicately braided it only reached their collar.

The leader of that group of dwarves was none other than Ancestor-King Redarik Greatgold, leader of the Federation of Dwarf Clan-holds, master of Karz Thang the City of Endless Stone, and he who sits on the Buried Throne. He was dressed in an impressive suit of gold plated ceremonial armor with red and black tunic and trousers underneath. Runes were carved into the surface of his armor, and I could feel magic lurking within a number of artifacts on his person, including his crown.

The headpiece in question was a band of a dark red metal with three polished orbs of amethyst each the size of an acorn set in a row on the front with a single massive diamond carved to look like the peaks of a mountain poking into the air from the rear of the crown. Though deceptively simple, the crown held incredible power, from potent defensive wards to magic negating runes. King Redarik wore it with ease, the royal accessory augmenting his aura of nobility and charisma.

That the Ancestor-King himself would travel hundreds of miles to attend such an auspicious occasion was proof of the alliance and friendship between the descendants of Hero-King Gregor and his own predecessor.

"I am most glad you were able to make it, King Redarik. It wouldn't have been a party without you," King Tiberius joked, earning a grin from the dwarf in question.

"You're right about that! And of course, it is lovely to see you again, Queen Amdora. Still as beautiful as you were on your wedding day."

"You flatter me, your majesty," the queen said, giving a pleased smile at the compliment. "And how is your dear wife? I'm sorry to hear that she could not attend."

"Yes, childbirth is not the best time to be traveling," the dwarf king said. "But she does well. We believe it'll be a boy, our third one."

"How are Rendin and Orrik, your majesty? Did they come with you?"

"Both are doing fine, though only Orrik made the journey with me, I believe he is currently wandering the dance floor. And who are these two adorable young ones? Could they possibly be the ankle-biters I once knew?" King Redarik turns his attention to Liliana and Julius, the two of them straightening up under his inquiring gaze.

"Indeed they are. Come, say hello, children," King Tiberius instructed and his two offspring step forward to present themselves.

"Greetings, King Redarik. It had been a long while. I am pleased to see you in good health," Liliana said with a curtesy, still keeping me close to her in her arms. Julius mimicked his sister, but with a short bow in place of the dress lifting bob of his sister.

"And it is a pleasure to see you both as well. Has it really been five years? Feels like it wasn't too long ago that you barely reached my beard. And now look! You're shooting up like mushrooms! You'll soon be towering over me in no time," the king chuckled.

The family chatted a bit more with King Redarik before both sides excused themselves and moved on to other guests.

After a few rounds of pleasantries with other dignitaries, we came across a group that look to be in an intense conversation. Both sides of the arguing people were easily distinguishable. The first was an older man in a dark green tabard and trousers, the outfit looking similar to King Tiberius's, with the notable differences that it lacked a cape and was designed for a man much larger and heavier. Where there had once been muscle, flab and the beginnings of a portly belly shoved it all aside, though the man still looked as if he could crush boulders with his bare hands. He had thick streaks of grey in the brown hair, giving him an aged, weathered look.

He wore upon his cape an emblem of a red stag on a green field and a yellow setting sun in the background. This man wore a crown as well, though made of a pair of silver and gold serpents that coil around each other before meeting at the center of the forehead, clutching a multi-faceted emerald that practically glowed with magic. Beside him were a pair of guards who kept reaching for weapons that were not there, and an older woman who was trying to discreetly pull his arm and drag him away from the confrontation.

She was dressed in a dark green dress, but had a much more conservative approach to fabric, as there was much less foof and frills than Queen Amdora's outfit. It looked wonderful though, and her gray hair was also done up in a bun.

The other party was not human. Though they were bipedal, they were much taller and thinner, with knife like ears and almond shaped eyes giving away their species. A pair of elves, one looking to be steadily growing more annoyed as he spoke with the crowned human, and the other possessing a bored expression as he watched it play out.

The arguing elf was pale skinned with blonde hair, and was wearing a silver-white toga-like robe above some kind of tight fitting light blue body suit. I had no idea what its purpose was, but it looks uncomfortable. A silk sash ties the ensemble together, while a choker of leather and gold inlay wraps around his delicate looking neck. Some sort of design was etched into it, and since I could see no magic in it I made the guess that it was an identifier of his rank or something similar.

The other elf was similar yet drastically different in his looks. For one, his skin was much paler than his comrade's, being almost snow white. His hair was also white but with an odd hint of blue to it. He wore silver-grey armor over a similar bodysuit though that was pale red, almost pink. The way his hand kept drifting to his left hip told that he was used to having a weapon of some sort hanging at his side, and it annoyed him having to be separated from it.

I shivered as we approached, for the lazy looking elf was barely restraining a killing intent as he watched the debate. Most unsettling was that his ire was directed at both the human and the elf, who I assumed he was tasked to guard. A flicker of his eyes informed him of our arrival, and he reached out and lightly tapped the shoulder of his companion, a jerk of his head and darting of the eyes pointing out our group nearing the argument. The blonde elf flickered his own gaze over to us, and disengaged from the conversation he's in with some muttered words towards the other human before stalking off over to us.

"Take a good look children. This is one of the representatives of the elves," Rene whispered to her wards their royal parents prepared to meet the diplomat. "For a bit of extra credit, what do you know of their nation?"

"It is a federation of the three major elven kingdoms and lesser countries such as the gnomes of Tantara. The main force in the

Domain is that of the so-called Grand Elves, one of the three elf tribes. Ambassador Roseknot is one of them, while the elf beside the Ambassador is one of the others, a Dire Elf from the frozen northern continent of Nora," My owner whispered back.

"Can you tell me why they call themselves the 'Second' Elfish Domain?" Their tutor then inquired.

"Oh, I know why it is called the 'Second!'" Julius murmured excitedly trying to get our attention. "Though the Second Domain is powerful, it is still a shadow of the fallen Grand Elfish Domain which was sundered by the same event that drove humans from Val'Narash."

"Excellent work, Julius! One of the sad but true stereotypes about Grand and Dire Elves is their excessive pride, and it leads to confrontations of all sorts. Not all of them are bad though. I know plenty who are kind and decent folks. It's just that the ruling elite seem to be bred rude." Rene looked over with a hint of disapproval to the elves as the conversation started.

"Greetings, King Tiberius," the elf greeted, plastering a smile onto his face. His control over his expression was that of a master, even I could barely tell that it was fake. My owner's father was not fooled either, though, but he gave a polite nod regardless.

"Ambassador Roseknot, it is a pleasure to see you attending our event in place of the Regent." With his own fake smile, King Tiberius greeted the agent and representative of the distant, yet massive, empire in the east of Par-Orria; the Second Elfish Domain.

"It is quite far from Grand City to Sanc Aldet, your majesty. He and his Consort have much to do in terms of running the Domain. Though they send their greetings regardless." If I could snort, I would, and I could sense that King Tiberius and Queen Amdora would have done so as well if it'd been permitted. Sure, the capitol of the elfish empire was even further than that of the dwarf's capitol of Karz Thang, but magical ships, enchanted carriages, and even new gnomish airships allowed for fast travel over long distances if necessary.

It wasn't an insult not to attend this event, as more than a few heads of state were absent from other nations in Orria and Par-Orria, but the ambassador's words held barbs in them all the same.

"Unfortunate, but understandable. It takes a lot of effort trying to take care of a bunch of crying children and selfish brats. At least when they have offspring of their own they will have obtained much experience in that matter. Regardless, I do hope you enjoy yourselves tonight, Ambassador Roseknot." The elf's features twitched slightly at the barb even as some bystanders snickered.

"I'm sure I can find a way to do so, your majesty. Even though there seems to more than just one kind of animal tramping around." Eyes full of loathing fell on me and I bristled unconsciously but restrained myself. It'll do no good to get angry at this pompous ass.

"If you'll excuse me," the elf said, stepping aside and walking off to go bother someone else. His guard gave one last glance back at us, or rather, me, before catching up.

"Sorry for having that unpleasantness boil over to you, my boy," the older human said, coming over to us now that his target of anger was gone.

"It was no problem at all, King Eric." King Tiberius responds with a comforting smile.

"You can call me 'uncle' you know, it won't kill you," the man smirked, trading a handshake with his counterpart.

Ah, I thought he looked familiar! I'd seen his portrait in the castle before, and now that I had something to compare to, Liliana's father did have some similarities to the older monarch, mostly in the hair, both color and curls.

King Tiberius just nodded noncommittally, before taking the hand of Brune's queen and kissing it in greeting. "Queen Sasha, it had been a long time."

"Indeed it had, you majesty. And may I say that you have some fine looking children," she said, looking over my owner and Julius.

"Thank you, I am very proud of them." He may have had a passive expression on his face, but I could indeed feel the fatherly pride in King Tiberius well up at the praise. A few more minutes of genuine pleasantries commence, though it wasn't much longer before the topic over the surly elf was breached.

"Children, I am sure I don't need to reintroduce you to your great-uncle, Eric Thardeen Naveros, king of Brune, do I?" He smirked at the indignant look Liliana and Julius shot him.

"Ah, Baroness Rene Bluemont. It has been a long time," the king said with a momentary flicker of panic when he saw his old tutor. She just smiled and bowed politely. She had the decency not to fuss over her old students when in public, something King Eric was noticeably grateful for.

After some more polite introductions the topic of the elf was brought up.

"What exactly was the ambassador berating you over?" Queen Amdora inquired to the ruler of Brune, who sighed in annoyance.

"A few days ago the spoiled little witch of a daughter for a wealthy elf merchant got it into her head that she wanted a Unicorn as a pet and mount," King Eric explained, a scowl appearing on his face. "And even though the stable masters and tamers warned her repeatedly about proper etiquette when approaching and riding such a magical creature, she ignored it all and ended up angering it. Next thing you know, she's been impaled and we have a frightened Unicorn tearing through the streets. Now the damned merchant wants reparations for his daughter's death! I keep trying to explain that it was her actions that caused the incident, but they refuse to listen to reason! Now I'm up to my neck in diplomacy and politics, and Roseknot wanted to give his two coppers on how it's all our fault and we should be reimbursing the elf..."

"She died? But I thought Unicorns were peaceful," Liliana interrupted, and the king of Brune, glad to get off that particular topic, was quick to explain.

"Unicorns are indeed peaceful, but they are cowardly and skittish things by nature. Spook them and usually they'll just run. But if you push too hard or they smell blood, then a Unicorn

224

becomes a very dangerous animal to handle. After all, they have a sharp horn on their head, and an uncanny ability to aim for the heart when defending themselves," King Eric explained to my owner. "Even the best of the beast handlers and monster tamers of my kingdom have a hard time training Unicorns. It's why most riders prefer Pegasi or regular horses over Unicorns. It takes a special person to properly raise one."

The monarch of Brune's words were full of pride as he regaled Liliana and Julius more about his kingdom's specialty.

"Ah, you should see it in the spring! The fields are blooming with flowers, and in the fall the forests turn into an explosion of color." Eric reminisced. "And because half of the country is covered in heavy forests which inevitably filled with monsters and magical creatures and the Starblind Mountains are a stone's throw away it has given rise to all sorts of people who raises and tame the wild beasts as partners and pets. We sell and breed the finest Pegasi, Thestrals, and elusive Unicorns in all of Orria!"

"And speaking of monsters, Liliana, it seems the rumors were true! You've got yourself a rare little companion," King Eric continued, looking down at me as I remained nestled in my owner's embrace.

"Yes, this is Jelly! Say hello, please," Liliana introduced, and I extended a pseudopod, waving it merrily in greeting.

"Oh! Such discipline! It seems to listen well, and for it to be able to create tentacles! And you haven't even had it a full year! Most beast tamers don't bother with trying to control slimes because they're normally too dumb to command and train. Usually only the more advanced sorts, like Healing Oozes, can be made into proper pets," King Eric praised, which inflates Liliana's ego a tad. I too am honored by the compliments, though the reminder that the rest of my kind are so different to myself brought my mood down a tad.

"He can do a lot more than just listen and wave!" Liliana said excitedly, moving away a bit to a clearer spot before letting me down. "Come on Jelly, let's dance! Show them what you can do!"

I wiggled in confirmation, and though I'd never admit it, I found it extremely satisfying to see the wide eyes and dropped jaws of almost half the party as they watched me expand and twist into my rudimentary bipedal form. With an exaggerated bow I offer my stubby little arm to my owner, and she giggles and took it in her hand. She began to lead me through a simple dance, which consists of simply shuffling back and forth. As I got more control over my legs, we sped up, our dance becoming a modified form of the Swan Step, with Liliana leading and myself following along. After a few minutes of being the center of attention, Liliana brought the dance to a close by giving me a twirl, then stopping and giving a bow towards her family the royalty of Brune. I mimicked her bow, and wild applause swept the hall. Some do so merely for the novelty of seeing a slime do the Swan Step with a princess, while others were impressed with my control over my body and Liliana's training. She and I, myself now back to my more comfortable spherical shape, head back to the two royal couples, when two new figures approached.

"That was both one of the most amusing thing I have ever seen, and one of the most impressive. Very few Ooze can move as well as yours can, and I have seen many of those creatures before." An old but strong voice carried over to us, and I could see Liliana and Julius' eyes light up as they took in the speaker and his companion.

One of them I recognized as Silas Revel, the half-elf who was the Guild Master of the entire Adventurer's Guild. He looked about the same as when I'd seen him last at the Reaffirmation of Faith, but in a richer outfit with golden charms and jeweled accessories dangling from his person, each holding potent magic within. He smiled kindly at my owner, taking her hand and pressing his forehead to her knuckles in the standard display of respect and greeting. He then took the hand of Julius and shook it warmly.

Both of the royal children had star struck expression at being so close to what amounts to idols for them. Of course, a great deal of that goes out to the retired adventurer's companion, and I had to say I was also impressed.

He stood a full head above King Eric of Brune, who was already a tall, imposing man. He had dark streaks of grey cutting through pale blonde hair, along with icy blue eyes that held great wisdom and pain, even as he smiled politely at us. Muscles like rocks were barely restrained by his black and gold evening wear, with crimson belt holding up his trousers. His boots too were black, but silver buckles laced with some sort of water walking spell added a bit of flair to his outfit.

This person was an adventurer without a doubt. And if his physical looks were not enough, then his blindingly bright soul would have given it away. What was most unusual was how it burned like a rainbow.

Every person, be they human, dwarf, or elf, had color and shape in their souls, representing what magic they were most attuned to, what god they pray to the most, and a number of other factors, such as age and innocence, which resulted in no two souls being the same in appearance. This man however had the mark of not only each of the Eight Elements of magic, but the presence of the entire Divine Family and a host of other gods and spirits swirling about in his soul. Even the most pious of the Clerics and Paladins I had observed at the display during the Reaffirmation of Faith had the power of at most two deities in their soul.

To have close to a dozen meant that whoever he was, this man was beloved of the gods more deeply than anything, or anyone, I'd ever encountered. And yet I felt no fear towards this man. Similar to how the presence in the church all those days ago had calmed me, so too did this man. I knew, with the very core of my being, that this man was not a threat, but the greatest of allies.

"Sir Tomas Nierz," Liliana breathed in awe, and I could see Julius, and even King Tiberius and Queen Amdora, become shocked and flustered by this man's presence. "The World Paladin!"

Chapter 14: Falling amidst the feast

"I'm honored that I am recognized so easily by a princess," the middle aged man said with a cheerful grin, which made my owner's face flare up in embarrassment. "But I am indeed he. As you said, I am Tomas Nierz, pleasure to be of service."

A short, respectful bow follows the adventurer's introduction, while he took Liliana's hand and presses his forehead to her knuckles in a formal greeting. This did absolutely nothing to reduce the red hue on my dear owner's cheeks, and even after he moves on to greet the rest of the royal family, Liliana had to fight her blush into control.

"Jelly! Meet Tomas Nierz! He is a human, and wields tremendous Divine magic gifted from numerous deities! He is an X-ranked adventurer, a feat only a handful of people have ever reached. There are less than a dozen X-ranked adventurer's in the world, and with over a million registered adventurer's, reaching this rank is impossible for normal people, no matter how skilled. One of the most active of these rare individuals, the World Paladin has vanquished monsters and demons alike, even saving the world once!" Liliana gushed, beckoning me forward while I was still in my Gel Doll form.

On Erafore, high ranked and popular adventurers earned more than just money. Fame was also a common gain. This meant that occasionally merchandise, such as books and toys based on these heroes, were made and they became a popular commodity among all strata of society. Some of the most powerful and renowned adventurers became akin to celebrities, and few were as famous as the man before us.

"I did not think you'd be able to attend, Sir Nierz," King Tiberius stated, my gaze able to see that while he was stoic on the outside, he was giddy like a boy about meeting such a famous person. Same for his wife, while Julius' excitement was visible and palpable.

"I finished my last mission earlier than I thought, and had some time to spare. Master Silas convinced me to attend, though I hardly needed much incentive for free food and good company,"

Tomas explained to the king, before giving some space for the Guildmaster to approach and perform his greetings to the royalty as well. I even shook his hand when I offered him my own!

"Might I ask where you found such a talented and obedient Ooze?" the World Paladin inquired once greetings were completed.

"The Gilded Parlor Pet Shop, down on Kaleidoscope Way in the Purple District," Liliana revealed, before hastening to add, "Though they said they just found Jelly out back in the alley one day and plopped him in a spare glass case."

"A common Ooze or not, I think the real praise for it, I mean his, talents go to the owner," Tomas said, offering his opinion, earning yet another blush from the princess. However, I noticed the legendary World Paladin and the elderly Guildmaster shooting the king a knowing look, which King Tiberius responded to with a nod. It seems that Sir Nierz and Sir Revel knew something about the bloodline magic of the Roans and Ar-Varians, if the flickering exchange of knowing glances between them and myself are any indicator.

I sincerely hoped this did not become a common event. Having people privy to, or at least suspicious of, my intelligence was testing my nerves. Not that I doubted or suspected the current, diverse group, but if high ranked adventurers could uncover this secret, what exactly was stopping a semi-competent criminal or villain from finding out? Their glances were not as subtle as they thought they were!

Silas Revel must have detected my mood somehow, because he turned to me and offered a fleeting placating grin. For my owner, I assumed she rationalized the gesture as an apologetic notion for talking down about me. I think.

Some people might find it surprising, but Liliana's mood was fairly stable and even most of the time, so getting an accurate read of her emotions was surprisingly hard, even for magically empathic beings like myself. A trait I assumed she obtained from her father, who was also a master of this mental craft. Unless she's blushing like a maiden or scowling like a drunken sailor, in which case her mood was painfully obvious to everyone.

Before I could muse any more, the World Paladin surprised me yet again but extending his hand to my owner with a tiny bow. The gesture was clear: he wanted a dance! Giggling like a giddy little girl, which I supposed she was, Liliana passed me over to Julius who took me eagerly, more for the fact he could hide behind me now than any other reason, and she lightly took the offered hand.

With fluid grace and practiced steps, the taller and much more solidly built man led the younger and more delicate princess onto the dance floor and into the Leol Waltz, their movements slowly matching up to each other's until they have a natural rapport going. They moved two-as-one, a term Rene Bluemont had used more than once to describe the way dancing was supposed to be when done between two competent dancers. And I could see where the term came from. Though they have only just met, my owner and the World Paladin could comprehend and react to the other's movements.

My owner was light on her feet and graceful, thanks to her upbringing and her own natural aptitude. Tomas Nierz had spent years on the hunt, slaying monsters and heretics alike in all manners of terrain and conditions. These two vastly different backgrounds are now complementing each other on the dancefloor, neither one of them leading but both of them following. It truly was an amazing sight, and I was glad to be able to have a front row seat to my owner's debut on the stage that was royal socializing.

As for the rest of the audience? Prince Julius might be young, but he looked up to his sister, and he could tell that she had poise in abundance. Her parents were immensely proud of her, for what parent wouldn't be glad to see their child excel? Guildmaster Silas Revel and the royal couple of Brune were also impressed by the display put forth, though one side appreciated the lack of wasted movements and how the dancers work astonishingly well together while the other appreciated the good breeding and excellent care that had gone into both participants.

King Rederik Greatgold of the Dwarves shouted his approval for the daughter of his greatest ally, while the two elves from the Second Domain showed not a single twitch in their facial expressions. Only their emotions scrutinized through my magical senses gave them away. Ambassador Roseknot had praise, albeit grudgingly so, for the two dancers and their steps, while his guard looked at the X-ranked adventurer with a combination of battle lust and respect.

As for me, I still had naught but adoration for my owner. Watching her dance was soothing in a way.

A little less than half an hour passed, and soon more guests begin to drift onto the dancefloor, dragging partners along. For the next hour the marble tiles of the Grand Reception Hall are all but obscured beneath twirling silks and fancy footwear. My owner and her first partner had split up earlier, going from one dance to the next, greeting and mingling with style on the dancefloor. Every so often Princess Liliana and Tomas Nierz reunited briefly, exchanging words. It looks like my owner had gotten control over her emotions and blush for the moment, as her face was smiling a serene smile regardless of who held her hands during the dancing.

Prince Julius had also been dragged into the dancing, much to his chagrin. Currently he was dancing with only a hint of awkwardness hand in hand with a girl of similar age and adorable disposition, whose father was a Senator of the Partaevian Empire's Council, if I recalled correctly. I had a few dances with Rene and Orleen in the fringes of the party crowd, and even Queen Sasha of Brune took me for a spin, as she referred to it, much to her husband's laughter and applause. Few others approached me that evening.

All of a sudden, a set of soft bells begin to chime all across the dance hall. Princess Liliana, Sir Tomas, and the other dancers came to a slow halt, the music fading, and everyone turned towards a corner of the room where two large double doors were creaking open, allowing a breeze of tantalizing aromas to waft through the room and fill it with watering mouths.

"It seems that dinner is now ready to be served. Shall we adjourn to the dining hall?" King Tiberius suggested, and many people eager to partake in a hearty meal nodded happily. Finger food and snacks were fine and dandy, but you needed more after dancing for so long. The Grand Reception Hall soon became a sea of silken waves as people bowed politely to their dance partners before heading off in an orderly rush to the next room. If I could, I'd lick my lips. No better time than a banquet to beg some nibbles from the guests!

Exiting the Grand Reception Hall was fairly easy, for myself and my owner, at least. As part of the royal family we headed in first before the others as a matter of protocol. I was back in Liliana's arms, snuggling down. I felt lethargic. Dancing took a lot of energy out of me. Added with the mental strain of keeping my bipedal form intact while doing, and it was a wonder I was not asleep yet! My owner was no less tired, but hid it well behind smiles.

Soon enough we all emerge into the warm and bright Great Feasting Hall, as it was known. The set-up was impressive, and far more dedicated than what went on back at the dance floor. Here, seven long and imposing tables have been moved in, one at the front of the room where the royalty and important guests would sit, while the other six were divided into two rows of three. Still put close to each other, but placed in a way to denote a person's importance. Naturally, the nobility and other high profile guests will sit close to the king, but not directly at his table. Each one was made of heavy dark colored wood that could probably survive a fall from the top of the towers without taking much damage. Heck, you could use these tables as impromptu battering rams they were so thick and massive!

Swiftly everyone started to take their seats. Though there was no official assigned seating, there was an unspoken hierarchy that everyone was quick to follow. Upper nobles at the front closest to the king, minor aristocrats and wealthy non-nobility to the further ends of the tables. Some jostling and elbowing goes on for the preferred spots, but for the most part the entire ordeal was soon over with minimal fuss.

Immediately to King Tiberius's right was Queen Amdora, as befitting her status as wife. To the king's immediate left sits Prince Julius, as his heir. I, held lovingly in the arms of the princess, sat with her two spots to the right of the king, on the right side of the queen. Further down on the right of Liliana was King Redarik of the dwarves and Eric of Brune as well as Ambassador Roseknot of the elves at the very end. Guildmaster Revel and Tomas Nierz sat close to the end of the royal table as honored quests on the left side. And finally at the very end of the left side Rene Bluemont sat, her seat assured thanks to her position as a noble and royal tutor.

241

And of course there are the all-important utensils, cutlery, and drinking vessels, just waiting to be covered in food and drink. Most of the plates and bowls were made of clay and ceramics, only a few made of precious porcelain from Distant Qwan, and those were reserved for those sitting at the royal table. Cups were made of ceramic as well, with only a single fluted wine cup per person being made of carefully cut glass. It was not an expensive material, as alchemists used the crystalline material to store their wares, but it was fragile, which meant it could became expensive quickly if one had to constantly replace them. Thankfully no one here would go about smashing containers and glasses on the floor. Not on purpose or while sober, at least.

Before the food was brought in, the king stood, raising a glass to the audience as they all turned to him.

"I wish to thank you all for gathering here tonight, to join in a festival of peace and unity. For centuries, the Adventurer's Guild had served all peoples and nation of Erafore. From hunting the monsters that prey on us, to researching ancient ruins to better understand the past and through it the present. Some see adventurer's as little more than glorified mercenaries, others as heroic ideals to emulate. Regardless of who they are or what they do, adventurers follow in a tradition of aide that was passed down by my ancestor. Tonight marks the one thousandth year of the Adventurer's Guild's operation. Tonight, I thank you in honor of those who have given their life for the world, and by praising those who continue to fight for all that was good and noble about Erafore. A toast to the promise of victory! *Tam ur varia!*"

"*Tam ur varia!*" Across the room these words were echoed back in an overwhelming roar. Tam ur varia: A promise of victory. Ancient motto of the Varian kingdom, spoken in the Elder Tongue of the first humans. I shouted these words as well, though only in my mind. King Tiberius' speech was a good one, and I appreciated the message. Something within me resonated with the final words, stirring feelings I couldn't properly identify. Did they come from my bond with Liliana? Were they a reaction to the magic that birthed me? I did not know, but I felt they mattered.

"Now, let us enjoy the feast!" As soon as this was said, the doors on either side of the room quickly flew open, and dozens of servants poured forth, each carrying platters of food or jugs full of liquid refreshment. The feast was quickly put on, and I could not help but wish for the ability to salivate, if only to show my appreciation for the scents I could taste on the air. The first course was served!

Mounds of leafy green salad decorated the tables, looking more like bouquets of flowers than random piles of fruits and vegetables. Bowls of soup, both creamy and clear, were placed down in front of everyone. Loafs of crusty bread loom like delicious towers. All in all, it was a splendid spread!

"Here you go, Jelly!" Liliana cooed, offering me a piece of bread. I devoured it gratefully, the gnawing hunger lessening slightly. She took a bite of salad, then daintily slurped up some soup, and soaked up some juices with the bread. This action was repeated all over the dining hall, the clatter of cutlery mixing with loud conversation.

"This truly is a magnificent repast, Tiberius!" King Redarik praised loudly, a sentiment echoed by most everyone else.

"Indeed, but it is not over yet!" King Tiberius assured, to yet more cheers. I wiggled in joy, and happily took a piece of bread that was offered to me by the princess. As I digested it, I noticed something in the bread. A bit of herb had been mixed in. Cautiously I examined it. Though I did not recognize the plant matter, I quickly saw it was harmless, just a little bit of extra flavor for the normally bland product. Like basil, in terms of taste. I shook myself in disappointment. I felt as if I was too paranoid right then.

After the incident with the Poison Oozes in the cellar, nothing had happened to threaten my owner's life. I felt as if this was just the calm before the storm, though. Still, no need to be utterly on guard all the time! Poison would not only be detected in food before serving it, but the numerous guards stationed around the room would be on guard for such foul play, especially for a feast like this one. I shouldn't worry too much!

Soon enough the first course's contents dwindled to little more than scraps, and the plates and serving containers were swapped out to be replaced by new, fresh food. If the initial round had had a fine fragrance, then this main course could only be

245

described as aromatic! Meat, meat, and more meat, with some token fruits and vegetables here and there. This was the staple of a human feast! For the most part, such massive amounts of animal's made into food would be rare. All sorts of carnivorous monsters stalked the lands and only large, well-protected ranches had any hope of producing large quantities of meat for sale. This was a luxury, and everyone here knew it, and appreciated it. I knew I was not going to let any of it go to waste!

Right now, I felt like I was in one of the Heavens! Tasty, succulent meat was being fed to me from so many different sources! Princess Liliana fed me a slice of glazed ham while King Redarik tossed me a chunk of sausage over from where he sat. Prince Julius shyly offered me a portion of his steak, Tomas Nierz flicked me a bit of chicken, and even Queen Amdora discreetly passed me a morsel of baked fish! This was the best night ever!

The seasoning on the meats was well made, though to my palate I felt it was odd that every single dish was using the same ingredient. Some sort of liquid? To the human tongue it was flavorless, but for one such as myself, who could detect even the faintest hints of other chemicals, I was able to tell that whatever this substance was it had been included in each meat dish. A niggling worry started to itch in the back of my mind, but again I pushed it aside. I was just being overly cautious.

"Careful not to feed it too much, my dear, or you'll have a tub of lard in place of a tub of slime," King Tiberius teased, earning an annoyed gurgle from myself and a snicker from his wife and daughter.

"He'll be fine. Won't you, Jelly? You're a big boy, yes you are! Big boys needs lots of food!" Liliana playfully chattered to me, earning amused chortles from those nearby. I politely ignored their ribbing, content to snack on whatever was given to me.

Only a few of the guests seemed put off by my continued presence, the rest just seeing me as another novelty the princess showed off. Still, the most notable person who seemed displeased was Ambassador Roseknot. I was not sure why, but he's been in a sour mood all evening. Work must be stressful. But he'd been focusing a lot on me ever since my dance debut, so I guessed he must not approve of Oozes as pets. Or in general. I decided to pay him no mind. No one else seemed to be focusing on the sour faced elf, so I assumed this was just his natural state.

An hour passed by, the time flying along as we all enjoy the food. It was delicious, without a doubt! The glaze used for the meats brought out the juices while the assortment of wines and ales brought the sobriety levels down. My owner sipped at her own cup slowly, much more so than the majority of adults. Her drink was just some watered down wine. She was not old enough for the strong, unfiltered stuff, but neither was she a child, like Julius, who was just drinking water. I dipped a pseudopod into a nearby mug and slurped up some of the booze within. It was not flavorful, and I could not become drunk as far as I knew, but it was refreshing none the less. Suddenly the hall started to quiet down, and I looked over to see why.

A giant cake, five whole layers and coated in sugary frosting. The icing was blue and gold with the royal coat of arms entwined with the Adventurer's Guild sigil skillfully drawn on the surface. Ah. That'll do it. Apparently it was time for dessert! The majestic beast of a baked good was slowly and carefully brought in on a trolley and set down before the king. It was his right to cut the cake and serve the first slice.

As I gazed longingly at the treat, something started to itch in the back of my mind. I tried to shake it off, but the feeling only grew more incessant. I grumbled, but then froze. This sensation was just like when the Poison Oozes appeared in the palace! I wildly began to scan the area, trying to pinpoint the source of the itching. Nothing in the shadows, nothing in the rafters, nothing beneath us, nothing behind us! The only thing my danger sense was reacting to was the… cake…

I focused all of my senses onto the approaching item. Nothing was out of place, though! No hidden weapons or monsters inside it, no toxins, no magic, not a thing that could set off my alarms like this. The servants were not the source, though I double checked to be sure. Over and over I stared into the cake with my assortment of senses, but still, nothing to tell me why I had reacted that badly to it! Oh, that was not ideal! The cake was now right in front of King Tiberius, and he was preparing to cut it! I had to do something, and soon!

My mind was starting to grow fuzzy from the incessant clamor that was my danger sense gnawing away at my thoughts. I started to quiver violently in Liliana's lap, and she was quick to notice this, as well as a few other people. Before she could do anything, I let loose a warbling screech and hurled myself from her grasp, barreling into the cake and sending frosting and cake bits flying. I immediately did the first thing that came to mind; eat.

Eat. Eat. Never stop, don't stop. It was a threat. Eat the threat, then it couldn't hurt her. Eat eat eat! For her for her for her!

My thoughts started to become erratic, and for some reason my "vision" was fading. I could barely hear someone screaming, but I couldn't tell if it was at me, or just a generic scream of surprise. I did not care. I ate. I ate. I had to. Save her…

The dining hall erupted into panic as the princess's pet Ooze suddenly started to shake and then leapt at the cake as it was rolled in before the king. It slammed heavily into the massive baked good and started to devour it with gusto.

"Jelly, what are you doing?! Stop it!" Princess Liliana leapt to her feet, shouting at her companion to cease, but it did not. In fact, it seemed like it could not. And then the Ooze started to turn pitch black. It was slow at first, but it rapidly began to darken in color, almost as if it was suffering from sudden necrosis!

"Everyone stay back!" Sir Blaine roared, striding forward and snatching the slime out of the ruined cake, all but throwing it back to the princess's arms.

"It's been poisoned!" Sir Renos, the representative of the Mages Academy shouted, and even more pandemonium set in.

"Impossible, I scanned the cake when it came it, there was nothing in it!" The Dire Sword commander argued.

"That thing was just a filthy animal, it probably just got sick gorging on the cake!" Ambassador Roseknot sneers, adding his own opinion.

"You take that back! He wouldn't do such a thing!" Liliana shouted, glaring daggers at the elf before turning her attention back to Jelly.

"And what would you know, pampered little princess?" The elf retorted, which caused King Redarik to stand angrily. The effect was somewhat dampened by the fact that only his chin was above the table edge, but not by much.

"Hold your tongue! Or do you want me to slice it out for offending my god-daughter?!" the high lord of the dwarves demanded, brandishing a table knife at the elf.

Amidst the turmoil, Tomas Nierz leapt out of his seat, vaulting over the table and swiftly approached the remains of the cake. He swiped a finger through the frosting and sampled it, swishing it around in his mouth, face screwed up in concentration. His eyes widened and he spat it out violently onto the floor, grabbing a glass of water and rinsing his mouth out before spitting that out onto the floor as well. That set of actions stunned the room into a degree of silence.

"Oracle's root, blended with sugar to hide the bitterness," the World Paladin announced, shocking the room even further into silence. He then looked around the room, magical runes and markings swirling about in his eyes as he examined the remains of the feast. He snatched up a chicken drum stick, peering at it, before dropping it to the floor.

"Raven's milk, diluted with water and added to the seasonings and glazes that were put on the meat." Tomas then picked up a scrap of bread from the ground, peering at it before saying, "Pink dragon leaf, ground up and mixed in with the flour."

His words stirred fear in the hearts of everyone present.

"Oracle's root: a bitter tasting golden hued tuber that possesses hallucinogenic properties if eaten after it had been soaked in water for a long time," Sir Renos started, listing off the ingredients and their effects in a wavering voice. "Raven's milk: a pale white alchemical substance used to increase the effects of healing potions, and utterly flavorless. Pink dragon leaf: a magical pinkish-purple flower that tastes a lot like basil and bestows a temporarily immunity to intense heat and cold."

"Alone, they are simple plants, useful for certain arcane practices. But when consumed together, the magic and chemicals within the three plants react violently, producing a chain effect not dissimilar to ingesting several hundred grams of cyanide and hydrochloric acid at once. The lucky victims died after a few minutes of searing agony. The unlucky ones had to watch as their own stomachs melted away and their liquefying entrails poured out on the floor all while screaming due to the pain," Tomas Nierz growled, glaring at the repast.

As soon as the ingredients and deadly effect were revealed, the other guards around the room leapt to attention, and started examining the food around them as well.

"He's correct. All three of those substances have been mixed in with the food. If the slime hadn't tackled the cake, we'd all be on the floor writhing and screaming." The lilted, accented voice of Ambassador Roseknot's bodyguard was soft and low, but it cut through the hushed chatter and was soon confirmed by the other knights and guardians in the dining hall.

"Seal off the kitchens and the surrounding areas! Round up all of the servants and chefs and anyone who went in or out of the kitchens today! NOW!" King Tiberius roared, his voice sending the Dire Swords into action.

"Daddy, Jelly isn't moving!" Liliana cried suddenly. Indeed, the Ooze was immobile. Worse yet he was slowly dripping onto the floor, dissolving bit by bit as the toxins tore him apart from the inside out. Tomas Nierz did not pause and pulled out a tiny vial of glowing purple liquid from a hidden pouch on his person. An Elixir, one of the most potent medicines known to exist! It was capable of curing even the most virulent of diseases and toxins, regenerate entire lost limbs, and remove curses.

Without hesitation the adventurer uncorked the vial and shoved it into Jelly, letting the healing liquid restore it. Slowly, the black color began to recede, and he stopped dissolving as well. But he remained unmoving, and where he was once blue, only pale, sickly white remained.

"The potion should have stopped the chain reaction for now, but I do not know if he'll fully recover," the World Paladin admitted sadly. Seeing Princess Liliana's devastated face, he quickly explained.

"Even after being cured from the Triarch Effect, as the combination of oracle's root, raven's milk, and pink dragon leaf is known, most people who survive fall into a coma. I'm sorry, but I just do not know if he can bounce back from this."

"Everyone, I ask that you all calmly return to your dwellings for the evening. For information will be provided as soon as it is available," King Tiberius cut in, his words carrying over the entire room. The guests all nodded and began to leave, some eagerly, some with curiosity, but all of them afraid.

"The Triach Effect?" Liliana asked, wiping tears from her face.

"Four hundred years ago, hundreds of nobles, rulers, rich merchants and powerful warriors perished in a wave of assassinations carried out by this very same technique. These actions drove the entire world in a massive, global conflict as no one could find a culprit and everyone blamed everybody else. The gods themselves fell silent, prayers going unanswered and their spells fading. Eleven years of bloody, vicious fighting then erupted, devastating the lands in tides of blood, steel, and spells." The World Paladin's words stirred shock from the royal children.

"The War of Fallen Gods!" Julius exclaimed from the other side of the table. Tomas Nierz nodded solemnly.

"Only thanks to a team of adventurer's was the truth uncovered; the entire war had been orchestrated by the World Rebellion, a legion of insane cultists whose only desire was to resurrect the ancient, primeval god of destruction and oblivion, Zard. By the time the cultists were completely hunted down four more years passed, half of a continent was consumed and destroyed by the emergence of a summoned fragment of the Dweller in the Void, and two whole gods were slain and a half dozen more maimed. The War of Fallen Gods, as it came to be known, was the single most devastating war since the Great Calamity that shattered Val'Narash and sundered the ancient Grand Elfish Domain three thousand years ago."

Uncomfortable silence fell on the dining hall, only a handful of people remaining within, waiting for news.

"Your majesty, we found a delivery manifest one of the chefs who tried to flee had in his possession," a Dire Sword called out, breaking the tense silence. He handed the parchment which was torn and stained with a bit of blood to the king.

"All the ingredients for the meal this evening came from the Edelstein territory, or passed through it on the way here," the royal guard summarized. Shock ran through the entire room and muted conversations were carried out by few individuals left.

Amidst the sea of worried and concerned faces, two stand out more than any other. One was that of King Tiberius, his face dark like a thundercloud, promising pain and retribution on the one who'd done this. A single name slips through his clenched teeth.

"Darpel!"

And the final face belonged to the most famous adventurer alive. Tomas Nierz's expression was coolly neutral, but within his eyes a violent tempest raged, as years of repressed hatred for the cultists of the World Rebellion simmered and stewed, eager to be unleashed.

One way or another there will be a reckoning. One way or another blood will be spilled!

Chapter 15: A shadow stained interlude

"You claimed that your plans would work! Yet they're still alive and now Tiberius is marching an army to my doorsteps!" A fist slammed down heavily onto a large wooden desk, papers and knick-knacks jumping from the impact. Behind the finely crafted piece of furniture a thin, sallow man sat with unbridled fury boiling in his brown eyes.

He wore dark blue clothes, all richly made and incredibly decedent. Streaks of grey cut through his dark hair, though few wrinkles decorated his face. Count Marik Yenfold Darpel, lord of the Edelstein region of Varia, and brother-in-law to King Tiberius Augustine Roan. A powerful man with an even temper, yet now hatred burned his soul.

"I have spent years waiting for my chance to strike! YEARS! I managed to hide my involvement with my wife's attempts at a coup, but it cost me time and resources! And now everything had gone to waste! All because of a single, worthless little monster!"

"It should have worked. The fact that the Ooze foiled yet another of our schemes means that you should have taken care of the animal when I first told you to do so." A second voice calmly spoke up, pointing out the reason for the failure of the various plans.

The voice was neither deep and booming, nor soft and whispery. There was no trace of an accent, or any sort of verbal, audible tick to give away identity. Even gender, race, and age were hard to identify, and only the fact that Count Darpel could see the speaker let him know that the person was a human male around middle age. The voice was utterly empty. A true, neutral voice that gave nothing away.

That emptiness worked in tandem with the man's appearance. All of his body was shrouded in a pure white hooded cloak with a golden mask, polished to a mirror sheen, covering the upper part of the face leaving only his mouth visible. Silver gloves made of silk covered the hands and bleached white leather boots encased his feet. Golden amulets hung around his neck and waist, held together by chains of platinum. Thick golden rings set with precious stones all but hid his gloved fingers. The jewelry radiated magic, creating an invisible heat and pressure that was at odds with the calm, collected man wearing them.

However, the robes were the most unsettling feature of the man's outfit. Scrawling lines of black ink slithered and writhed across his body, forming terrible curses, unholy verses of dark scripture, vile truths, and shameful secrets. They were never at rest, and always seemed to be new when one tried to focus on them for too long.

"Once is a coincidence. Twice is an accident. Three times means an active interference," the man continued, sitting peacefully in a chair in the corner of the count's study. "The Rose Worms were too subtle. The Poison Oozes were too brazen. And either of those foiled plans can be explained away by mere animal instinct on the part of the pet monster. But the Triach Effect served up at the feast should have been undetectable. Not even trained beasts can detect it since it is three components uniting as one that creates the danger. Yet this Ooze managed to uncover the threat, and now our efforts are spoiled and the king is aware of them. So, what shall happen now?"

"Now? Now we go to war because of this!" Darpel screamed at the robed figure.

"We? I'm afraid this is all on your head, Count Darpel. I have given what assistance was required, both in this matter and in others, as per our agreement. But I never said I would take the fall with you." The man in the golden mask rose from his chair which caused a torrent of swears and curses to be hurled at him.

"Bastard! You're just going to up and leave me?! This is your mess too!"

"Indeed it is. Already some people will begin to suspect me and my order's involvement in the failed assassination. I wanted you to plant the tainted food in the private meals of the royal family, to make a quiet but none the less deadly statement, but you insisted on having it become a grand, bloody spectacle during the most auspicious festival of the year. Dozens of nobles and notables would have died, and while it would have advanced the plans greatly, now we both must deal with the fallout in our own ways."

"The Triarch Effect is far too infamous these days, and gives away my order's involvement. The elves will hunt me. Though few still live from the last time I and my people arose the memories of death and humiliation linger. They will focus much of their power on eradicating us for good this time. And do not forget the World Paladin, whom once suffered at my hands. His wrath will not be quiet or subtle. So now we fight. You have your battles, and I have mine." The robed figure stepped away, raising a hand to the door knob, before pausing.

"Of course, I will honor our alliance, short as it may have been. A handful of my followers will aide you in battle. They will slip in amongst the mercenaries you will no doubt hire to bolster your own troops. You'll never know who they are, in case you or they are captured. But I will help. I never lie, and I never break a promise."

"A cultist keeping their word. What will the gods think of next?" Darpel sneered. He quickly regretted that action as the room became filled with tension and the ozone tang of raw magic. His guest did not turn back to face him, but the reply was chillingly direct.

"Mortals lie. Mortals steal. Mortals cheat. Such is the way of all sapient life. No species is exempt, no culture free of these sins. And yet me and my own strive to avoid such things, in spite of our admittedly devastating goals. Why? Because it gives us pleasure to know that no matter who we murder, maim, and harm, we still maintain the moral high ground. We do not lie. We do not steal. We do not cheat. We just kill and kill and kill. Without malice, without ill-will, we deal death and destruction equally to all. The world shall rebel, and the heavens shall shatter before us. And it will happen without us resorting to the petty tactics of those who seek to preserve this worthless existence."

The man in the blasphemous white robes turned his head slowly to stare at the count, and the noble couldn't help but shiver in terror. For reflecting in the golden mirror was not himself and his room, but a landscape of fire and death and looming oblivion, presided over by an eldritch being composed of nothing, with infinite-yet-zero mouths and eyes.

Darpel choked back a scream at the images, nearly retching in fear. The Hierophant of the World Rebellion turned away with a disdainful air, opening the door and exiting, softly closing it behind him.

Wiping his lips free of spittle and froth, the count shivered before grabbing various documents and calling for his servants. Things were about to become very dangerous for him and his territory, and not all of the threats came from his brother-in-law.

Chapter 16: A new member of royalty is born

It was dark and cold all around me. It was a terror I thought I had long ago forgotten and escaped. The damp chill reminded me too much of the alley I was born in. How long did I live amidst the trash and refuse, the cold stones slick with moisture? I remembered hands, plucking me from the ground, and then being tossed without care into a glass tank. I remembered a time of darkness and isolation. I could not see beyond the confines of my tiny prison. How long did I spend, before I was saved, and shown the light of love?

I recalled the first image to ever grace my newborn soul; a kind, caring face with eyes that wanted only to see smiles and happiness around her. Love. For the first time in my miserable existence, I felt such an emotion, and directed at me no less!

How long did I drift in the blackness, seeing nothing, feeling nothing? A day, a week, a year? I did not know. I could not even properly pinpoint when exactly my mind "woke up" to process coherent thoughts and ponder the nature of this emptiness. I shuddered. I was afraid. Afraid of being lost and alone, of becoming unwanted by my savior...

It was at that moment, as those thoughts sent shivers through my body, that my surroundings, once dark and gloomy, started to lighten as color rushes in to fill me. It was slow, and as the color returned so too did other things. I felt wet, as if I was submerged in liquid of some sort. I didn't have enough control to focus on examining what it was, just enough to know that it wasn't hurting me. Then came sound. Footsteps, oddly muted, rumbled around me, the vibrations shaking me about in the pool of liquids. Then voices, low and distorted, but growing clearer with every second.

"My lady, you need to rest. Pacing around and worrying won't accelerate the healing process."

"But Orleen, he nearly died trying to protect me! To protect my family! I, I just don't want to lose him!"

"He'll be fine, my lady. Don't worry. Didn't Mage Petrus assure us – I mean you – that Jelly would wake up eventually? He just needs time to recover."

I could hear my dear owner's voice and that of her maid, and I smiled inside. Liliana's concern for me warmed my core, and I wobbled happily. Even Orleen, for all her gruffness towards me, had a note of worry for both the princess and myself that made me chuckle at how far we'd come.

I wiggled around and started to struggle, trying to get their attention. Gods, I wished I could talk! My movements caused the liquid I was immersed in to slosh around and splash to the floor a bit, which seemed to alert my two worried visitors. Instantly I heard the sound of two pairs of footsteps rushing towards me, and moments later a pair of soft and small hands pluck me from my resting place.

"Jelly!" Liliana cried ecstatically, clutching me to her chest in joy. I felt small wet droplets impact me, and I realized she was crying! I snuggled closer to assure her that I was fine. My vision started to clear up and improve as my senses trickled back into awareness. I noticed a few new things. First off, I could see. As in, actual colors and shapes, not just what my magical echolocation told me were shapes and colors! Second, my range had increased, but now I could see through two sources; the echolocation but also an "eye" of sorts, which seems to have formed from my core! It had transmuted in a pseudo-eyeball that I was using to perceive the world around me as a human might, which was something I didn't think was possible, yet clearly was.

Now I had to rotate and move the "eyeball" to look in a direction like a normal life form. Supplemented by my extrasensory ability as an Ooze, this was an incredible change!

I explored my body and mind to see what else had changed. I felt that I was producing a new form of gel inside my body, like when I assimilated the Poison Oozes. The concoction didn't seem to be toxic, but I kept an eye on it regardless. Thirdly, I seemed to have a higher density of magic in my body than before. Checking it, I could not believe my senses!

Mana! All living things produced this energy, even Oozes, but in the past my mana had been thin and watery. Now, it was thick, more abundant, and more akin to a human's; vibrant and filled with colors and a purer grade of power. I wondered if I could cast spells?

"I'm so glad you're OK, Jelly!" Liliana sobbed, and I turned my attention back to my owner. "When you ate that poisoned cake and everything started to go wrong I was so worried! Thank the Divine Family for your safety!"

Poisoned cake? It wasn't poison, I remember that much. More like an alchemical reaction between different substances that made a 'BOOM!' Still, it had hurt like the Hells themselves had forced their way into and out of my body, and I didn't normally feel pain!

"It's a good thing Oozes don't need air or have lungs, else you'd be hugging poor Jelly to death right after he's healed," Orleen joked, making Liliana "eep!" in shock and she let me go slightly.

"Sir Tomas Nierz identified the stuff in the cake as a mixture of substances that creates something called the Triarch Effect. He also said that your danger senses alerted you to what was in the food. He was kind enough to feed you an Elixir to heal you from the damage!" My owner continued, explaining a bit more about what happened. I nodded, or at least tried to. Dang, not having a neck was annoying! And I never thought I'd say that.

"Father investigated and uncovered who tried to assassinate us." At this, Liliana's eyes turned wet. "It was Uncle Darpel! I don't understand though, why did he and Aunt Liliana want to do that? I just…"

She broke down a bit more at this reveal, days of tension and worry finally coming unwound and she let her tears free. I patted her arm comfortingly with a tendril, and she sniffed and recollected herself.

"It seems Uncle Darpel tried to help his wife, father's oldest sister, take control of the kingdom in a coup. Failure was the outcome though, and he was only spared death because he and his wife had been very careful not to give themselves away fully. There had been too little evidence for a summary execution. For years Darpel kept to himself, biding his time."

"Father has already mobilized the army and marched on Edelstein. The fighting was fierce, but he's already wiped out most of the opposition. Uncle Darpel was slain on the battlefield, and now Cousin Einrik is fighting against father."

The princess wiped her tears away, and sat down on the bed. Ah, so we're in her bedroom! I quickly took a look around, something I'd forgotten to do when I'd first woken up. Everything seemed the same, with maybe a bit more mess lying around. The only real change appeared to be a tin tub at the foot of the bed filled with Healing Potions, and of a high grade quality! I realized that must be where I'd spent my coma resting. It must have been expensive, filling the whole container with the potions.

One other thing I noticed was that I felt different. Stronger, naturally, but in the reflection of Liliana's mirror I could have sworn I had changed color.

"It's been three months already, and winter is going to arrive shortly. I hope father will be back before the snows start and he gets trapped out in Edelstein," Liliana went on to say, which snapped me back to the conversation.

Three months?! I'd been unconscious for three months?! I shivered, suddenly realizing how close to death I'd gotten. My owner felt this and quickly pulled me tighter to her.

"It's Ok, everything is OK, Jelly. You have to be brave with me now. Father will be fine. Just fine." I relaxed and wrapped tiny limbs around her in a facsimile of a hug.

What did three months really matter to me? In that time, my precious owner had lost an uncle, nearly lost me, and could possible still lose a father. Her suffering was so much more than mine.

Within my core, I burned with rage. How dare they? How dare they?! Why did they do this, how could anyone let someone as kind and pure as my owner be hurt so badly like this?! When I find them I would rip them apart!

Inside, I had a gnawing feeling that this was not the end, merely the beginning of something much worse. But she had me. I would stand by her side and never let her go! Nothing would hurt her so deeply again, I swore this on the Divine Family!

Upon that declaration, I heard five voices whisper into my mind, "We'll be waiting for your call." Startled, I looked around trying to find a source of the voices, but could find none. Not even a trace of mana.

When nothing else happened for a bit I tried to relax and burbled contentedly. This was a good spot, right here in her arms. Warm and soft and suffused with kindness.

"Orleen, could you call for Sir Goyn? I want him to check up on Jelly, now that he is awake and seems to have changed colors," Liliana instructed, and her maid bowed before heading out. Oh, I actually had morphed? Interesting.

Petrus was here? Hadn't seen him in a while, it'd be good to be able to again! I wobbled happily, and waited patiently in Liliana's arms for the wizard.

He arrived soon enough, looking flustered and out of breath, until his eyes landed on me and he brightened up.

"You gave us all a fright, little one. I am glad to see you awake and in good health," Petrus said, a tired but genuine smile on his face. "My lady, do you mind if I hold him for a bit? I need to check his condition."

Liliana paused, struggling against letting me go. But I patted her arm tenderly, and she sighed sadly before passing me over.

"Alright..." Petrus started to fuss over me, peering into my core with a magical magnifying glass, taking samples of my outer body, and feeding me various potions and concoctions. As he worked he spoke to the princess and Orleen about various subjects, ranging from the situation in Geldstein to the latest advances in magical theory. Whenever the conversation drifted to magic and spells Petrus' eyes sparkled with intensity and his words were full of awe. He truly loved magic with all his heart. His animated passion was infectious, and by the end I could tell Liliana was hooked. I knew that in a little bit she'd be asking her mother and father for permission to study more complicated and advanced spells.

After a little while Petrus' mood turned... well, it couldn't be called solemn, but there was something tense in the air. He started flipping through thick tomes he had brought after a while, muttering to himself. The wizard was pulling them out of his robes even though they shouldn't be able to fit. Based on the magical energy I 'saw' hanging around his pouch, I concluded it was a Bag of Holding. After a bit of mumbling and searching the books, he passed me back to my owner's grasp and massaged his forehead.

"Well, to alleviate your worries, my lady, Jelly is perfectly healthy. In fact he is even better than before."

"How do you mean?"

Petrus steepled his fingers, unsure of how to explain.

"Princess, what do you know of the various types of Ooze?"

Liliana thought for a moment before speaking. "Well, I know about Green Ooze because you told me about them, and how various kinds can form based on where they live and what they eat. Other than that, I've read that rarer types of Ooze can only be born as such, and that much about this particular species is unknown because of their nature as semi-solid magic."

"Exactly," the mage said happily. "So, in your research, have you ever heard of a Royal Ooze?"

Liliana shook her head, as did Orleen. I merely wobbled left to right. Necks and heads were useful sometimes.

"To be honest very few have. You see, there have only been three confirmed sightings of a Royal Ooze in the past two hundred years, and no more than three dozen in the entirety of the Academy and Guild's history or records. There have been twice that many unconfirmed sightings, and dozens more wild tales and the like. But the point is they are extremely rare, and extremely powerful." He smirked a bit at our shocked expressions before continuing.

"A Royal Ooze is deep purple with a golden core, and with flecks of gold floating around inside it, mainly concentrated around the center. It had the power to command all other kinds of Ooze, from the lowest ordinary ones to the vast Pond Ooze. It can actually cast spells, and not just use spell-like abilities. Royal Ooze can produce incredibly toxic slime or potent healing gel on command, and are able to dissolve even dragon scales in their gullet. The smallest one recorded was seven feet wide and eight feet tall. The biggest was over a hundred feet all around."

"What does this have to do with Jelly?" Liliana asked even as a hint of understanding came to her and myself.

"I suppose we'll have to change the records around," Petrus mused with a smile. "Jelly here is not just the smallest Royal Ooze in history, he is also the first one known to have evolved to that stage. He is also, from just a cursory glance, easily a C-rank Mage in his own right. With training that could rise to B or even A-rank in just a few years of training."

"Wow." The princess held me up and looks at me, smiling in pride. "I always knew you were special. Now I know just how much so!"

"His diet won't change, and as long as you do not overfeed him he shouldn't grow to massive sizes. Just keep magical items away from him, as they may cause his growth to be unstable. Other than that, treat him as normal," Petrus said happily, glad to see a genuine smile on my owner's face again. From what I'd gathered from his talks during my examination, he had been put in charge of setting up various wards around the palace and acting as a liaison to the battle mages on the field, keeping the king informed of what happened in the capitol and the queen of what went on during the pacification. During that time he probably hadn't seen my princess smile too often.

"I need to double check the wards, and then I have a report to send to the king," Petrus said, standing. "If you want me to send the king a message, I will do for you."

"Thank you, Petrus. I will compose a letter you may send him," Liliana replied gracefully. Her attention had become focused on me, but she was still aware of her surroundings and how to act.

Petrus gave a bow before exiting the room, and Liliana flopped onto the bed with a sigh. It was filled with pent up exhaustion and relief, and she snuggled up to me. I could see her eyelids start to droop, so I got comfortable. A nap couldn't hurt. I'd just rest here with her for a bit. No one would hurt her with me around. So I swore.

Chapter 17: Magic in the family

"Hello Jelly. I'm glad you're feeling better," Prince Julius greeted happily. It was early evening now, and after waking up hungry from her nap, Liliana had decided to go down to dinner and bring me along.

Her brother was sitting in the private dining room, eating a light meal alongside Rene. It seemed he had not had a very large appetite since their father marched off to war. According to Liliana's chattering the heir had been melancholy and blue for many days. Joy returned to his face though as Liliana carried me into the room.

I jiggled in my owner's arms and understanding my intentions she released me, letting me squish my way across the table. I hopped into Julius' lap and gave off a purr like sound. More like a 'glug-glug-glug' to be honest, but it's the thought that counts.

"I'm glad to see you're OK," Julius admitted, holding me close for a hug. "I've been so worried. I don't want to lose anyone."

"Dad will be fine, Julius. He's really strong! He won't be hurt and he'll come home safe and sound," Liliana said, comforting her brother. I could hear the anxiety in her voice though. She said that to assure herself as well as Julius.

Rene smiled tightly, a note of sadness in her facial expression as she watched her pupils struggle with their emotions.

"What would you like for dinner, Jelly?" Julius asked, turning his attention back to me. I gave the shoulder-less version of a shrug by bobbing my body up and down and side to side. It sort of looked like I was making a circular motion. Thankfully Liliana was as attuned to me as ever, and she smiled and offered up a hearty slice of roast pork. I reached over and plucked it from her fork with glee. Almost dying was hungry work!

"Liliana, I heard that your pet has recovered." The doors to the dining room opened up and Queen Amdora entered in a swirl and swish of her royal gown. She had long dark bags under her eyes and not even her makeup could hide the weariness and worry she felt.

283

Still, a genuine smile graced her features as she saw her children cheerful for the first time in a long while.

"Do you mind?" the queen asked, and she held out her hands to Julius. He seemed to know what his mother wanted and a quick nod and smile from his sister made him lift me out of his lap and hand me over to Queen Amdora.

In her hands I felt her repress a shiver at touch of my soft and cool body, but she held me close and gave me a hug. Surprised, I stayed still, unsure of what was going on.

"Thank you." It was quiet, and if I hadn't had such capable hearing it would have been missed. Those two simple words filled me with her gratitude, and I finally understood what she was trying to convey. She was not Queen Amdora of Varia right now. She was simply a mother who'd almost lost the lives of her children and husband. I had saved them with my actions, and she was giving me her appreciativeness. Not out of obligation but true heartfelt love for her family.

"I see that Jelly has grown a bit, and changed in color. Has something happened?" Queen Amdora inquired as she passed me back to my owner. She reasserted her stern aloofness, but I knew she was concerned for me as well as for her daughter that I stayed with as she asked that.

"Sir Goyn told me that he has become a Royal Ooze now," Liliana said. She quickly explained the significance of that to her audience, and the queen grew thoughtful while Julius was content to stare in awe at me.

"So, on a bit of side note, mother, I was wondering... do you think I could be permitted to learn magic? Like what Sir Goyn does?" Liliana asked, holding me in one arm while gripping the hem of her dress in nervousness. "If I understand more about magic, I could learn more about Jelly and help him and maybe help you and father and..."

"I don't see why not." Queen Amdora cut off her daughter's rambling, and everyone stared at the prim and proper queen. No had expected her to capitulate that quickly. It usually took a lot more begging and pouting to get what my owner wanted when it came to large, complicated requests.

The queen scoffed at the surprised expressions on everyone's faces, bar mine. Not having one saved me some trouble once in a while!

"I'm wounded that you think I'd be so cruel to shoot down my own daughter's dreams, especially when I myself am a registered B-rank mage," Queen Amdora said in mock hurt, her children and servants becoming sheepish.

"But in regards to this matter, as long as you follow your instructors orders, keep up with the rest of your studies, and stay safe, I see no harm in letting you try your at hand at this."

"Thank you, mother!" Liliana exclaimed happily, rushing to give her a hug. I end up sandwiched between the two, and once again found myself glad I had no need to breathe.

"Just be sure to remember my conditions," my owner's mother said stiffly, trying to hide her own emotions. I wasn't sure why she bothered though. It was a turbulent time for the kingdom and royal family alike. I thought she could at least smile a bit more often.

"I do believe it is time for dinner, my ladies," Orleen interjected and the princess separated from her mother. Queen Amdora just flashed the maid a thankful nod before settling down into her chair.

The food was delicious as always. Or at least I assumed it was. I still had a limited grasp on taste. Sweet things and magically infused substances were still the main source that granted me a moment to sample that special sense. Other flavors remained dulled and muted to non-existence. Still, I could actually tell they were there now, and that was better than nothing. I could only hope that that particular sense would grow in time and with use.

Dinner that evening was a quiet affair. The joyful energy gained from my reawakening buoyed the small family, but without the overwhelming presence of King Tiberius the meal felt as if it was missing a vital component. They tried their best though and ate dinner with tiny smiles and small talk scattered throughout.

Finished at last, the royal family bid each other goodnight, and returned to their quarters. It had been a stressful few weeks, and with the tension bled out of them lethargy set in.

Some stifled yawns later and Liliana was ready to prepare for sleep. As she removed the clothes she'd once worn I snuggled up into one of her pillows. I doubted she would let me out of her sight or cuddle-grasping range so I settled down, content to spend the night with my dear owner. Things would improve. There was hope for that.

"I heard from Petrus Goyn that Jelly has recovered. I hope the mood at the palace has become better for it."

In her private chambers Queen Amdora sat in a large stuffed leather chair facing a thick wooden desk. Atop the surface were several stacks of papers, some half empty ink pots, and used quills, though the queen's attention was on a mirror-like object that thrummed with a faint whir of mana.

What resembled a hand mirror was propped up on a tripod of legs made from delicately crafted silver. Underneath the legs and mirror a glass orb hung, clouded with flickering bolts of blue and green lightning and nestled in a cage of enchanted metals.

A scying glass, a tool designed for long ranged Clairvoyance spells. Fairly cheap to make but astronomically expensive to use and maintain due to the amount of magical energy needed to power it even for a few minutes, but it was worth it for instant battle reports, immediate calls of aide, or advanced warnings of impending attacks. However, it was currently being used for a much more selfish and personal reason.

The queen, stripped of her fine clothes and jewelry and wearing only silk negligee, smiled happily down at her husband's grainy, static laced face that hovered in the mirror's pane.

"Indeed, Liliana's pet did awaken late in the afternoon. I assume young Mr. Goyn also informed you of what he has become?" Her tone became strained a bit as did her husband's expression.

"He did. An honest to Cynthia Royal Ooze… I had him send me as much information on them as he could, and it should arrive soon, but from the basics he told me I worry we're going to have trouble housing it if it grows," King Tiberius said. His own face was haggard and his beard was scraggly and surrounded by stubble. Weeks of fighting, marching, and campaigning had taken its toll on him. But his eyes remained strong and lively, with a hint of fondness now present as he gazed lovingly at his wife.

"I too am worried about his eventual size. But at least now some of the nattering lords and ladies in court can cease their blathering on Liliana's choice of pet. How many of them can claim to have raised one of the rarest monsters in the world?" Amdora mused with a chuckle. Tiberius laughed as well.

"Also, Liliana asked me a question at dinner. She wanted to know if she could start learning magic," the raven haired queen revealed, causing her husband to sigh.

"And what did you say?"

"I said she could as long as she keeps up with the rest of her work and duties. And doesn't make messes. And stays safe."

Tiberius barked out a laugh at the last two stipulations of his wife's conditions, and continued to do so as Amdora's face turned red.

"If she takes after you we'll have to buy a whole new wing for the palace! And magic-proof the rest!"

"That was long ago! I was younger and more reckless then!" the almost bare queen protested to her husband's amusement.

"You only stopped blowing up the place because Liliana was nestled in your belly! If she hadn't stopped your rampages, we would have had to live in a much smaller, more humble abode," Tiberius teased causing his wife to huff.

"I don't regret giving up the life of a mage, you know. Liliana and Julius are the lights of my life now. That's why... I'll be more lenient with Jelly from now on," Amdora said, and the mood turned somber.

"Keep an eye on him but don't worry too much. If these past few events have shown us anything it is that he will protect our children with his life," Tiberius urged and she nodded.

"I should be home soon. We've tracked the remnants of Einrik's forces down, and are preparing for confrontation. Come tomorrow evening I'll be on my way back to you and the kids," Tiberius said after a short lull in the conversation. He was careful not to say any sensitive information over the mirror.

It was hard but not impossible to eavesdrop on magical communications, and if there was one thing the king had learned from fighting his brother-in-law it was that he could not underestimate the mages at his disposal. More than a few of the mercenary spell casters had been powerful. Much more so than anticipated, which had caused severe casualties in the first few engages against Edelstein's troops.

"Be safe, Tiber. My children may be my lights but you are the lamp that protects them and lets them shine. Return to me in one piece."

"I will, my Duchess of Destruction," Tiberius said with a tiny smirk. Amdora just returned it before leaning down to the pane of enchanted glass and planting a quick kiss onto the image of her husband's cheek. He chuckled and returned the gesture before undoing the spell and severing the connection.

Amdora settled back in her chair before getting up and striding over to her dresser. She spent a few minutes digging around in the back of it before dragging out a large oaken chest. It was surprisingly light for its size, and was wrapped in bands of rune engraved brass. A muttered incantation later and the lid popped open, revealing a much larger storage space than it should have had.

Carefully removing a wand made of willow and capped with an amethyst wrapped in a silver band shaped like a lotus blossom from within the enchanted storage space, the bedroom attired queen smiled fondly at it before removing a tiny packet of leaflets and loose parchment bound in twine.

"It's been a while since I've had a reason to look at these," Amdora whispered to herself. She twirled the wand and watched with a judging eye as the mana flowed through it. Nodding in satisfaction she then untied the collection of parchment and looked over the neat, handwritten spell formulas and instructions.

"A proper mage needs a proper set of tools. I hope Liliana does not mind hand-me-downs and heirlooms," the queen said with a smile full of memories.

Chapter 18: To apprentice a princess

I sat in my owners lap, bouncing excitedly. After Liliana had

spoken to her mother yesterday Petrus had been asked to become a

temporary tutor for the princess in the ways of magic. As a

practitioner of barriers, wards, and other defensive spells he was

deemed to be the best choice to begin the training. Teaching her

basic theory as well as low simple protective charms would go a

long way in preparing her for a more thorough magical education.

The two of us were in the small, comfy classroom that

normally was used for history lessons. The large blackboard, tiny

mound of chalk stubs, and shelves lined with books were so very

familiar to the two of us, but now seasoned with the spice of

excitement. I was as interested in magic as my owner was, and if we

could both learn magic together it would make everything more fun

and enjoyable.

"A pleasure to see you again, Princess Liliana," the thin and

sallow mage greeted as he walked into the room. In his arms were a

number of books, parchment piles, scrolls, ink pots and fresh quills.

He seemed excited as well, eager to pass his knowledge on to a willing pair of ears. He plopped his load onto the desk at the front of the room and grinned over at my owner. I myself was partially hidden under the table, but he knew I was there and offered a wave. I returned it with one of my pseudopods.

Ever since I'd awoken I had felt that my control over my transformations and limbs had improved. I could now make eleven tentacles at once and maintain my bipedal shape for up to three hours straight.

"Before we start, what do you know about magic?"

"Magic is a fundamental force of nature. It is typically undetectable by normal senses and exists within everything, even if not everyone can use it," Liliana recited.

"Correct. All living things have magic, and by extension mana. This is because mana is generated by the soul. And all living beings have a soul. Some creatures, like insects, have barely recognizable souls, while a more complex and self-aware organism like a human has a larger soul and corresponding pool of mana. This is because intelligence has been correlate to the quality of a being's soul. Sapient entities will be superior over an ordinary animal," the mage revealed, drawing some crude diagrams on the board, showing stick figures that described relationship between magic and the soul.

"So the next thing to ask about is spells. How do they work, and how does a person cast them?"

"Chants and incantations are the most common, while the other popular method is to draw runes and ritual circles or magical diagrams and patterns that act as instructions for the mana to follow, thus forming spells. The latter method is typically used for enchantments and magical tools and artifacts," my owner announced and Petrus nodded with a smile.

"Very good! But I'm sure you also know that if someone has cast a spell enough times, they slowly begin to memorize it? Eventually a mage only needs to recite the a few parts of the whole incantation, and eventually a well-trained mage can cast spells nonverbally. All they have to do is think of the spell, remember what it means to them, and let the mana in their body remember how it works."

"Now before we start flinging magic willy-nilly I want to know what spells you can perform, and how well. Please show me," Petrus instructed and Liliana nodded before holding out her right hand and squinting her eyes. One, then two glowing spheres of pale yellow-blue light appeared above her palm hovering an inch off over the flesh.

"A good show of the *Dancing Light* spell. A bit dull and not as bright as some but you can create and maintain two at once, so that puts you ahead of the curve in that regard. Anything else?"

At the mage's question Liliana nodded, dispelling the orbs before sending out a pulse of greyish light from her palm outwards to the ceiling. She then used her left hand to release a second wave, this time with a pale green color to it. I used two pseudopods to applaud her.

"*Detect Magic* and *Detect Poison*. Both very well done. I see you've practiced with them before," Petrus noted with a pleased glimmer in his eyes. Liliana just gave an embarrassed smile. I wasn't sure why though.

"Both spells are vitally useful for anyone. The first spell can check on magical objects or anomalies or beings, the color of the pulse changing and highlighting objects that carry a certain level or type of magic. All living things have magic, so the spell merely looks for active spells, enchantments, or large concentrations of it. It is very useful for a mage or anyone out on long travels. *Detect Magic's* one downside is that it only pinpoints magic and does not automatically detail what that magic is," Petrus explained, jotting his words down on the blackboard.

"As for *Detect Poison*, I know that the life of an aristocrat can be dangerous, and courtly intrigue means that everyone of a noble or distinct peerage would want to know this spell to avoid assassinations. As for commoners, it is useful to avoid dangerous plants and animals which can appear without warning beyond the city's walls. Of course it cannot detect all threats. As the near fatal events at the Adventurer's ball could attest to not everything that could kill you was toxic at first glance," the young tutor warned. "Now, what else can you cast?"

The next spell my owner prepared was barely noticeable. A flicker of brief mana and she turned her head to face a corner of the room.

"*Find North*?" Petrus inquired, and the princess nodded still facing the wall before turning back to her teacher.

"Very good. *Find North* is a very simple spell, only able to point out the direction in question. The easiest to cast in fact. Quick question: Do you know about how we measure mana, in both people and in spells?"

"Mana is measured in Points, correct? All humans have some mana that they can use, and it grows with use and practice. As for spells, *Detect Magic* requires five 'points' of mana to be cast, same as *Detect Poison*. More complex and powerful spells need more mana, and thus use up more 'points,'" Liliana explained and the older mage nodded.

"An average human has fifty to two hundred Mana Points, though most do not have the training to use a spell more advanced then Cantrips, which rarely exceed twenty Points worth of power," Petrus elaborated, and Liliana hastily scratched some notes out for herself. He nodded in approval before continuing.

"We use this method of rating the 'price' of a spell and the capacity of an individual because it makes it simpler and easier to group and organize new spells, be they invented or rediscovered, and to group and organize mages for different classifications and rankings. And like anything, the more you use it, the better you get with it. One's mana capacity increases over time and with training. Like a muscle, if you use magic often you will be able to do more with it."

"Now, for the final part of your demonstrations I want you to perform the most powerful spell you have. It does not matter if it is an offensive spell or not. I will block it and neutralize any problems you have." The adept mage stepped out from behind his desk and took a stance in front of the pair of us. My owner rose from her seat and placed me on the top of the desk before facing her tutor.

Liliana then nodded her head at Petrus' order and then clasped both her hands together. I felt a tingle run through my non-existent spine. I opened my 'eye' wider and tried to peer at my owner as she prepared her spell. I had not felt anything like it before, and judging from how it felt this was a more potent spell than a mere Cantrip.

Petrus threw up a shimmer green disc of solid magic, a barrier of some sort, as a bolt of flickering yellow-blue energy slammed into it. A deep 'whump!' echoed through the room as spell struck shield, the dart-shaped projectile creating a bright burst of light and sparks that pattered harmlessly on the stone floor. My owner's spell shattered across the surface, inflicting no visible damage.

"A most impressive *Magic Arrow!*" the princess' tutor praised, dismissing his shield spell once he was sure the spell was completely gone.

"Mother thought it was best that I know some spells to protect myself with," Liliana said with a hint of red to her cheeks. "I don't have much experience with it though. Did I do well?"

"Very well, I should say. It wasn't the largest or most powerful version of *Magic Arrow* I've ever seen, but it was competently formed and well-aimed. A bit more practice and you should have a good offensive spell if you ever get into trouble," Petrus said cheerfully, praising his new student. I wobble in joy as well, impressed by my owner's attack. I wondered if I could perform that spell as well. It looked easy enough based on what I'd observed from Liliana.

"*Magic Arrow* is just a blob of pure magical energy shaped into a projectile and fired off like a crossbow bolt. Nothing fancy or complex about it."

As I pondered on how to go about training my own magic and spells, Petrus spoke directly to me.

"I know that look. You may not have visible features or expressions but even I can tell that you're thinking about doing experiments on your own."

I jerked in shock, flopping around a bit in surprise before 'facing' the mage, giving off a sheepish and apologetic aura.

"You're a Royal Ooze now, Jelly, and clearly of higher intellect than any other of your kin. That means you are also going to be my student while I teach Princess Liliana," the mage stated. "You have a lot more mana than she does, but far less control or understanding. I will be teaching the both of you how to perform magic the proper and safe way."

"Will mother allow this?" Liliana asked. Petrus shrugged.

"I see no reason why she wouldn't. True, it is unconventional, but he has actual power now, and needs to be able to use and control it. She'll likely request me to teach him regardless as having an unstable mage is as dangerous as letting a child swing a sword, if not more so," the Academy student turned temp teacher explained. "He won't be an official student of course. Not even the most progressive or open minded professors at the Academy would allow a monster as a student, even if it has clear levels of abnormal intelligence."

"I understand," the princess said softly, slight disappointment emanating from her. I cooed softly, soothing her. Her empathy was truly astounding.

"Speaking of being a student, I guess I should mention this now," Petrus said getting my owner's attention back. She took her seat and looked on attentively.

"As you are not yet an adult you won't be able to officially be a student of the Academy. However the queen has requested I give you a crash course on the most basic topics a First Year would receive in the Gen. Ed. Course. I have a feeling she wants me try and enroll you in the Academy early so you'll need to be better than average to do so. She also wants you to create a special research project to work on as you learn with me."

"Research project?" Liliana asked and the mage nodded.

"Indeed. The Academy requires all students to work on a special research project after they choose the type of magic they wish to study. We do this because learning magic is far more difficult and dangerous than learning history or math. The administration needs to see proof every year or so that you are taking your lessons seriously. Queen Amdora wants you to get a head start on this so you won't be left in the dust by the older students when you do attend," Petrus cautioned. His warning and the requirements made some sense, but I felt annoyed on Liliana's behalf. I was so glad I was a monster and didn't have to take tests or study in the normal style. It looked boring.

"Don't worry, princess. You have the perfect research project already," her tutor said trying to cheer her up. She just looked confused before understanding.

"Jelly! He'll be my project!"

"Correct again, princess! He is a rare Royal Ooze. Very little is known about living ones, and this is the first time to have one as a specimen so readily available for study!"

I shrank in on myself, suddenly afraid. The glint in both Petrus and my owner's eyes was unsettling, and I worried I may have fallen in with a bad crowd. There's nothing worse than being used as a science experiment. Oh, the things I do for love…

Chapter 19: The way to learn magic

It was a brisk, chilly afternoon at Palestone Castle. The sun had sluggishly crept up the sky and done the bare minimum of shedding some warmth onto the city of Sanc Aldet. A blistering, biting wind tore down from the mountains and the inhabitants shivered slightly in their thick clothes. Winter had finally arrived in Varia and the first snowfall of the season was fast approaching.

King Tiberius had not yet returned from his pacification of Edelstein, but he was reportedly on his way back. According to the gossip I'd overheard he had stopped off at the fortified city Bastiongard to see an old friend before marching his forces back home.

As for the brief war, it ended in total victory for the king and his forces. Count Marik Yenfold Darpel and his son Einrik had both been slain on the fields of battle and the rebellious territory beaten down. Most of the soldiers and levies had surrendered quickly, as without their lord to command them they saw no reason to fight against the rightful king. Now came the lengthy process of rebuilding Edelstein. That including find a new Count to take over. None of Darpel's immediate family or close allies and advisors could be trusted and their statuses and privileges hung by a thread. A more loyal noble needed to fill in the gap and restore proper order. To that end extensive investigation was being undertaken.

As for King Tiberius' sister, the count's wife had escaped and gone into hiding. None knew where she was but there was a bounty on her head; dead or alive she was worth a thousand gold coins. It was rare for the royal family to offer such a large prize for anything, and already people were scouring the lands to find her. No second chances for her.

In regards to me and my owner, we wiled away the growing cold learning magic under the tutelage of Petrus Goyn, Senior Apprentice to Master Renos of the Varian Royal Mages Academy.

Petrus was a fine teacher. He gave concise explanations of the theories we studied and answered any questions to the best of his ability. While not an expert on every subject he knew plenty and his eclectic array of trivia about historical magical figures and events kept Liliana engrossed with every lesson.

I was less focused on the lectures and more keen to get my pseudopods on the practical side. I was learning slowly and I itched to see visible improvements.

"You've proven to be skilled at basic Cantrips, so for today's lesson we'll be learning several spells, two of which are stronger versions of the ones you currently know. First up, *Detect Good* and *Detect Evil.*"

"Will these spells let me know who is going to try and hurt my family?" Liliana asked, looking up at Petrus from her desk. I sat on the top of my own table since Petrus had thought that having me sitting in the princess's lap all lesson would be distracting for both of us.

The thin and sallow tutor shook his head. "No, they won't. Contrary to popular belief, these two spells are designed for detecting, locating, and analyzing Light and Dark based magic respectively. It would be impossible to fully create a spell matrix or ritual algorithm that could properly discern such things as 'good' or 'evil.' Morality is sadly very flexible and up to interpretation, and magic works best in absolutes. Some gods, like Kardale, can grant their disciples the power to see through lies and uncover sins, but only to an extent. Kardale's tenants say that murder is an evil, and so one of his Paladins could locate a murderer with magic. But another god, like Vandalore, would view murder as an act of good and loyalty, and so would not have a spell to see murder as 'evil.'"

The mage's casual mention of the infernal God of Murder and Betrayal made my owner and I shiver in our seats. A magic user saw gods as just another source of magic and spells, but to Liliana who had been raised to see gods as something more, offhanded references to dark entities were more shocking. My owner's fears and upbringing carried over to my own mindset.

I was fairly certain I had met two of the Divine Family during the Reaffirmation of Faith, and the thought of something out there being a dark and corrupt version of such purity revolted me.

"Then why is it important to know them?" Liliana asked and I bobbed in agreement, both of us controlling our earlier disgust.

"Because they can be used to get a more accurate read on certain kinds of magic. Tell me, what are the Elements of Magic?"

"There are eight substances and elements scholars believe relate to magic. They are Fire, Water, Wind, Earth, Energy, Dream, Light, and Dark," Liliana recited automatically.

"Exactly! And each Element has its own subtypes of magic. Healing spells and exorcism type techniques belong to the Light Element, while Necromancy and spells used by Demons and Devils all fall under the Dark Element. With *Detect Good* and *Detect Evil* you can quickly tell what kind of foe you face, the sort of magical tools you should use, or the preemptive knowledge that there is a threat or safe zone ahead," Petrus explained. "Of course, the odds of you ever actually needing to use them are slim. I just want you to be able to practice them, as they are considered Level 1 Spells, much more difficult and expensive in terms of mana to perform."

Petrus handed the young princess two small squares of parchment upon which looping, elegant handwriting could be seen. Liliana nodded her head and began to mumble under her breath the incantation for the two spells inscribed in front of her.

"As for you, Jelly, your senses are several times sharper than a humans, and you seem to have the 'Detect' series of spells incorporated into them naturally. Therefore I want you to practice the *Summon Water* cantrip. You've had trouble with it so far and I want you to be able to master it before I teach you any more advanced spells."

I nodded, slightly annoyed at myself for having to constantly practice such a basic spell. Out of all the Cantrips, *Summon Water* was the most mana intensive and required a great deal of concentration. Rather than conjuring the water from another source as its name might imply, *Summon Water* was a lesser form of Hydromancy and it gathered stray moisture and excess water from the air to create up to a gallon of pure, clean, fresh water. The most desired spell for a farmer to learn, and one all commoners adore as it gave them quick access to cheap and healthy liquid nourishment.

And out of all of them Liliana and I have studied, this one was a poor match for myself. Why? Because an Ooze's body was full of water as well as magic with very few solids and other substances or elements to bind my form together, and *Summon Water* desiccated me whenever I used it. My body would shrink as moisture was sucked from my gooey flesh and it caused me genuine pain.

The only way I could figure out to use the spell was to create and extend a pseudopod, alter its composition so it was thicker and less gel-like, and then focus on creating the Cantrips formula on the tip of the tendril. In this way less fluids were sucked out of my body when the spell gathered the water.

I had no mouth and no way to form words of any kind so I was taught by Petrus how to mentally speak the incantations or use my mind's eye to imagine what the runes and spell diagrams looked like.

It was a high level ability normally only taught to advanced mages and used by extremely magical beings. Making a mistake resulted in various calamities for the caster, with death being just one of the possible outcomes. But the tradeoff was a faster casting time and opponents not knowing what the incoming spell was until it had been unleashed.

"Now, watch what I'm doing and how I form the spell," Petrus instructed, and I bobbed up and down.

One aspect about my transformation to a Royal Ooze was a greatly enhanced boost to my talent to subconsciously analyze whatever I observed. It worked best on magical objects, thanks to my connection to my semi-solid mana body. But it could interact with others as well.

Before, I had to physically touch something to understand its composition. Now I was able to scan things from a glance. Magical artifacts revealed their basic spells and natures and when observing someone casting a spell I could decipher the exact sort of spell just by watching them. With this new trick I could quickly grasp what I needed to do to cast a spell. The actual act of creating the spell was still difficult for me, though.

Focusing back to my task at hand, I started to mentally draw the 'patterns' of the spell I had seen Petrus use with my mind and allowed my internal energy to flow towards my extended limb. It thickened and took on a consistency like toffee, and then I felt a ripple in my inner workings as the mana inside my body and the spell diagram I mentally envisioned reacted with the free flowing Ambient Mana of the air and room. Slowly tiny droplets of water condensed and floated a few centimeters off of my tendril, held in place by my magic. I winced as I felt pricking sensations cover my exposed limb as stray fluids were drawn out of me.

"Yes, I see your still having a bit of trouble keeping the spell from targeting yourself," Petrus mused as he took a closer look at me and my spell. "This is probably because living flesh acts as a natural barrier against minor magical backlashes, which is why even an ordinary person doesn't dry themselves out when using *Summon Water*. But because you do not have 'flesh' in the conventional sense, your body is free game to the spell's ravages. When using it, try and form the spell a bit further from yourself, so it isn't actually touching you."

I grumbled at my mentor's observations. Hopefully in time I could find a way around this, but until then I endured.

After a few moments of dull pain I deposited the tablespoon or so of water I managed to create into a copper pot Petrus had provided for me. I wondered what he'd use it for. Boil it for tea maybe? I felt weird thinking about someone drinking what was partially made of my own essence.

While preparing for the next set of exercises, I pondered why I felt disgusted by someone drinking me, but not by cannibalism? I hadn't felt that way after consuming the Poison Oozes, so was it double standards or something due to my link with my dear owner?

"Not a bad amount, Jelly," Petrus praised, looking into the container. "There's a bit more in here than last time. Once you work around your issues with the spell you'll be a master at this! Control is everything in magic, after all."

The mage turned tutor wandered over to check on the princess's progress, humming and hawing as he looked over her work. Time passed slowly in the tiny, cozy room. But eventually our session ended with Petrus and my owner and I rose from the seats to move on to the next classes. I bobbed and slithered around Liliana's feet, nuzzling her ankle as we walked.

Liliana could no longer carry me. In the days since I'd woken up from my coma I had steadily grown. Soon I was the size of a large dog, not unlike one of the hunting hounds King Tiberius kept in his menagerie of animals and beasts.

There was a slight feeling of sorrow from both me and her about this fact. I missed being small and cuddly. I slept in a modified dog bed nowadays rather than on a pillow next to my owner, I made a sloshing sound when I moved, and I had an increased appetite as well. That latter part I sated with rats and mice I hunted in the cellars at night, not wanting to disturb Liliana or her family. Apparently non-magical animals like rodents and roaches can scurry into the palace without being hindered by the barrier and wards. There's fewer of them about than a place without the magical defenses, but still plenty for me to feast on.

Hopefully my size would stabilize soon. I really did not want to be any larger. Allowances had been made for me recently due to my growth spurt, but that was thanks to me saving so many people's lives at the feast. If I got any bigger I'd have to move out of the palace. Maybe a nice kennel of sorts… no, no, I shouldn't think like that! I have to be close to Liliana! I have protect her!

"Come on, Jelly! We don't want to be late for history," Liliana said kindly as she reached down and patted my head. I burbled happily in agreement, and oozed on after her. I wondered what todays lesson would be about?

A trio of figures moved through the pre-evening crowds of Sanc Aldet's central plaza. They were ordinary looking humans, consisting of two men in their twenties and an older woman in her mid-forties. Clad in simple brown traveling cloaks with lowered hoods they attracted no attention, and since they had no visible or badly concealed weapons the City Guard paid them no heed. All in all the group was, to an outsider looking in, a mother and two sons out shopping.

But the three figures had sharp, focused eyes that watched everything, and they seemed to communicate without a word or sound uttered to the others. Their gazes were fit more for adventurers or mercenaries used to the sight of death and suffering.

They moved silently and swiftly though, their footsteps leaving no sounds or marks, even in the puddles of brackish water here and there or the heaps of garbage on the corners. Up flights of steps and steep ramps they tread, moving up to the elevated Purple District. The trio shied away from straying too close to the Divine Family's cathedral, but made it look as if it were a natural avoidance rather than a deliberate aversion.

Through much better kept streets they slipped, before sliding into the shadows of an impressive restaurant. The scents of spices and cooking meat were pleasant, and masked what happened next.

First, one of the young men doubled over and clutched his stomach before spewing out torrents of blood onto the cobblestones.

However, the liquid did not stay put and lashed out, wrapping around the trio's cloaks and stained them red while bestowing them with corrupt blessings. Thanks to the restaurant, the coppery tang of blood was hidden from any wandering noses.

As the first man wiped blood from his lips with the back of his hand the second bared his arms and winced as black bones ruptured the flesh and formed elongated knives and short swords. As the weapons appeared the scent of rotten wood filled the air. The older woman and bloody lipped man reached out wordlessly and dragged the weapons from their comrade's limbs, squelching sounds faintly echoing in the air. The man's arms fell limp at his sides, before the flesh writhed as something squirmed below the surface and the bones were restored.

Lastly, the sole woman of the group reached into the depths of her cloak and removed a small, purse like bag. Completely innocent looking, but a mage would be able to detect the magic suffusing it. Opening the bag the woman removed three glossy black masks, each one made of polished obsidian with a pair of eye holes cut into them and several runes of concealment etched onto the surface. They should not have been able to fit in such a small place but the tiny sack was in fact a magical container, a *Bag of Holding*. A minor one, only able to store a few dozen pounds worth of objects, but easily worth many tens of gold coins. It was sufficient to hide the various tools of their dark trade, and woman passed the masks out to her two partners while placing the last one over her own face.

The cover of night quickly arrived, and with the winter chill no one who did not have to be out and about dared to brave the dropping temperatures. A perfect time for crime to be committed. The trio looked to each other knowing glances. Each knew what they had to do.

"For the glory of the Hierophant, who speaks the words of the Void," the woman intoned.

"Let his will be done," her younger companions replied, covering their own faces. The three then flipped their hoods up, and in an instant a chilling aura filled the back alley.

"Let the world rebel!" The assassins hissed before leaping onto the roof of the restaurant and start to run across the roofs to their destination; the royal dwelling of the Roan family and their abominable pet.

Chapter 20: crimson and ebony deaths

"Dinner time!" Liliana cheered, practically skipping down the hallway.

"Dinner!" Julius echoed, keeping pace beside his sister with a wide smile. Lessons had finally finished for the evening, and the two royal children were walking side by side enjoying each other's company. I was glad to see that the two of them had such a close and friendly relationship. I'd heard stories about sibling rivalries before, and of course there was the more recent and close to home example of their own father's traitorous sisters, so it was refreshing to me and the other older servants to see them act so kind to each other.

Maybe it might sour as they age, but for now it was adorable to see little Julius acting in tandem with his beloved older sister.

As for myself I was following behind them and their ever present maids, since I was too big to squelch along next to them and I did not want to annoy their maids with my movements or presence. Even though Orleen, my owner's personal maid, was much more used to me than Julius' I kept back a bit for her sake. I think the prince's maid's name was Jean. She was fairly young, a decade less than Orleen, and was versed in the various arts and tasks she needed to perform but being around Oozes had not been part of the training.

"Please calm down, your highnesses. I understand you're relieved after a hard day of studying, but try to maintain a level of decorum," Orleen begged as Jean nodded her head in silent agreement.

"Yes, of course Orleen," Liliana replied, eyes downcast and her tone chastised. She really is a good girl.

"Oh, and if Jelly breaks another chair I fear your mother will be most displeased," the maid warned.

Only Julius chuckled at that. Liliana just rolled her eyes.

"Yes, yes, it was a mistake! I know he's been getting bigger recently, you don't have to keep bringing it up!"

"I'm only trying to get you to be cautious, my lady. And he isn't just 'bigger,' he's the size of a hunting dog! This level of growth is not normal. So please do not be surprised when your mother forces Jelly outside to live in a kennel."

I gurgled in annoyance at that. But I had to admit I was growing larger much faster recently. My ascension to a Royal Ooze being the likely culprit.

As we were walking Jean suddenly stiffened and stopped walking. I almost bumped into her because of her abrupt halt. The rest of the party froze in confusion. A second later a blaring alarm started to ring in my head!

My *Danger Sense* was going off like mad, klaxons echoing in my mind and I stretched out my perception, whose range had increased drastically after my change. Instantly I detected three objects hurtling towards our position! They were less than a dozen feet away! Outside the walls of the palace, certainly, but how could they move so far into the barrier around the royal dwelling?!

There were countless wards layered on top of the ancient stones, many of them so old they had been laid millennia ago by the original builders of the castle, and so powerful their effect permeated the very nature of the building, even though the old lode stones and building materials had long ago crumbled to dust and been replaced hundreds of times since.

How was it then that this trio of rapidly moving figures had gotten through these defenses without detection until just now?!

That answer has to wait as the invaders slam into the surface of the palace and seem to melt, dissolving into the stones and flowing through the cracks before appearing before us.

Blood spurted out of the walls, two geysers in front of us and one behind. The thick crimson fluid hurt my 'eye' when I tried to look at it, and I soon come to the solution as to how they'd gotten past the fortress-level barriers; dark magic, and lots of it!

The blood twisted and bent and morphed into dark red bipeds which further solidified and transformed into a trio of people wearing carmine robes with tar black masks covering their faces and clutching ebony hued weapons.

The cloaks seemed to be saturated with bizarre Dark Element magic with the trait to liquefy the wearer and then reform them.

Impressive magical resistance was also woven into their nature. That might be a problem for something like me. They fluttered menacingly in the breeze created by their owner's appearance.

In their grasp each assassin bore a wickedly sharp short sword and knife, one in each hand. They were black as tar like the masks, but had no sheen to them. Further, the blades were writhing with Dark Element magic as well, but of a slightly different sort than the robes. They would tear life force from their victims and give it to their wielders. Lastly the weapons seemed to be made of organic materials of some sort, but I was unable to accurate analyze them thanks to their cursed nature.

Finally was their masks, which were the secret to their infiltration. Potent runes of hiding and concealment had been scrawled onto the exterior and interior of the mask given the wearer an unparalleled ability to be ignored by living creatures and magical spells designed to keep people out. In the eyes of the spell matrices, the people who wore these masks 'Did not exist.' And that was also a part of the curse.

Each and every one of these enchanted items damned their user. The cloaks would permanently turn their wearer into a puddle of gore if they continuously used the effects. Turned to a pool of immobile blood and bile, but still able to perceive the world.

The blades would slowly rip and tears at their wielders if they did not take the lives of others. The longer they were held, the more it hurt their owners. Even sheathing them or tossing them away would not stop the life drain. They had to be destroyed or purified, and neither option was easy, for they possessed a hardness rivaling steel and a Darkness akin to a demon.

Finally, the masks. In exchange for allowing the wearer to hide from anything, the person who put them on slowly was erased. Their own memories and recognition of 'self' was eroded, eventually turning them into mindless husks that could only hunt and kill from the shadows. It also melted their faces if removed by anyone but the user, so wearers could not be identified by facial features.

Alone, each artifact and its curse was heinous enough for summery execution on sight or knowledge of possession. Together, though, these three items made it clear these souls were disposable. Death did not matter to them, for they were already dead men walking.

Only a few seconds had passed since the trio of assassins had appeared in real time. In that miniscule frame, Orleen had whipped out a pair of long dagger that had been hidden in her stockings and jumped in front of her charges while Jean conjured up a shimmering wall of magical energy between the two royal children and the assassins in the front. As for me, I threatened the assassin who had popped up from behind by growing three waving tentacles and prepared to cast *Magic Arrow* from their tips if my opponent approached.

None of these preparations gave the assailants pause. With unnatural dexterity and grace they lunged forward to try and kill us and the targets behind us.

In a single blow the barrier Jean had created shattered, the pulsing black blade in the left assassin's grip rending through the magic. The maid did not despair though, as she raised both hands and sent a gale force wind to slam into the duo in front of her. It knocked them back and gave Orleen a chance to leap in front of Princess Liliana and Prince Julius. There was no chance of trying to escape from the front. We were trapped between attackers in the middle of a hall with no doors, windows, or side corridors.

As for the figure trying to strike me, my first two spells went wide, the assassin skilled enough to dodge them even though they were fired faster than a crossbow bolt at short range. They crashed into the wall and cracked the stone. The third *Magic Arrow* did land a hit though as it impacted violently onto their right leg, drawing a gush of blood and charred meat. The person, a woman based on her figure that I gleaned from her under her robe, staggered and I took that chance to wrap my appendages around her to try and pin her down.

It failed though as she flicked her two black weapons in a blur of skilled movements and sliced my tendrils off.

In the admittedly short time I had lived, I had never really felt pain. When I ate the Poison Ooze, I did not feel the effects of their toxins. When I over exerted myself trying to form my bipedal form and cast magic, it was nothing more than a tingly nuisance. Even when the Triarch Effect ravaged my body and I suffered greatly it was over relatively fast and I was too focused on trying to protect my owner that I barely recall the sensations of agony I should have had. But now, I knew what pain was.

The curse that dwelt in the blades sent my mana into shock and I froze from the sudden experience of 'pain.' My severed limbs flailed around on the floor before melting into a purplish slurry, and the stumps did not instantly regenerate as they should have. I felt a large sliver of mana get torn from me and become assimilated into the cursed weapons.

Retracting my tentacles, I nursed the stumps with some healing juice. As it turns out, a Royal Ooze secretes powerful healing fluids akin to a Greater Potion of Healing. With Liliana's help in studying my new abilities, I had discovered this vital trick. Rapidly healing myself with my own body was nice, and I could mend the wounds of others by dribbling it from myself onto them.

It didn't seem to work well to counteract the curse's effects, though. At least, not that quickly. I couldn't afford to be distracted though, as the crimson robed woman began to slash away at me. Moving my body like a slippery snake I avoided her blows easily. She was talented though and started to mix up her attacks and combine different movements in an attempt to confuse me.

Slash then stab, feint from a lunge into a fierce upwards cut. Thrust both blades at the same time but have them move aside at the last minute and attack at an angle. Step back once to lure in the opponent, then follow up with a barrage of lethal hits.

Had I been a guard or one of the lesser knights I would have been dead several times over from her tricks. But I relied on a different set of senses to observe the world, and so when I analyzed her form and read her attacks it was easier for me to dodge. I can see everything at once if I wanted to, and so I did not have to be restricted to a single field of vision like humans or other beings with two eyes.

Worried about how Orleen and Jean were handling the two other assassins, who looked to be male, I was relieved to see they were holding their own, if only barely. Jean hurled the foes back with bursts of wind and telekinetic shoves while Orleen countered any wayward blows from the dark blades with her enchanted daggers, keeping the cursed weapons away from my owner and her brother.

But they were faltering. No matter how strong they were, the two of them were still maids, and their combat training was limited. Enough to become a deterrent to a common thief or rapscallion, but against trained killers?

No matter how much I wanted to help, I could not. For one, the person I was squaring off against was several degrees more powerful than the twins, and could overwhelm Orleen and Jean with ease. I had no choice but to hold off the assassin woman and pray for the maids.

I wasn't worried that much though. Alarm charms blared through the castle, activated by the presence of unauthorized Dark magic. The cursed artifacts may have allowed them to pass through the wards around the palace, but now they were drawing the attention of the interior defenses. And drawn by the magical detection spells, dozens of Dire Swords were rushing up to engage the assassins. I knew this thanks to my enhanced senses. Oddly enough Queen Amdora was also running towards the conflict as well with Petrus and her own personal maid Karina in tow. I saw the queen carrying a wand I'd never noticed before, and it glistened with power. I made a mental note to stay away from my owner's mother if she started swing it around and casting spells.

"Get away from the prince and princess!" Oh thank the Divine Family! A Dire Sword had appeared from down the corridor in front of the maids and behind the two male assassins. He dashed forward and clashed with one of them, allowing Orleen and Jean to focus solely on the other mysterious killer.

As for me, I had to keep holding off the woman. My Magic Bolts were slower than her reflexes and I dared not to approach her terrible swords with my bare appendages. So I keep her back and on guard by flinging bolts of magic here and there to make sure she cannot get close.

After a few more instances of me blocking her movements she became annoyed at my efforts and decided to just rush through. Crap!

Her body rippled and her entire form seemed to take on a crimson tint. A coppery tang of blood filled the air, and it was only through my magical senses that I saw what happened to the assassin. The red robe activated its special power and turned its wearer's body into a semi-liquid state. She attempted to slip past my defenses like this, and to my shame it worked.

I managed to score a single hit on her left arm as she darted past, but in her blood-form it did nothing as she just reformed, completely unharmed. Even worse was that the wounds I'd inflicted on her earlier in the battle also healed up!

Growling I lashed out violently, but it did nothing to her impervious body. The assassin retaliated with her blades in response to my pathetic attempts and severed two more of my pseudopods.

Warbling in pain I flinched and retracted my stumps into myself. She was too close to my owner! Orleen wouldn't stand a chance against this woman! And the other guards were still hurrying to arrive!

In desperation, a crazy thought struck me as I helplessly watched the assassin's body sway and wobble like blood-scented jam. I jabbed out with one more pseudopod and pierced the hip of the female invader. She didn't react though as the cloak would protect her from physical damage. If the tentacle had been made for physical attacks, it would have.

Summon Water! I crafted the basic Cantrip in my mind and activated it on the tip of the limb currently imbedded in the assassin. At once there was a noticeable effect. The enchanted blood turned darker and thicker around the point of penetration, and for the first time the woman let out a noise of shock and pain!

My plan worked! *Summon Water* draws in moisture, but normally it would be impossible to take any from a human even if I touched their skin while doing the spell. Unless, of course, I pierced their flesh or there was nothing between me and their precious bodily fluids. Sucking up the water in the assassin's own blood I dealt a sudden spike of damage to the woman which couldn't be negated easily even with a cursed artifacts help.

I drank down the water I had gathered eagerly, using it to slightly replenish my own mass. It wasn't much, but this way I could regain some of what I'd lost to her cursed blades. A fitting compromise.

Her cry of surprise shook her two companions who'd apparently never seen or heard their leader injured before. And that moment of hesitation was enough for Jean to crush her opponent under a wall of telekinetic weight and for the Dire Sword to hack off the left arm of his own foe. The tables turned on them in our favor!

Victory did not last for long though. The older woman tore herself away from my appendage and hacked it off while returning to her solid human form. The other two assassins did the opposite, letting their cursed capes transform them into blood to escape their situations. Jean's opponent slipped out from under the crushing barrier and tripped up the Dire Sword while the assassin took that chance to reattach their lost arm and retaliate by plunging both of their weapons down into the swordsman's body. The longer sword-like blade tore off the guard's own left arm in revenge and the dagger-like weapon sunk into his chest plate and punctured a lung. From behind the second male killer stabbed both of his weapons into the royal guard's back, the sword jutting through the front of the body, slick blood dripping off the grotesque black blade.

He collapsed. The first casualty of the battle. Thanks to my special sight I was able to see the soul fade and become torn. The Dire Sword's life energy suffused his murderers. But thanks to that sacrifice, help finally arrived.

"Get away from my children!" Sensing danger I tossed myself forwards, wrapping around Orleen and the two royal heirs while being careful not to accidently engulf and digest them. It was a good thing I do so. A spear of pure flames shot down the corridor from behind me, setting a nearby tapestry ablaze as it passed by. The woman assassin dodged it by throwing herself flat to the floor, and it soared past to slam violently into the male intruder standing directly in front of the fallen Dire Sword. His companion had been facing the direction of the spell and had a moment more to react to it and was spared death.

The spear of fire pierced the back of the unlucky assassin and carried him several feet before the heat combusted his flesh and clothes. He tried to liquefy to escape the damage but the flames were too hot and he could only utter an inhuman scream as the cursed blood boiled and turned to noxious steam.

My flesh bubbled and popped due to the heat that passed by me. Clouds of purplish smoke rose up like a haze and I hastily uncoiled and dropped to the floor to try and recover some of my injuries. I learned something new as well. Damage from fire? It really hurt. Not even my squishy body was immune.

"*Burning Lance!*" Again a second Level Four spell was hurled down the passage way, but it was sliced to pieces by the female assassin. Despite that the faces of Liliana and Julius lit up in relief and joy. Even the maids and I were happy to see her. There, striding down the carpeted path like a well-dressed cake of motherly rage was Queen Amdora, a ruby colored wand in her right hand, held out like a rapier towards the assassins. Behind her Katrina and Petrus could be seen, the latter shaping a barrier spell while the queen's maid drew several throwing daggers from somewhere.

And, to add to the firepower that was assembling, a quartet of Dire Swords appeared from further down the hall with swords drawn and ready to defend their liege lady and children.

The last male assassin tried to run past and reach the children in the confusion but was struck down by another burst of wind from Jean, and sent sailing towards the running knights. They bellowed a war cry and made their blades shine with brilliant white light. With holy magic etched onto their weapons the cursed artifacts of the assassin stood no chance. His black sword and dagger shattered, his cloak was ripped to tatters and his body hacked into bloody chunks.

As for the woman she looked around her and saw how hopeless the situation appeared. She reached down to her waist and slipped her hand into a bag at her side, likely to grab a last resort weapon.

I didn't let her. Instead, I shot forward and slammed into her left side. I did not stop though. I made my body as acidic as I could, so when I touched her I just kept going, my form transmuted into a giant stomach that melted and devoured her when I landed on her. She was cut near clean in half, part of the robe and whatever it was that she'd reached for dissolving as easily as her flesh and bones. I slid off, having carved a great gouge from her left hip to her right glute, severing her spine and causing great torrents of blood to gush out along with blobs of offal.

But something I'd consumed made me pause, and I felt a sense of vertigo overtake me. My vision swam and I felt nausea for the first time. What on Erafore had I just eaten?

Thankfully, my sudden disability didn't give the last assassin a chance to react. Why? She was too busy gurgling and choking on her own bile and pain from my attack. She spasmed and twitched before groaning and falling still. Anyone else might have kept up their guard, fearing a feint, but I could see that her life had fully vanished. She was dead.

"Liliana! Julius!"

"Mama!"

I turned my attention to gaze at the heart warming reunion between Queen Amdora and her precious children. Petrus started casting spells to heal Jean and Orleen while also checking over the royal offspring. Katrina took up a position near her lady while watching the corpses with a wary eye.

"Are you both okay? None of you are hurt?" Queen Amdora inquired, checking over her babies.

"We're fine, mama. Jelly, Orleen, and the others protected us," Liliana confirmed, wiping tears from her eyes as she tried to put on a strong front.

Now that the tension was gone, there was finally a time to shed tears. Julius openly cried, relief and belated terror staining his face as he desperately clung to his mother and sister. My owner also had tears shining in her eyes and even though she tried to act strong I could tell she was badly shaken.

"Was that your magic? I've never seen you use anything like that before," Liliana asked her mother in between sobs. Her voice was sparkling with awe, but her mother only had embarrassment when she was forced to reply.

"Well, yes, it was," Queen Amdora stuttered. It seemed she had wanted to hide this side of herself from her children. I wondered why, but decided I did not care at the moment. I was still disoriented from whatever it was I'd made my meal, and still trying to sort through it all.

"Teach me!" My owner demanded of her mother, to which Petrus chided the princess.

"Learning such a dangerous spell comes after you can properly create a shield! Not before! We want to keep the palace intact to some degree!" Her pout was adorable. The atmosphere was calm and comforting, and tension fled the area as the Dire Swords started to clean up the remains of the battle and the assassins. I was so out of it, I didn't even notice what came next until it was too late.

"Oh my. Such a touching scene!"

Everyone froze, hands going to weapons and mana gathered for attack spells. With shaky motions everyone, even myself, turned their gaze to stare at the dead woman.

She was still dead, I was sure of that. Blood and organ loss not being issues easily overcome. But now something dark and unholy was filling her empty shell, animating her and forcing the ruined form to rise to their feet and turn to face us.

Billowing out of the corpse was a heavy, dark pressure, completely foreign to me. It was so thick I was choking on it, my mana going wild with fear and I felt I was far too close to this 'thing' than was safe. A few countries over might be prudent. A whole continent would be even better! It wasn't just me, either. Petrus, Jean, and the queen all felt the same unearthly power pouring out, and they were just as terrified. A scent of urine filled the air. It seems one person wasn't able to withstand the terror.

"Who are you?" Queen Amdora demanded, overcoming the sudden pressure to glare at the puppet-corpse.

"I am the owner of these failed assassins. It's a pleasure to finally meet you, Duchess of Destruction Amdora Tein Roan," the figure uttered, giving a mocking bow to the queen. The movements were sickening as its gaping wound flapped obscenely as it did so. Droplets of thick, flesh colored liquid dropped onto the floor from beneath the mask.

I was so very glad I could not vomit. If I could, I likely would have lost my lunch at the sight of the assassin's melted face dripping onto the blood slicked marble. Oh, wait, something just plopped out of the wound. Was that her liver? Oh sweet Cynthia it was!

"For what reason did you dare to attack us?" Amdora demanded, tightening her grip on her wand. It seemed hearing that nickname infuriated her. Geeze, unknown puppet master! Stop making the already furious mage-queen even angrier!

"It was a contract, nothing more. The request of the demented sister-in-law recently driven from her home."

"So it was Countess Darpel, then. What now? Will you continue to attack our family?" the queen demanded, to which the possessed corpse shook their head.

"No. This was just to complete an agreement we'd had with her husband before his death. To be honest we weren't going to kill your children. Just kidnap them. Hostages are much better for leverage than corpses. However since we have failed there is no more reason for me and my associates to continue this. For now," the masked remains explained, the obsidian face covering starting to slip a bit as the features holding it in place sloughed away.

"Then leave, and never darken our home again," Queen Amdora snarled, to which the corpse just laughed in response.

"We'll stay away for the moment. But the world shall rebel. And at that moment, we will see you one final time." That ominous warning given, the dark presence faded letting the pile of meat collapse to the floor once more.

"Search the area! Secure the exits! No one enters or leaves the city, let alone this palace, until I say so!" Queen Amdora shouted, before wrapping Liliana and Julius in her arms. With surprising strength she hefted them up and cuddled them close to her chest and proceeded to walk back to their bedrooms as the Dire Swords scrambled to obey.

"What about the bodies?" Karina inquired, giving a disgusted glare at the remains.

"Burn them." Was the curt response to Katrina's question. The maid bowed in acknowledgement.

"Shall I set up additional barriers this evening?" Petrus inquired. A stiff nod was his reply and he started to weave enchantments into the air, reinforcing the various wards. He bent down to examine the remains of the assailants and the spells they had used, recoiling from them.

"Dark magic, and lots of it. They were wearing the spell *Blood Dress*, which allows one to infuse their own blood into garments to become pseudo cursed items. It grants high resistance to all forms of magic and accelerated healing, as well as allowing the wearer to turn into blood themselves."

"And they were using *Black Bone Armament* to fight with. It's another forbidden Dark Element spell that take's a person's bones and physically alters them into weapons. The blades end up possessing Necromantic powers that steal the life force of whomever is wounded by them, transferring magic and life force to the person who wields the weapon." Upon concluding his examination Petrus' face was simultaneously green and pale.

"Inform the Temple I want Exorcists up here to cleanse their corpses and to purify the castle. I refuse to let their taint stink up the place any longer than necessary," the queen growled.

I kept my distance from the bodies, feeling ill just being close to the tainted magic.

"Jelly…" Liliana began, gazing at me with worry, but was cut off by a grunt from her mother. Orleen hastily picked me up, and I was grateful for her help. I still felt woozy and unsteady.

"The two of you are sleeping in my room tonight," Queen Amdora announced to her children and smiles filled their expressions.

"Sleepover?" Julius asked, and he got a nod in confirmation. Slightly cheered up, the mood that had settled over them lightened a touch. Still, uneasiness remained, and there likely would be a few nightmares to tend to the next few days.

Chapter 21: A triumphant return

It had only been a week since the assassination attempt, and the effects from that were still rippling throughout the entire city. Rumors had swept the populace about the attack, and by now the assassins were everything from Dragonslave Fanatics, Orc Separatists, and, my personal favorite, Gnome Revolutionaries. But the point remained that there had been an attack, and I had helped foil it. That was something that had been circulated amidst all the rumors, and I gained a degree of fame thanks to that.

Oh, and speaking of myself, something very strange happened in the aftermath of the incident. I had actual started to shrink in size the morning after, and I'll admit, I panicked a bit. So did Liliana when she woke up and found me bouncing around the room and half my previous mass.

After a checkup from both Petrus and Queen Amdora, they announced I was completely fine. In fact, I had just broken several laws of magic!

"I just don't understand this!" Petrus moaned, flipping through various tomes as I sat on a table, my owner hovering nearby. The queen just sighed at the young man's actions.

"When you attacked the female assassin, you practically tore her in half. In the process of ripping into her, you must have consumed a very unique item; A *Bag of Holding*. Enchanted to hold far more than it normally could with space bending magic, these items are expensive but well worth it. Nobles, merchants, as well as adventurers, all sorts found them useful for storing and hiding important artifacts." Queen Amdora was the one who explained this all to me and my owner while the mage had a mental breakdown.

She had actually started talking at me like I was a person, now, and it made me grateful. It seemed the queen could not deny that her daughter's pet was as intelligent as she was.

"What happened when you ate it seems to be that you assimilated its magic into your own being. You now have the same ability that a Bag of Holding does, though in a very odd way."

That explained the nausea I had felt after devouring a portion of the invader, as well as why my body shrunk.

I now had a dimensional 'hole' or 'pocket' inside my core, where I could store physical objects as well excess mass. In this way, even if I grew to the size of a horse, I could suck it all up and put it away in storage for later. If I got injured I could quick reintegrate excess mass to heal myself, and I could keep important items like potions on hand in case of emergencies with my owner.

Needless to say I was ecstatic. I had been so worried about my constant growth, and a solution was practically offer to me. Also, it gave something else for Liliana and Petrus to investigate about me. There was already a vast list of things they wanted to experiment with. What was one more?

The start of winter also heralded the victory of King Tiberus and his march back from the Edelstein region.

The king returned to Sanc Aldet just as the first snows began to fall. It was a close thing, as the weather had been growing colder and windier with each passing day. As it was, when the triumphant army led by the victorious king marched up the Red Road into the capitol, tiny flakes of snow fluttered down onto the gawkers and parade watchers and dusted them white.

My owner and the rest of the royal family were waiting for King Tiberius just outside the outer gate of Palestone Castle, dressed in warm, sensible finery. We were surrounded by numerous Dire Swords who formed a cordon around us, as well as taking up hidden positions here and there. Furthermore, Sanc Aldet had been in lockdown for several days and had only been eased open when word of the returning king was brought in.

Liliana's father rode up to his home on a beautiful black and white steed. A roan, befitting the family name and coat of arms.

"That's *Ergesel*: Trample, in the Elder Tongue. He is the royal steed, descended from the roan of the same name that my ancestor King Gregor once rode. Supposedly there's a bit of Dire Horse in it," Liliana explained to me under her breath.

As she saw her father approaching a wide smile began to split her face and for the first time in a long while not a trace of melancholy could be seen on her.

With a cry of joy, the king brought his mount to a halt in front of the palace gates and leapt off, leaving Ergesel to the stable hands that rushed out to lead him away.

"I'm so glad you're all safe!" King Tiberius exclaimed, striding forward and gazing lovingly at his wife and children. He was still in public, with many high profile figures around him. He couldn't go around hugging them and nuzzling them, no matter how much he wanted to.

And he really wanted to. I could see his desire to sweep his queen off her feet and play with his adorable children who were staring at him with relief and unbridled joy. But for the sake of his image, he restrained himself.

"Your Majesty, we should move inside for now. It is growing colder and it would be unwise to keep Prince Julius and Princess Liliana out in the snow for too long," Sir Blaine suggested, keeping pace with his lord at his back. It had been a while since I'd laid eyes on the commander of the Dire Swords, and he looked fine. He was limping though and his right arm moved stiffly. Had he been injured on the battlefield? I couldn't recall any gossip about that, so it must have been suppressed, or at least gone unnoticed.

"Excellent idea," King Tiberius agreed and hastily ushered his family back into the palace.

"Oh, dear, I'm so glad you're safe!"

"I'm so glad you're safe as well!"

Finally out of sight from the citizens and in private at long last, the king and queen throw aside all pretenses of decorum and throw themselves into each other's arms, noisily making out and coming close to groping each other.

Liliana blushed violently crimson and turned away while Julius gagged and looked ill. The maids and various servants all studiously looked somewhere else while maintaining an air of 'oh, us? No, we're not embarrassed. Not at all.' Very classy.

The only people who did not seem bothered by the blatant display being put on by their royal lord and lady were myself, Sir Blaine, and Queen Amdora's personal maid. My excuse is because I have no concept of love and desire beyond caring for my owner, and human notions of courtship have always baffled me. The captain of the Dire Sword and Miss Karina just had a stoic look on their faces. They'd seen this before, being the personal guards of the Roan family, and so very little the royal couple did surprised or shocked them anymore.

"Oh, I'm so glad you're home," Queen Amdora uttered in a breathy whisper, separating partially from her husband.

"I am as well. I'm just happy to make it back before the snow arrived," King Tiberius replied before pulling closer.

"Perhaps you should change out of your armor if you're going to continue this. And maybe relocate to your quarters," Sir Blaine spoke up, a single eyebrow raised at his liege.

"You're right, of course," the king murmured, finally realizing where he and his wife had been getting intimate, and who exactly was watching.

"Liliana, Julius…" Acting not as a king at that moment but a concerned and loving father, Tiberius Augustine Roan lowered himself slightly and opened his arms wide, a clear invitation to his dear children.

At once his prince and princess leapt into them, tears of loneliness, fear, and love bubbling up after a long absence. He gave them both a firm and gentle hug, only reluctantly letting them go.

"I missed you both so much," Tiberius confessed, smiling down at them. The expression took a sorrowful tint as he recalled the incident just days before.

"You've been very brave. I'm so proud of you." His praise brought joyous grins to his children's faces and I burbled with happiness of my own, the pleasure of my owner being my own source of bliss.

"Is it finally over?" Julius' innocent question brought a faint frown to the king's lips, but he nodded none the less.

"Yes. Count Darpel and his son are dead." It might have been blithe and cold, but it was a fact that that man had been the cause of a lot of grief for the family.

But I knew, as did the king and queen, that the countess had survived and fled. She had been the one to dispatch those dark magic assassins, and I had no doubt she would try again once she found out they had failed.

Liliana Roan Darpel. The thought of her brought my gut to a boil. Despite being a sibling of the king and sharing a name with my dear owner she was truly a wretched human being. I'd have to be even more vigilant. No harm would come to my owner if I could help it.

"By the way! I do have some good news. Varda will be coming down after the Winter Solstice to visit," King Tiberius said, bringing smiles to his children's faces.

"Will he be here for my birthday?" Liliana inquired, childish innocence and hope in her eyes.

"He will. I know he won't miss it. You and Julius mean the world to him," the king assured, while I wracked my mind trying to connect a person to the name. Varda sounded familiar, but where had I heard it?

In the end I couldn't remember and contented myself with relaxing in my owner's arms as the family moved to the dining room for an early dinner. They were happily discussing what they'd do this winter together.

There were two events that were coming up this season. One was a religious festival based around the winter solstice. It was a day uniquely celebrated by humans, dwarves, and even elves. Each species did it differently, but the point was the same. That is, praying for survival in the depths of winter.

The second event was something I was personally excited about. The first day of spring, which was Princess Liliana's birthday! Since that date was also New Year's Day based on the human and elf calendar, the whole kingdom threw a massive celebration in honor of both the end of winter and the birth of the eldest child of the royal family.

I giddily wondered how she'd like my present. Ever since I'd found out about the date, I had been preparing a gift. It wasn't much, as I had no money to my name, but there were some things unique to an Ooze like myself that were impossible for ordinary humans to obtain. As such I was confident that my owner would find it pleasing.

Dinner passed by quickly and the rest of the evening was just spent cuddling on the massive bed in the royal quarters. It had been a trying time for my owner and her sibling being separated from their father for so long, let alone having assassins come after them. After all that tension drained away, they were left exhausted, and fell asleep quickly.

The king and queen stayed awake just a bit longer, as did I. Listening in on their whispered conversation might have been rude but it was about the campaign, a scandal at some place called the

Tower of Chains, and lastly about the implied threat on their family. I felt it was my duty to listen in.

"Tiberius, I want to enroll Liliana in the Royal Varian Mages Academy," Amdora mentioned, slowly stroking Julius' hair.

"Do you really think that's a good idea? Having her so far from home might be too lonely for her, plus she only just started her magic training…"

"Liliana is nearly an adult, Tiberius. She'll be fourteen when spring rolls around, and then it'll only be one more year before she's legally an adult, and thus will either have to start looking for a fiancé or find some sort of respected career to keep her independence," Amdora countered, her voice still low and calm in spite of her words. "Plus, there are few other places as safe as the Academy. You'd have to be either stupid or suicidal to attack a place with an X-ranked guardian."

"Lastly, she's my daughter, after all," the queen said softly, gazing lovingly at her daughter. "She's picked up magic like a sponge in water, and has a great desire to learn more."

"At least she's kept the collateral damage to a minimum," Tiberius joked, only to be rewarded with a slap on the arm and a pouting glare.

"You destroy part of a garden and wreck two wings of a mansion and no one lets you live it down," I heard the queen mutter under her breath. Her husband didn't appear to hear it, but could see the look on her face none the less and moved to comfort her with nuzzles.

"If you truly think she'll thrive at the Academy, then we can talk to her about it in the morning. Classes only begin in mid-spring so we have time to enroll her, and let Petrus catch her up on the bare minimum for passing the entrance test."

Queen Amdora nodded happily at that, snuggling closer to her husband and children. A look that was a mixture of fear and relief washed over her face as she observed the rise and fall of two tiny chests.

"I was scared, Tiber. So very scared. When those three... scum... breeched the defenses and came straight for our children, I thought I'd have a heart attack! And their magic! I haven't seen anything that dark and corrupted before! Petrus looked them over and claimed they were using Curse magic. If such people come after us again, I'm afraid I won't be able to save them next time."

The king carefully extracts his right arm from the pile of sleeping adorableness and wraps it around his wife's shoulders. I too inch closer and vibrate in a soothing manner next to her side. Blinking back tears Amdora allows herself to relax in the safety of her family's embrace.

As they finally let themselves succumb to the call of dreams, I thought about what I could do to protect Liliana. My magic was not enough, though I improved day by day. My own abilities as an Ooze were still fairly new and unknown to me, and I needed to practice with them some more. There were other avenues of training open to me, but they would need more time and effort than what I had at the moment. For now, all I could do was continue to be my owner's companion. There was time to grow, but now was a time to heal first.

Chapter 22: Under the light of truth

Snow piled up on the streets, upon the roofs, upon the people. Winter and it's 'gifts' had come to Varia's capitol, and in a great deluge that stunned me.

Since I was technically a newborn, this was my first experience with 'snow' as well as the biting gales that howled down from the mountain slopes. I was honestly shocked at how cold it got, and had I not been filled with an inordinate amount of mana my semi-liquid body would have turned into an ice sculpture.

Had I been in my old body and out in the streets I would have frozen to death on the first snowfall. Even inside the palace I would have been sluggish and in danger of icing over on some of the colder nights. Thankfully as a Royal Ooze I was slightly more resistant to the cold, but only to the point that I would not freeze solid in minutes. Now it would take hours. Lucky me!

I stayed as close to the fireplaces, furnaces, and boilers as I could whenever my owner and I had to leave the comfort of our warm beds or her arms. This of course meant that the maids and staff were almost tripping over me each time they tried to tend to the various heat sources. Which in turn meant they would lift me out of the way or shove me aside. Had I been an animal with vocal cords I might have hissed and growled at anyone who tried to take me from my tiny, temporary sanctuaries. As it stood the most I could do was wobble in anger and maybe make a tendril to gently slap them on the wrist when they did so.

Oh how I wished for eyes at that time, so that I might glare at those who dared to disturb me!

Alas, I did not spontaneous grow eyeballs. I did focus on more of Petrus' lessons though. The one with the *Self Heating* cantrip had made me jiggle with joy. It proved harder than I'd thought however, as heat based magic reacted poorly with my semi-liquid form. First the element of Water, and now Fire. I am truly a deprived soul!

It took much more effort and mana to construct a working *Self Heating* spell than it should have. Annoying. Truly annoying.

What's the use of having more magic than most other humans if I cannot even use it to stave off the chill of winter?

"Looks like Jelly is extra grumpy this morning," Princess Liliana teased as she carried me in her arms. I grumbled good-naturedly and sunk into her body heat in bliss, willing to put up with her jokes for the sake of not freezing.

"If I had to be awake when it's this cold and early, I think I'd be grumpy too," Prince Julius mumbled to himself, earning a glare from Queen Amdora and a chuckle from King Tiberius, the couple walking slightly behind their children.

The royal family was dressed in thick layers of winter clothes, though as befitting their wealth and status they were ornately decorated and made from the finest materials available.

In addition to the expensive Hycon wool and Dire bear fur, the clothes had numerous defensive spells woven into them, capable of withstand a barrage of Level Five spells!

I spent some of the time analyzing the unique enchantments in the clothes and was impressed, but fairly confident I could pull them off on my own with just a bit of study and practice. Shield spells, barriers, and wards came easier to me than any other magic, and Petrus and the queen had noticed this.

Queen Amdora was participating in the magic craft lessons as well now. After she and King Tiberius had discussed sending my owner over to the Mages Academy the queen had spent more time with her daughter, teaching her the various tricks and spells she had picked up in her youth. It was amusing to find out that her nickname, the 'Duchess of Destruction,' was actually a well-known one in the kingdom! Seeing her flesh red with embarrassment when Liliana found out was utterly priceless! Thank the gods I cannot laugh, or she'd have blasted me in a fit of abashed pique.

My owner had been so excited to hear that she'd be allowed to attend the premier magical finishing school and academic center in all of Orria! Well, it was the only one in the northern part of Orria, and until three hundred years ago it was the only one in all the continent. But the point still stood!

Ever since that announcement, my dear princess has been studying even harder, and absorbed all that was being offered to her. Come spring, she'd pass the entrance exam with flying colors!

On a side note, I was worried Julius might feel neglected by his mother focusing on his older sister over him, but King Tiberius stepped in and has made sure he has lots of time to teach and play with his son.

It seemed that government slowed to a crawl during the winter months. Letters, packages, and reports were slowed, travel became difficult and limited, and while magical means of communication do exist, for the most part they're saved for emergencies. So with most of the bureaucracy stalled, King Tiberius had more time to spend with his family. Seeing the two of them joyously sparring with wooden swords in the exercise room gave everyone a happy expression on their faces.

"Alright, quickly get inside! Don't let out all the warm air!" Queen Amdora ordered, ushering her family into a small shrine in the center of the gardens. This was the reason we were outside in the first place.

Located in the expansive courtyards of the palace is a small, worn looking building. It carried a somber, almost depressing aura, and the fairly basic looking stone and old fashioned architectural style made it feel as if it was displaced in time.

Glancing around the inside, the interior could best be described as austere. There were no windows, nor were there any carpets, tapestries, or gilded displays of wealth. Only nine rows of pew made of stone that had been smoothed and polished by generations of posteriors, and a raised platform that held a collection of religious icons and paraphernalia at the very end were set-up. In brackets along the walls small glass lamps had been placed in alcoves all over that filled the area with an even, steady illumination.

"The Shrine of Ar-Varia," Liliana muttered under her breath in reverence. "The ancient clan that founded the kingdom of Varia built this easily overlooked building millennia ago as a place to pray for and lay to rest the deceased."

371

"Beneath its unassuming exterior is a vast network of catacombs that house the noble dead of the royal family, and it acts as a vault for the most precious and valued artifacts of the kingdom. These chambers extend throughout the entire mountain that the city rested upon, and also acted as anchors for a complex array of spells and runes that prevent or limit natural disasters. From avalanches to earthquakes, this small, tucked away shrine is the focal point for numerous defenses for the wellbeing of the entire city," King Tiberius explained to us, more for my benefit than that of my owner.

He had come to understand I was vastly more intelligent than he had first thought as he had observed me in Petrus' lessons with his daughter. The king had no issues with it, much to my relief.

"It also serves as the local site of prayer for both royalty and the servants and guards. The ground floor was converted long ago into a tiny church of sorts, with benches for visitors to rest at and a set of statues and icons of the Divine Family, as well as the other sanctioned gods and goddess of humanity. Any member of the staff, be they maid or knight, can access these facilities any time of day if they so choose," Queen Amdora continued, teaching her children the history behind the shrine. "Access to the lower levels was, of course, restricted, and it was impossible for an ordinary person to even detect the hidden entrance."

I could spot the superbly wrought wards as I looked around. Anything that even tried to circumnavigate their way through the countless barriers or attempt to usurp the spells would be met with instant, lethal force. I shivered at the sight of the *Backlash* runes and *Revenge* curses layered upon every part of the array. It was a necessary precaution. If this place fell, the whole city would be at risk.

It was the religious aspect and duty of the Shrine of Ar-Varia that the royal family was here for. It was the morning of the Winter Solstice.

First we'd wake early, fast and pray to the Divine Family for success and survival, and confirm New Year Resolutions. Then there'd be a large luncheon where everyone in the castle was invited to partake. The day would end with one final round of prayers and the lighting of devotional candles. Normally there would be bonfires, but in a city it was safer to limit the amount of open flames as much as possible.

As was tradition, before dawn on the day of the Winter Solstice the king led the rest of the palace staff in the annual rites of this event. Princess Liliana and I were preparing for a day of religious devotion alongside the rest of the family.

I didn't mind the hustle and bustle, and was only slightly bitter about the brief moment of biting cold. I sort of liked the feeling of community everyone had at this time. Though the king and by extension the rest of the royal family would never directly mingle with the lower servants, at least normally, today was a special occasion. King Tiberius offered a smile to the various guards and male staff, while Queen Amdora politely spoke to the women about this and that.

Whatever could be said about the king and queen of Varia, they cared for and respected the commoners and their servants.

Slowly, a hush fell over the assembled people, and soon seats were found and claimed. Up at the front was where Liliana sat, sandwiched between her parents on a bench. In the nave before us, a set of five familiar looking figures stood. Icons of Cynthia, her husband the Knight-God, and her children Selika, Kardale, and Nia. Cast from gold and silver, they shone in the candle light.

There was a sixth icon standing with them, a statue made of green jade. It looked like an elderly woman, stooped with age and wearing a shawl while being supported by a cane. I didn't recognize this deity. Something about the statue put me at ease though, as if I was in the presence of a doting grandmother.

King Tiberius moved to the collection of statues and knelt before them, silencing any remaining conversations in the tiny chapel as he prepared the tools and rituals for the ceremony. A sealed lead box that wafted with fumes of chilled air was placed next to King Tiberius by Sir Blaine alongside a marble bowl. A grateful nod was given before eyes focused intently on the altars.

"Water to ice," the king intoned, solemnly removing a carved block of ice from the box. He placed it into the bowl, which had been put in front of the icon of the withered crone. The ice had been carved to resemble an avian. It looked like a chicken perhaps, or maybe a swan?

"Ice then turns to water. The seasons change. Life gives way to death and in turn becomes more life. The cycle is unending. We are blessed to witness it."

"Gaea watches with all four heads." The crowd spoke along with the king, words coming to their lips. We all watched as the ice dripped and melted.

To my surprise and shock, the statue of the crone began to melt and run like wax, much like the frozen offering in front of it! I extended my senses towards the two objects, but quickly retracted them.

They blazed with piercing light, too bright for me to even glance at while using my magical sight. The shining energy felt calm, peaceful and benevolent though. It meant no harm to anyone, and thin wisps of this power drifted off of the two objects and infused themselves into some of the people around us.

Curious, I examined the people who'd been 'touched,' and found that their body had taken on some new qualities! Small wounds and afflictions, like a cough, a few bruises, or sore joints, were slowly eased away and healed by the altered mana that had been gifted. I looked carefully but saw no evidence of danger. Relieved I turn my attention back to the event going on, and see that where the icon of the old woman had been, now there was a new one, slowly appearing from the shifting material.

A young girl in a simple dress, bare foot and with vines woven into her hair. A playful smile on her face beamed out at the devoted mass, and I felt a surge of magic well up. The small ice sculpture finished melting into the bowl, and it glowed with white and then green light, flashing and filling the entire room with a spectacle.

Through some manner of divine blessing, the water had become imbued with potent properties. Mainly of healing and plant growth, but if it so much as touched the flesh of a being saturated in curses and dark magic it would burn like acid. I had just witnessed the creation of Holy Water!

Reverently, King Tiberius held aloft the bowl now filled to the brim with what was essential a high grade magical potion. Showing it to the crowd, he then placed it back onto the altar in front of the morphed icon. It would probably be collected later, if the vials I detected in the lead box was any indication. For now though it was left alone, and the king of Varia turned to the statues of the Divine Family.

"Mere words cannot express our thanks, oh mother of mercy," Tiberius said, bowing his head to the golden statue of Cynthia.

"So instead we offer up our actions of the year to prove that we have lived properly according to the Tennent's of you and your family. We strove to be kind, courteous, respectful, lawful, and worthy of love and further blessings. Please, see to our safety in this coming year. We are your servants, now and forever more. Praise be to the Five."

"Praise be to the Five," intoned the mass, and I thought the words aloud in my head alongside my owner's more verbal response.

Once more ethereal, blinding light poured out of the statues, unseen by all save myself. I was ready this time, and quickly looked around the room for some other effects to occur.

Again, thin tendrils of magic swept out, briefly caressing the people in the chapel but instead of healing wounds, as the first light had done, this one instead bolstered the various wards and protection spells that were layered on everything. From the secret entrance of the royal catacombs to the personal enchantments in the clothes, there was a faint but still noticeable improvement to them. I smiled to myself as I saw the wards around my owner grow stronger.

'Thank you,' I thought, pleased that the one person I cared about the most was even safer.

"You're welcome."

I tensed in Liliana's lap, looking everywhere for the source of the voice. There! At the statue of Cynthia!

Before my 'eyes' the light that filled the room condensed and took on form. From the icon she stepped forth, shedding the confinement of the mortal material that was her likeness and stood before me in radiant beauty. Awed, I could only stare as Cynthia herself appeared.

Skin like liquid gold. Hair like the magenta sky of twilight. Clad in robes of endless, shimmering white. And looking upon me with eyes of dancing, swirling cosmos and full of love and affection and forgiveness that was wider than the world and deeper than the oceans. This was a goddess. This is what it meant to be blessed by that which is divine. All I could do was stare. In shock. In disbelief. In awe. In reverence.

"You have struggled and suffered greatly in your short life, noble Ooze," the Goddess of Light said softly, gazing at me with adoration and respect and love.

"For your owner, your benefactor, you have endured harshness most men would break from. Selflessly you have thrown yourself into danger, never expect or wanting reward for your actions. As long as Liliana was safe, nothing else mattered."

Cynthia stepped forward, daintily stepping off of the platform and walking over to me with collected and measured footsteps. Out of the corner of my 'eye' I saw that the world seemed to have frozen in time. Nothing moved, not even a single mote of dust.

I returned my gaze to the Patron of Humanity as she stood in front of me, my body still clasped in Liliana's lap. To my shock she squatted down, her dress shifting like moonlight on the surface of a lake. Once she was level with me, her beatific smile faded somewhat.

"But beneath that selflessness, there was self-destruction. Everything you've done was enacted with a desperate desire to repay what you see as a debt. You believe that you owe your life, your mind, and your soul to Liliana Augustine Roan. That there is no chance you can repay this impossible gift. Not even with your life."

Tears gathered in Cynthia's eyes, and she smiled sadly at me. I dared not breathe. I dared not move. Her words cut deep into me, but I did nothing.

"Your love is touching. But it is poisonous too. You harm yourself and Liliana with it. You give and give, and that is not healthy. That is not what she wants. And you know that. Yet you persist."

Reaching out Cynthia picked me up, somehow moving me from Liliana's lap into a cradling hug in her bosom. If I had been a man, I would have been suffering from a severely embarrassing biological reaction being so close to her chest. Hells, even if I'd been a woman I'd have issues! She was perfection incarnate, in every meaning of the word.

"It is alright to live for yourself. It is alright to be selfish. You have earned that if nothing else. You do not have to stop loving and serving Liliana, but do not destroy yourself doing so. There is still much for you to see and to learn. You have only just scratched the surface of the wonders that this world holds."

She planted a single kiss upon me, and a tingle of energy traveled through my core. I felt magic of some kind, searing with divine intent, suffuse my being. Her smile became one of understanding and acceptance, and she returned me to my place in my owner's lap.

"Do not be discouraged, do not give in to the fear and hate you will face. For your sake, and for Liliana's: Live. Live and do not regret a single day. After all, you are important to more people than you can possibly imagine."

Her piece said, Cynthia rose and returned to the statue, giving me one final smile before she sank back into the precious metal, her divinity fading and her presence dissipating. The unearthly magic that had been in the air returned to whence it came. Before the last of the magic vanished though, I saw another figure of light watching me, in the shape of Nia. She waved shyly at me with a soft smile before vanishing along with her mother.

I could have also sworn that I saw the statue of the barefoot girl wink at me, mouthing the words 'you lucky dog!'

For some reason I felt that the best option was to ignore Gaea's manifestation and not her give any reason to continue teasing me.

Time resumed and the world reasserted itself. I sighed to myself and snuggled closer to Liliana, barely listening to the rest of the ceremony.

I had been given a divine revelation. Cynthia herself had sought me out, and given me advice. I felt... odd. Honored was too weak a word for it. Reverent was too zealous. She had wanted to help me, and so did, forcing me to confront the truths I had been trying to hide from and ignore all this time.

I was too devoted to my beloved princess. Even medicine can become poison in a large dose, but I had refused to see that. That said, I would not stop caring for her. But, I would start to try and live for myself as well. Moderation in all things. Balance being the key for a successful life.

It was time to change. But how? Perhaps the answer would come to me in time as I explored my options and the world. For now,

I wanted to spend the rest of the day basking in the warmth of my dear owner.

"Love you, Liliana."

…Um, why had it gotten quiet? Why was the queen staring at me with bugged out eyes? Why did Orleen just faint? Why did King Tiberius just face palm so hard that the people in the back row could hear the impact? Most importantly, why was Liliana staring at me with a mixture of shock and joy?

"Jelly, did you just talk?"

Wait, what?

"Talk? Jelly, talk?"

Hold on, was that me? Was that tiny, childish voice… mine?

"Talk? Talk! I can talk! Lili, look! I can talk!" I began to excitedly bounce up and down in my seat in Liliana's lap, and a grin that lit up the world broke across my princess's face.

"You can talk! This is amazing!" Liliana jumped to her feet and began to spin me around, hugging me close.

As I rotated past the statue of the Mother of Mercy, I felt a whisper of familiar intent brush across my mind.

'Happy belated birthday, Jelly. I hope you enjoy the gift from myself and Nia.'

If I could have smiled, I would have. This was a present more wondrous than I could have ever hoped for! I started to laugh in sheer exhilaration and Liliana joined in. Her joy radiated out and embraced me, and I embraced it back.

I was going to live my life for two now!

Chapter 23: A Promise of new beginnings

Several days had passed since the Winter Solstice and my ability to talk was obtained. To say that people were shocked would be a gross simplification and understatement. Petrus was almost foaming at the mouth in his desire to examine me and find out how and why this had happened. Sir Blaine had the look of a man who'd found a new, valuable asset or threat to palace security. Orleen was completely flabbergasted and kept her distance, unsure of how to deal with me now that I was marginally more human-like.

Julius was amazed and eager to play with a new friend. Queen Amdora was surprised and annoyed that I had undergone yet another change. King Tiberius just seemed like he wanted a stiff drink. And more than a few of the serving staff had worried looks, since now that speech was possible, the next logical question was "how long has that slime been able to think? And how much gossip has it overheard?"

Oozes were stupid. Incredibly so. An ordinary Ooze would just keep moving forward in search of food. They did not stop unless they detected prey, or something blocked their way. In many cases, they'd tumble into pits, even over cliffs and just stupidly roll their way into danger and thus death. Larger, more specialized Oozes had more instincts, such as lying in wait for prey and using ambush tactics, but they could be easily tricked or avoided. My kind could be dangerous, and many a person had underestimated us to their detriment. But in the end, an Ooze was barely cognizant and aware.

So when one of them suddenly can not only talk, but do so in sentences with mostly proper grammar and form coherent thoughts and beliefs, it would only be natural for people to wonder when exactly I had become so smart.

The look King Tiberius gave me when I first spoke said that he'd had his suspicions the whole time. He wasn't the only one, come to that. The queen, her personal handmaiden-slash-assassin, Sir Blaine, even Julius to a degree! Petrus as well, once he stopped twitching with research-gasms, had that same understanding look.

My owner had been the only one not to show surprise in any way shape or form. In my opinion this was because she was a forgiving and understanding soul. Or it could be due to the bond she had made with me when she blessed me with my soul and thus had always known to a degree. Either one was likely.

But for all the whirlwind of commotion I had caused business continued on in the same fashion as before. Governance of Varia had to be done, learning was required, and the palace needed to be kept clean. In that vein the rest of winter passed. Only as it drew to a close did activity kick back up.

The first day of spring, the 1st of Thaw Month, was the day my owner was born. It was the time the snow and ice began melting, but this close to the north and backed up against the mountains Varia and its capital of Sanc Aldet rarely started to be free of winter until the next month.

Still, the weather was warmer and travel became easier, and several guests arrived for the princess' big day the day before. Among them was the largest human I'd ever met.

Varda Ornleif, the Royal Headsman, Warden of the Tower of Chains. A massive mountain of muscle and scar tissue, who'd served as a highly placed member of the Dire Swords before his elevation to his current vaunted rank. It was his duty to manage the largest prison in all of Varia, the infamous Tower of Chains, and to execute any and all traitors to the crown.

An ordinary commoner, Varda had saved King Tiberius from an assassination during the young king's own coronation parade, and later risked his life to save Liliana and Julius from an act of arson, barreling into a building awash with magical flames and suffering countless burns to rescue the two. This selflessness earned my respect and him several rewards including a surname and honorary nobility status, and the moment I saw the love and concern for the royal children I knew he was an ally in my own quest to keep my owner safe.

When he arrived the massive man was greeted by the wide smiles of Liliana and Julius, and King Tiberius who treated the shaved bear of a man with a cheerful clap on the back. Queen Amdora gave a demure smile of fondness as well for Varda as he bowed and kissed her hand in fealty.

"Varda! It is wonderful to see you again!"

"It is an honor to be in your presence once more as well, my queen," Varda rumbled, his voice rough and heavy.

"Come now, old friend, no need to be so stiff! Or do you want to make my darling children sad?"

At a prompt from their father the prince and princess stood in front of the Headsman and began to pout, lips trembling and eyes water.

"Apologies for my rudeness," Varda said slowly before sweeping up the royal brood into his arms, giving them a crushing hug.

"We missed you, Varda," Liliana whispered into his shoulder, and a multitude of emotions cascaded from him.

"I as well, my little Lily and brave knight," he said softly before returning them to their feet.

I stood close by, looking at with awe at the man. I still could not get over his size! While I stared eyes flickered over to me and appraised my position next to my owner

With a slow blink of his eyes he shifted his gaze away from me and towards some of the Dire Swords, giving a salute to Sir Blaine who returned it. I was floored.

No curiosity, no wonderment about how an Ooze was a pet for a princess. Nothing at all. He just accepted it, apparently shrugging it off as more Roan Family eccentricities. It seemed he knew the royal family intimately if he could just consider me as another part of their oddness, which was both galling and hilarious. Not even my childish voice could surprise him.

"I'm sure you remember Baroness Bluemont, Varda," King Tiberius said motioning to the elderly woman behind him. The tower of human flesh and muscle nodded politely.

"A pleasure to see you again," Varda intoned, to which the ancient tutor smiled lightly.

"Oh, indeed. I am so glad you could come to the princess' birthday. It means the world to her."

"I'm honored." Those were the final words on the matter and attention turned to the baroness who'd began to fuss over the children and myself.

Rene Bluemont had never left. After the ball she continued to come by, still teaching Liliana and Julius etiquette but with less frequency. Apparently the Bluemonts had a manor in Sanc Aldet where she had stayed the winter.

"Is there anyone else coming today, or should we shut the doors?" Rene inquired as she pet me on the head. She gushed over me, cuddling and fondling me like I was a toddler ever since I had started to speak. I tried to protest at the treatment but to no avail. From the sympathetic looks King Tiberius and Prince Julius gave me, it didn't matter to Lady Rene how old you were; everyone was a child in need of pampering to her.

"We are waiting on one more guest," King Tiberius said, his wife nodding in agreement. I perked up. It was a lot of fun meeting new people.

Before anyone could ask who exactly it was that was coming, a faint argument could be heard from beyond the hallway. It quickly drew closer, revealing an elderly man, stooped with age and supported by an old, unadorned wooden staff.

His robes were creased and starched yet showed their age in the frayed edges and bleached grey look that could only come from countless washings. He wore his beard short and neatly braided in the dwarf style. The same went for the hair on his head; It was tightly done up in a style identical to that of his beard.

A herald ran in front of the advancing man with an annoyed glare before clearing their throat.

"Introducing Archsage Arnolt Cantos, Lord of Magic and Headmaster of the Royal Varian Mages Academy!" As he entered his very presence filled the room with overwhelming magical power that pressed down on my senses and nearly blinded me the first time I took a peek at him.

"Archsage? The Archsage?! Oh no, what should I do, I'm not properly dressed for this!" Petrus uttered under his breath, panicked.

"Who is this man?" I whispered up at the mage, who calmed down enough to answer my question.

"Arnolt Cantos, also known as the Lord of Magic, Slayer of the Dragon of Weeds, Champion of the North, and Master of a Thousand Rituals, is an X-ranked mage and head of the Academy! He runs it all and hardly ever meets with anyone!"

"I've never personally met the legendary headmaster before, but he could shake his head in disapproval once and utterly destroy the future of anyone who displeased him," Petrus explained to me quickly.

"As long as you don't make a fool of yourself by panicking I doubt he'll do anything to you," I hissed back, and my rational words caused the thin mage to take a deep breath and collect himself.

"Greetings, Archsage. I'm honored that you accepted our invitation," King Tiberius said with a respectful bow of his head which was echoed by everyone else, family and servants alike.

Varda and Rene did so as well, though the former was expressionless as always while the latter had a strange smile on her lips, as if she knew the man in front of her before he'd been so powerful and was remembering tiny embarrassing stories and details.

"It was a pleasant surprise, and an excellent chance to get out of the office for a bit," Arnolt replied with a small shake of the head. "Could have done without the fanfare though. I get enough of it back at the school."

He swept his gaze over the assembly, his piercing gaze lingering on myself and my owner for a moment. That look then was given to Rene, who exchanged a wink with him. The Archsage's stern look faltered at that and he unconsciously reached out and rubbed a small gold and silver band on his left ring finger.

Oh! So that was their connection!

He recollected himself quickly, and the old mage cleared his throat.

"When you wrote that you wished for me to observe your daughter's talents and find a place for her in my school I was curious about the abilities the Duchess of Destruction might have bred into her child. I vividly remember her own time at the Academy. I pray that the princess has better control over herself," the Archsage said with a knowing look at the queen. She responded by blushing, huffing, and looking away. King Tiberius nodded his head with a smirk on his lips and turned to escort their final guest into the castle.

We made our way towards a room where tea had been set-up, with myself hopping up into Liliana's arms to avoid walking.

"Regardless of lineage, know that we do not often accept students before they are adults. Only exceptional talent and circumstances let me dance around the rules," the ancient sorcerer continued, stating without actually saying that Liliana would have to work hard to impress him to earn a spot in the Academy.

"My wife and I feel that Liliana would not only be safe at the Academy but her burgeoning talents would blossom in that environment," Tiberius began only to be cut off by a snort from the old man.

"Your daughter has a tongue and she is right beside you. Why not let her tell me what she wants to do."

Everyone stopped walking, frozen in mid step. For a moment the Archsage's annoyance had bubbled up and almost felt like a rush of killing intent. It had faded as soon as it had appeared but left everyone, even the stoic Dire Swords, shaking slightly.

Swallowing a nervous lump in her throat, Liliana turned to face Arnolt, locking gazes. I too looked up at him and fixed him with determination. Even held in her arms I would hold my own against this man. Our futures hung in the balance, and it would be for the best if we showed him what we were made of.

"Greetings, Archsage Arnolt. I am Liliana Augustine Roan, First Princess of Varia. I wish to attend your school in order to improve my magic and pursue the knowledge I seek. I can pass any test you give me," Liliana said, starting off with a bow before introducing herself. It seemed to please the headmaster as he fiddled with the braiding in his beard for a bit.

"And what is it you wish to study? While you will have to take general classes, it is up to students to choose a subject and not just learn about it but to explore it to the fullest potential." He waited for her answer, expressionless.

"Oozes. I want to study Oozes. I want to learn about their habitats, their diets, their migration habits, their magic, and their uses. I want to explore these creatures like never before," Liliana claimed, sparing a brief look down at me before matching Archsage Arnolt's gaze.

"Why?" It was a simple question, but it would decide her fate. I knew this, and she did too. She took a deep breathe, steeling her nerves, before replying.

"Do you see this figure in my arms? This is a Royal Ooze. And he is my dearest friend. When I found him, he was just a regular Ooze in a pet shop. But he quickly became so much more than that to me. And to others. He found a Rose Worm infestation that could have hurt the gardeners if left unattended. He saved me and an entire party from a poisoned cake. And he fought and won against a cultist of the World Rebellion. He has nearly died for me." Liliana paused for a moment as emotions clogged her throat, but she pressed on, buoyed by a supportive tendril I laid across her arm.

"I want to understand him more. I want to know more about what he is, where he comes from, and why he is so unique. Jelly has done so much for me, and that has only made me more curious. From what Petrus has taught and I myself have investigated, Oozes are actually fairly lacking in extensive study. The common ones are so basic they need no real research, and the rare ones are found in dangerous places so few can study them. And yet they provide so much for us! They can be 'milked' for special fluids to make countless potions and their cores can be processed into magical gems! I want to change what the world knows about them, and how they are seen." She looked up at Arnolt, proud and almost defiant. "That is why I want to learn about Oozes."

"Purpose and conviction are the two things a mage needs. More than mana, more than vast repertoires of spells. Without those, they will never achieve their full potential." The expression of the Archsage did not change, but a pleased glint danced in his eyes for a moment, before he turned his searching gaze onto me.

"And what of you, Ooze? Tell me, what do you seek in my Academy?"

"I want to find more ways to protect my princess," I responded, speaking up for the first time today. I wasn't really surprised that he had figured out I could talk. "But I also desire to learn more about my kind and this world. I have been alive for less than a year, and I know there is more for me to see and explore. If I can control my innate powers and become smarter and stronger I can not only help others but help myself."

"Why?" Again, he inquired as to my deeper reasons.

"That's it. I have no greater goal, no deeper meaning to my existence. At least, not yet. I know so little, that until I can learn more I am less than a blank slate. In my pursuit of power and in my duty of protecting my princess I feel that I can find greater meaning to my life. I need to grow, Archsage. And I believe I can do that beside my owner at the Academy."

A long silence filled the hallway we had found ourselves in. I had no eyes with which to maintain eye contact with, but I focused intently on his eyes none the less, and got my meaning across. Slowly, he began to nod, fiddling with his braided beard once more.

"Only a truly wise man can claim that they know nothing and understand they still have so much more to discover. There is much worth in what you seek, Ooze." Another glimmer of brightness flickered in his eyes and he reached out, patting me on the top of my head.

"I expect to see the two of you at the Academy before tenth of Seeding Month for obtaining your quarters and planning your classes. Lessons begin on the fifteenth of Seeding. I'll write you up a list of items you'll need before arriving and pass it to you before I leave," Archsage Arnolt said, sliding his hand up to pat Liliana on the shoulder. "I expect great things from the two of you."

"Oh, and I'll also be sure to give your parents the tuition bills before I leave," the aging sorcerer said with a teasing tone in his words, looking over at the king and queen as he did so with a sly look in his eyes.

"Bills? As in, plural?" King Tiberius asked, confused.

"Of course. I have two new students that need to be paid for."

"Jelly is a pet," Queen Amdora tried to argue but was cut off by a chuckle.

"He can speak, form coherent sentences, has hopes and dreams, and can cast magic. Ooze or not, he'll be learning from my teachers and using up my resources. That is a student in my books."

A wicked chortle escaped the Archsage which was soon echoed by Rene Bluemont as she reminisced about her ex-husband's old habits. Their laughter only grew louder as they saw the horrified look on the king's face and the disbelieving ones for the rest of the adults.

And that was how my owner and I met Archsage Arnolt Cantos, Lord of Magic, Headmaster of the Royal Varian Mages Academy, and infamous Great Miserly Mage, a man who would fight for every single coin he could scrounge up and would even extort the rulers of a nation for money if he could get away with it!

Oh, and we got to attend the greatest school for magic users in the world. Which was neat. It was an exciting day, all in all.

The rest of the day passed by quickly, as much of it was taken up with setting up the Archsage in his quarters and some minor housekeeping matters for the birthday feast.

Liliana and Julius -and by extension me as well- spent the remainder of the afternoon with Varda who took the time to stroll through the chilly garden.

"Heads up!" A patch of fluffy white appeared on the back of Vard's black hood, and he slowly turned to look at the guilty prince who'd hurled the snowball.

Julius' grin faltered when the Headsman bent down and deftly made a much larger snowball of his own.

"Heads up." With a squeal of fear Julius tried to run but he barely got five paces before he was nailed by the orb of frozen water.

"Take this!" Now it was Liliana who tossed a missile at the larger man with a wide smile. He chuckled and proceeded to craft a second snowball. He didn't have time as two of them sailed forth and struck the pair. Eyes turned to me and I waved my two tendrils in a jaunty wave.

"Combat has been joined!" I cried and a smirk lit up Varda's face. He threw his half formed projectile while Liliana furiously made her own.

"Traitor!" She replied as I began to rapidly grow extra tentacles and craft half a dozen snowballs at once.

"Quick Jelly! To me!" Julius shouted and I leapt, joining him behind a snowbank and the two of us began to our wintery battle against the other two.

"My tentacles are good for some things, but sadly making snowballs is not one of them," I complained.

After being playing around for a while, we decided to head inside obtain something warm to chase away the chill.

"At least you have a lot of them. You really pelted them! It was like a blizzard out there!" Julius cheered, making his sister stick her out her tongue at us.

"I still cannot believe you'd betray me like this, Jelly!" Liliana pouted, mock disappointment in her voice. I gave an approximation of a shrug.

"All is fair in love and war," I replied. Huffs and a roll of the eyes were my response.

"Here." Our talk was interrupted as Varda presented a trio of mugs full of cider. We all grinned at the hot, frothy fruit juice and eagerly took the offering.

I sighed in contentment from the warmth that filled me as I drank. The days were still cold and my body was still more susceptible to it so having something hot melt the ice that had formed here and there on me was more enjoyable.

"Delicious. I am so glad Cynthia gave me the ability to taste things as well as speak," I murmured.

"I still cannot believe you couldn't taste things before that. I mean, besides potions," Liliana said, patting my head in sympathy. "It must have been hard."

"I can safely say that I fully understand why people are so enamored with this sense," I admitted, finishing off the cider.

I was finally able to enjoy food as a normal person. I silently hoped for strawberries to start growing. The first thing I'd ever tasted was a healing potion which had tasted of strawberries to me thanks to my connection with my owner. Soon I would be able to sample the real thing!

"There'll be plenty of things you can sample soon. After all, dear sister's party is tomorrow! They'll have plenty of goodies to try," Julius promised me and my owner nodded.

A tantalizing aroma filled the air and attention was drawn to it.

"Now Jelly, try not to hog the entire cake this time," Liliana scolded as our gazes fell to the large pastry that was being formed in a different section of the kitchens. I merely bobbed up and down, not deigning to respond to her joke. Julius at least got a laugh out of it, though there was an undercurrent of fear that surfaced in the two children as they remember the last cake they'd seen.

"Don't worry, you two. A professional assassin never tries the same trick twice," Varda spoke up, trying to comfort them. I just shot him an incredulous burst of annoyance. Was that really the best he could come up with? Gods help us if he ever had offspring of his own.

Thankfully, before any more unhelpful remarks could escape the Royal Headsman's mouth, Julius' maid Jean walked up to our tiny group that was hiding near the kitchens. She shot our guardian an annoyed look for taking her master out of her sight.

"Dinner will be soon, so perhaps it would be in your best interests to get ready for it?" she sternly informed, and we all nodded hastily. We did not want to try the patience of the queen or Rene by not being properly dressed in front of the legendary X-ranked mage.

The evening meal was larger than usual, as there were three additional guests to eat with, and the smaller, more private dining room usually used by the royal family was replaced with a larger area that had more space and a wider table.

"Do you really think our Lily should have wine? I mean the strong stuff," Queen Amdora worried.

"She's nearly an adult, dear. Besides, if she goes off to the Academy I have no doubt the 'strong stuff' will be all she can find. Best to wean her onto it now," King Tiberius pointed out, placing a bottle of fine looking vintage on the table near her.

"If you weren't so handsome I'd be more put off by your flippant attitude," the queen said dramatically. My owner's father just winked and the princess gagged at her parent's flirting as she took her place at the head of the table.

The rest of the family and guests gathered quickly, the allure of free food drawing them quickly. Conversations started to suffuse the room in a pleasant hum.

"How has the Tower been since I last saw it?"

"It remains standing. Now that the slimy weasel paper pusher is being transferred I expect to see efficiency increase several fold," Varda claimed, informing the king of the various issues at the legendary prison he operated.

"And what of the… other matter?"

"I am fine. I will get over it."

"We are here for you, Varda."

"So, Rene, I was hoping you had some ideas for Julius' lessons once his sister heads off to the Academy. It would be a shame if his concentration were to drift at that time."

"Oh, not to worry, your majesty. I've done this before, and I have a few good ideas for the Crown Prince."

A shiver ran through Julius' spine, and he looked towards where his etiquette tutor was plotting his upbringing.

After a wary look at the women he turned back to the side of the table where he, his sister, Petrus, and myself were conversing with Arnolt Cantos.

"...And that is why the Alchemist's Guild no longer uses powdered Mandrake in hair regrowth potions."

"Did he ever recover?" Liliana asked with genuine concern and the Archsage nodded.

"Oh yes, once we managed to shave all the excess hair from the places it wasn't supposed to grow. And take care of the ingrown hairs," Arnolt assured, taking a bite of soft white bread in-between sentences. "He actually got married a year later to a woman who didn't mind the whole 'Lumberjack crossed with a bear' look."

"Really?" I asked, incredulous. Humans were weird.

"There's someone for everyone, little one. I learned that, if nothing else in my long life," Arnolt stated.

"You're X-ranked, correct Sir Arnolt?" Julius inquired. The man nodded as he swallowed a mouthful of stew.

"Indeed, I obtained that lofty rank in my younger days. And you can just call me Arnolt, or Archsage if you desire formality."

"Yes, of course Si- I mean Archsage Arnolt." The ancient mage heaved a sigh but continued to listen without interruption.

"You've clearly seen a lot. What can you tell me about when you slew the Dragon of Weeds?" Julius continued and the old man looked his age for a brief moment.

"It was the most terrifying battle I have ever experienced. You face a few Wyverns and Lesser Dragons and expect to be able to take on a real dragon. But those earlier fights were just warm ups at best. A true dragon has a mind shrewder than a dwarf and magic stronger than an elf. But worst of all, they have the battle lust of an orc and the desire for wealth and power that surpasses a human."

"Its name was Yalmoro, and it was a Green Dragon able to grow forests with a swing of its tail and every exhale spewed spores and seeds of toxic plants that would choke and strangle."

"Why did it attack Brune?" Liliana asked and the Archsage scratched his chin.

"Because it wished to claim the Dullwilds, one of the most ancient and magical forests in Orria, for itself. Brune just so happened to be nearby."

"And how did you slay it?" I leaned in as I inquired.

"There were at least a hundred other adventurers from C to A-rank, with half a dozen S-rank there, myself included. Half of them perished in the battle, and in the end it was I who sealed its movements with my spells and dealt the final blow. I earned the adulation of the survivors and the praise of Brune and Varia. But I lost all but one of my companions in doing so."

"I'm sorry for your loss," Liliana said with a bow of her head and the mage smiled before patting her on the head fondly.

"You remind me of when my own little brats were adorable. Now they're all old and cranky like myself," Arnolt said with a chuckle.

"How did you deal with the sorrow and regret afterwards? Did it hurt?" the princess asked in a hushed tone.

"I kept their memories close to me. And I took in all the rage of being worthless before a much more powerful being and turned it into motivation. I realized I had neglected many important aspects of my training as a mage when I was boy. I had scorned the basics for more flashy and deadly spells. But that was what cost me my friends." He took a deep gulp of wine to steel his nerves before speaking on.

"I wasted so much mana on big spells early on when I should have taken care to figure out its weaknesses and probed its movements. And then, do you know how I slew Yolmoro, the Dragon of Weeds?"

The royal children and myself leaned in, enraptured.

"The final blow was done with a single *Magic Arrow*. My spell went through the remains of its right eye, which was ruined thanks to the enchanted axe of Borin, my close companion. I splattered Yolmoro's brains inside its own skull with the only spell I could cast because I had wasted all the rest of my powers earlier."

"Eventually I climbed my way to the top of the food chain at the Royal Varian Mage's Academy. I tore apart the curriculum and insured that future generations would not make the same mistakes I did," the Archsage said with a sigh as the past weighed upon him.

"That is why students now are required to perform in-depth research projects to fully explore and understand their magic. It is why I make them exercise their muscles as well as their brains so they can be sound in body and mind. It is why I expect the best from all of them. Because I do not want them to suffer like I did."

"I'm honored to hear this," Liliana said slowly and I nodded. "This only makes me want to become a mage even more."

Companionable silence descended on our section, Petrus in contemplation over the man he'd idolized and myself deeply engrossed in thoughts of magic. Liliana though was thinking over everything her soon-to-be headmaster had spoken of. Her emotions were stable, but they were focused on preparing her heart for her own time as a student.

"You have a very clear mind," Arnolt praised my owner as dinner finished. "Some mages and thinkers will claim that a sharp wit is one of the best tools, but in my experience only someone who can think their own actions through and see past their own knowledge can improve. Based on what I've gleaned so far, I am relieved to see my initial thoughts have been vindicated."

Liliana blushed deep red at hearing the praise, her complexion also partly due to a few cups of wine.

After dinner I morphed into my bipedal form and helped Orleen carry her off to her room. It was her big day tomorrow, and she'd need all the rest she could get for that.

Cuddling up with her amid the soft pillows of her bed, we drifted off to sleep as one.

The next morning was a subdued rush of activity. An early bath was prepared and my owner, still bleary eyed from sleep and wine, was scrubbed and cleaned by a group of maids in her luxurious bathroom.

It was amusing to see my owner manhandled into the tub and then lathered up and scrubbed. I let out a faint laugh at the scene, and earned a glare from the drowsy princess.

My laughter quickly vanished as some of the maids shared a look before pouncing on me, beginning to do the same to my body that was being done to Liliana's. It was utterly demeaning, and the little coos and comments from the bathroom attendants didn't help. I was not 'cute,' and I have never been a 'dirty boy!' Their giggles and my owner giving me her own amused snort made me grumble out loud. Honestly, sometimes I think women are as odd as I am, and that's saying something!

Half an hour later and smelling faintly of roses and lavender my owner and I stepped into the dining room for breakfast. The rest of the family and guests were there already, having set up gifts and a brunch beforehand as a surprise.

"Happy birthday, my dear little Lily," King Tiberius said, tenderly embracing his daughter.

"Thank you, daddy," Liliana replied, breaking formality for the moment and giving him a squeeze in return. I slithered over to the table while the rest of the people went and offered hugs and handshakes to the newly minted fourteen year old. Morphing into my bipedal form, I took the time to remove my gift from within the strange magical storage space I now possessed and grinned in my mind. She was going to love it! I gently placed it in the pile already waiting near Liliana's chair.

"Impressive technique. I've never seen an Ooze mimic human form before. And that Dimensional Magic I sensed just now... how did you obtain it?" I turned to see the Archsage watching me intently and shrugged.

"I devoured a *Bag of Holding*. It was quite delicious," I noted, remember the taste of the artifact's magic. "Not unlike grapes with a hint of chocolate."

"You continue to impress me." With that, Archsage Arnolt turned away and moseyed over to the table, a sheen of eagerness in his eyes as he looked over the breakfast spread.

I shook my head. What a strange old man!

The morning meal passed by quickly, and I leapt over into my owner's lap as soon as it was finished. It was time to open gifts! And I wanted the best seat in the house!

There was quite the assortment.

"This is from me, Lily. A grimoire of rare and obscure magical beasts and how to tame them, what their components can be used for, and more," King Tiberius said as he passed over a thick tome bound in pale purple leather. I could tell that whatever monster had been used to make the cover, it had been no easier foe to bring down. It reeked of magic, and the various preservation spells inside it created a medley of confusing sensation for me.

419

"In my family, it has been traditional to pass this down from mother to daughter when they go on to practice magic," Queen Amdora said, trying to keep her tears from spilling out. "My mother gave it to me when I was going to the Academy, and she got it from her mother, and so on and so forth. All the way from my ancestor, Camilla the Crimson Bloom. I know you will do fine. You're my daughter after all."

The artifact was a wand made of willow and capped with an amethyst, the purple gem held in place by a thin piece of silver made into the shape of a lotus flower. It gleamed in the light of the dining room, clearly well taken care of and full of experience.

"Thank you mother," Liliana said, having no compunctions about tears. She wrapped her mother in a tight embrace and the pair spent a moment of bonding only parent and child can.

"Since you'll be at school the next year, I thought this would be nice to have some supplies." Her brother showed off an impressive assortment of quills and inkpots.

"Maybe you should keep them, Julius. After all you need all the help you can with math. Don't want to fall behind on your own studies, do you?" My owner teased, earning some chuckles from the rest of the people.

"Oh, come here, brother! You know I love you! Thank you for the thoughtful gift. I'll be sure to use them well," Liliana promised, dragging the ten year old into a hug which was quickly joined by their parents.

"Tiberius said you'd been practicing needlepoint. I thought you could do with some more bits and pieces for it," Varda explained as he revealed a knitting set, with many unique and expensive colors of thread, including Royal Purple and Turquoise Blue.

"It's lovely, Varda! Thank you!" The much smaller girl hopped up and wrapped her arms around his tree-trunk like neck while the Headsman patted her back gently.

"What good luck that my gift compliments this," Rene said with a grin. "This is a very popular book on knitting techniques and simple objects like scarves and mittens."

When the baroness' grin fell on me and was joined by Liliana's I wondered with a hint of worry if my owner would try and make me a sweater or something else to wear.

Not that I wouldn't like a gift from her, but I draw the line at wearing anything that has tassels. And those were what my owner included in anything she sewed. I think she believed they looked cute and fashionable.

"So, I wasn't sure what would be an appropriate gift for a princess, so I got you a set of healing potions and medical supplies. The Academy is as safe a place as you can find, but you know what they say, better say than sorry!" Petrus said with a nervous chuckle. He placed a collection of vials onto the table in front of Liliana. "As you can see there is a Minor Healing Potion, a Major Healing Potion, and a Grand Healing Potion!"

From left to right, the trio of potions shone, taunting me. Pinkish red, to a darker crimson, to a hue not unlike liquid rubies. But although I looked longingly at the tantalizing drinks, I restrained myself. They weren't mine. I had better control than in the past. But they did look really tasty...

"I also have this, the directions for casting the *Parchment Preservation* spell. A must have for any student, Academy or otherwise." Petrus handed over a folded piece of paper, and when Liliana opened it I could see the intricate runes and magical array along with written instructions for properly using the Level One spell.

"Many thanks Petrus. I'm sure we'll see each other on campus soon," Liliana said with a bow towards the mage.

The skinny apprentice just blushed and turned away while scratching the back of his head while grinning. The Archsage gave Petrus a pat on the back as he stepped up. I saw the young mage wiggle in pleasure at being acknowledged and I wished him all the best.

"It isn't much, but I hope you don't mind some primers on the general study subjects all First Year students had to take. That way you'll be able to review and catch up to where all beginner mages are supposed to be." The Archsage offered up the princess a small assortment of worn tomes and books, each one easily half a century old. But despite their tattered nature they had been well loved. I could see the care that had been put into them over the years.

"Amazing... I'll be sure to take good care of them," Liliana promised, bowing to Arnolt. He just smiled and waved her off, but I saw the approval in his eyes.

"And this is mine," I said, presenting the final gift. It had taken lots of effort and I had started work on it after the Winter Solstice had passed. With a kind smile down at me, she picked up my gift, which I had placed inside a basic leather pouch.

"You didn't have to get me anything, Jelly," Liliana protested.

"I didn't think you could afford anything," King Tiberius said under his breath, earning a sharp jab into his side from his wife.

A gasp slipped past Liliana's lips as she stared at what I was giving her. From the crowd there were similar intakes of breath.

It was a ring, a simple band of opaque, glass-like material that was etched with a few runes. However, it was more than just a pretty accessory. It radiated a pale, ghostly light that felt alien yet soothing. Magic oozed around inside it, frozen yet flowing.

"I made it myself," I explained. "I separated and crystalized a fragment of my core and then shaped it with my magic."

Her jaw dropped, as did that of Queen Amdora and Petrus. After all, what I had done was take a fragment of my own being, my soul, and turn it into an accessory.

"Jelly…"

"I understand it seems like a lot, but I want you to have this. You will always know where I am when you wear it, and I will know your exact location in turn. If either of us are in danger, we'll know about it instantly."

"But most importantly, if you channel your mana through it, the runes I have carved on the ring will act as a summoning catalyst and drag me through time and space to your side. No matter how far I am, I shall always be nearby. It'll shatter afterwards though, as such a powerful summoning ritual will put too much magical strain on it. The backlash will reduce the ring to powder after a single casting. But it'll be an excellent last line of defense."

"Do you like it?" I asked, tilting my body upwards in an approximation of looking at my owner's face.

"Oh Jelly, I love it!" Liliana squealed, slipping the ring onto her right hand immediately. As soon as it was on, the magical aura faded and it no longer could be detected without magical senses.

"Thank you so much! I'll treasure it always," she claimed happily. A brief but loving nuzzle later, and I was aglow with pride.

"Well, it seems we've gone over the initial presents. I believe there are some well wishes from the king and queen of Brune, as well as from King Redarik Greatgold as well..." King Tiberius spoke up, distracting everyone.

In the hubbub of new items being brought it, I slipped out of my owner's lap and waddled over to the Archsage. Those runes had been a last minute addition, and one that I had shamelessly begged the Archsage for.

"Thank you again for helping me with my gift," I began, but he waved me off with an impatient hand.

"No need to thank me. You paid with a lot of Extract, which will go a long way towards crafting some high-end potions. So why are you really over here, Jelly? I thought your profuse thanks from last night had been sufficient to convey your gratitude," Arnolt said with a pondering look in his eyes as he examined me.

"Teach me." I made my request without preamble. He blinked, taken aback. He recovered quickly as he peered down at me.

"My lessons will be neither easy, nor cheap. I am a powerful man, and thus extremely busy. You have to give me good incentive for me to teach you personally." And so it began, the bargaining phase.

"I can produce more than just Soul Slivers and Ooze Extract," I began. "I can also help you discretely clean up any 'messes' that might appear on the campus. After all, who would suspect a slime?"

"Why should I take your offer?" Arnolt inquired. From the beginning, I knew he'd accept. After all, I could provide rare materials and various esoteric services a man like himself could appreciate. However, he had to act the stoic, had to hear me give an offer and then a reason as to why I wanted this. So I obliged.

"My owner is in danger, and I must protect her." It was simple and selfless. So pure that it was either a lie, or I was just that altruistic. And we both knew which one it was.

"You know, that little brat with that rainbow colored soul spoke highly of you when I last saw him," Archsage Arnolt mused. Ah, so Tomas Nierz had mentioned me before. It made sense that two X-ranked individuals would know each other.

"He claimed that for such a tiny creature, he'd rarely seen such massive reserves of courage and loyalty."

"I did what I felt was right." Not an excuse, just a statement of facts. Arnolt nodded silently, before glancing over at my owner and then his estranged wife.

"I know a bit about that too, you know. Fine. Call me a sentimental old man, but I cannot deny such zeal," the Archsage sighed, accepting my deal.

"As soon as you arrive at the Academy, I expect you in my office at midnight. Our lessons will begin then."

I bowed before hurrying back to rejoin Liliana as she opened the rest of her gifts. I could hear the elderly sorcerer sighing, but I also 'saw' him smiling faintly.

Things were about to change. I could feel it in my core. Enemies of the court and the world itself were moving, and I feared I would soon have to take a role in these conflicts one way or another. Because no matter what happened, I would die before I let my love suffer.

This, I swore. On the Divine Family, on my life, on the miracle that is my owner.

"And we await the day you call upon us, and the day we call upon you. The World Rebels, and heroes will be needed."

The voices faded, and I knew I was on the right path. It was time for a new chapter in my life.

Made in the USA
San Bernardino, CA
26 November 2018